SIXTEEN TONGUES

Annotated Screenplay

By Scooter McCrae

Happy Cloud Media, LLC
www.happycloudpictures.net

ALSO FROM THE HAPPY CLOUD SCREENPLAY COLLECTION:

NOTLD 90: The Version You've Never Seen by Tom Savini
The Shatter Dead Collection – By Scooter McCrae
The Resurrection Game Scrapbook – By Mike Watt
Splatter Movie: The Director's Cut – Annotated Screenplay – by Amy Lynn Best
Demon Divas And The Lanes Of Damnation – Annotated Screenplay – By Mike Watt

Printed in the United States of America

Layout and interior design by Ryan Hose.

First Printing, 2022. *Sixteen Tongues – The Screenplay* © 2022 Happy Cloud Media, LLC. All rights reserved.

ISBN 13: 978-1-951036-33-1

Happy Cloud Media, LLC
Publisher: Amy Lynn Best
Editor: Mike Watt
Cloud Logo Copyright © Happy Cloud Media, LLC
www.happycloudpublishing.com

FROM THE CREATOR OF SHATTER DEAD

SIXTEEN TONGUES

SIXTEEN TONGUES

NEVER DOUBLE CROSS A STRANGER IN A XXX WORLD

Adrian Torque is a renegade cop who has lost more than half his skin to a terrorist explosion. His scarred flesh has been replaced with the tongue meat recovered from all the people who died during that violent act, and now his borrowed flesh is beginning to remember that agony.

Ginny Chin-Chin is an assassin chasing down the doctor who altered her by implanting a clitoris under the fold of each eyelid. As she struggles to suppress her violent impulses, each blink of an eye is a scream of over-stimulation that only the blood of her enemies can satisfy.

Alik Silens is a computer hacker hunting 'the datastream' for the identity of her brother's killer. Burnt out and exhausted from the endless pursuit, the only person binding her emotional seams together is her lover, Ginny.

And now in The Sappho Motel, a run down S&M franchise where even the strangest desires can be met for a price, the lives of these three double-crossed people are about to intersect in a frenzy of vengeance-fueled sex, bullets and borrowed blood....

SPECIAL FEATURES

Behind The Scenes Featurette, Make Up & Costume Tests, Deleted Scenes, Visual Effects Breakdown, Two Audio Commentaries, Music Only Audio Track, Music Video and Trailers

A SUB ROSA STUDIOS RELEASE SEEING EYE DOG PRODUCTIONS PRESENTS A GEM-IN-EYE PRODUCTION
"SIXTEEN TONGUES"
JANE CHASE CRAWFORD JAMES ALICE LIU
VIDEOGRAPHER ROBERT FERAPPLES PRODUCTION DESIGNER DAN OUELLETTE EDITOR RICK O'SHEA VISUAL EFFECTS BY MECHANICAL WHISPERS
SPECIAL MAKEUP EFFECTS BY REAPERDUCTIONS MUSIC BY GEEK MESSIAH ADDITIONAL MUSIC BY CEREBELLION
PRODUCED BY ALEX KUCIW WRITTEN AND DIRECTED BY SCOOTER McCRAE

Rated "17" by the IDRB
Recommended for ages 17 and older

Running Time: 80 minutes
Color, Stereo 2.0; 1.33:1
www.sixteentongues.com

"If You're Looking for Something Truly Transgressive, SIXTEEN TONGUES should test the Threshold of Even The Boldest Viewer"
— MORIARTY, Ain't It Cool News

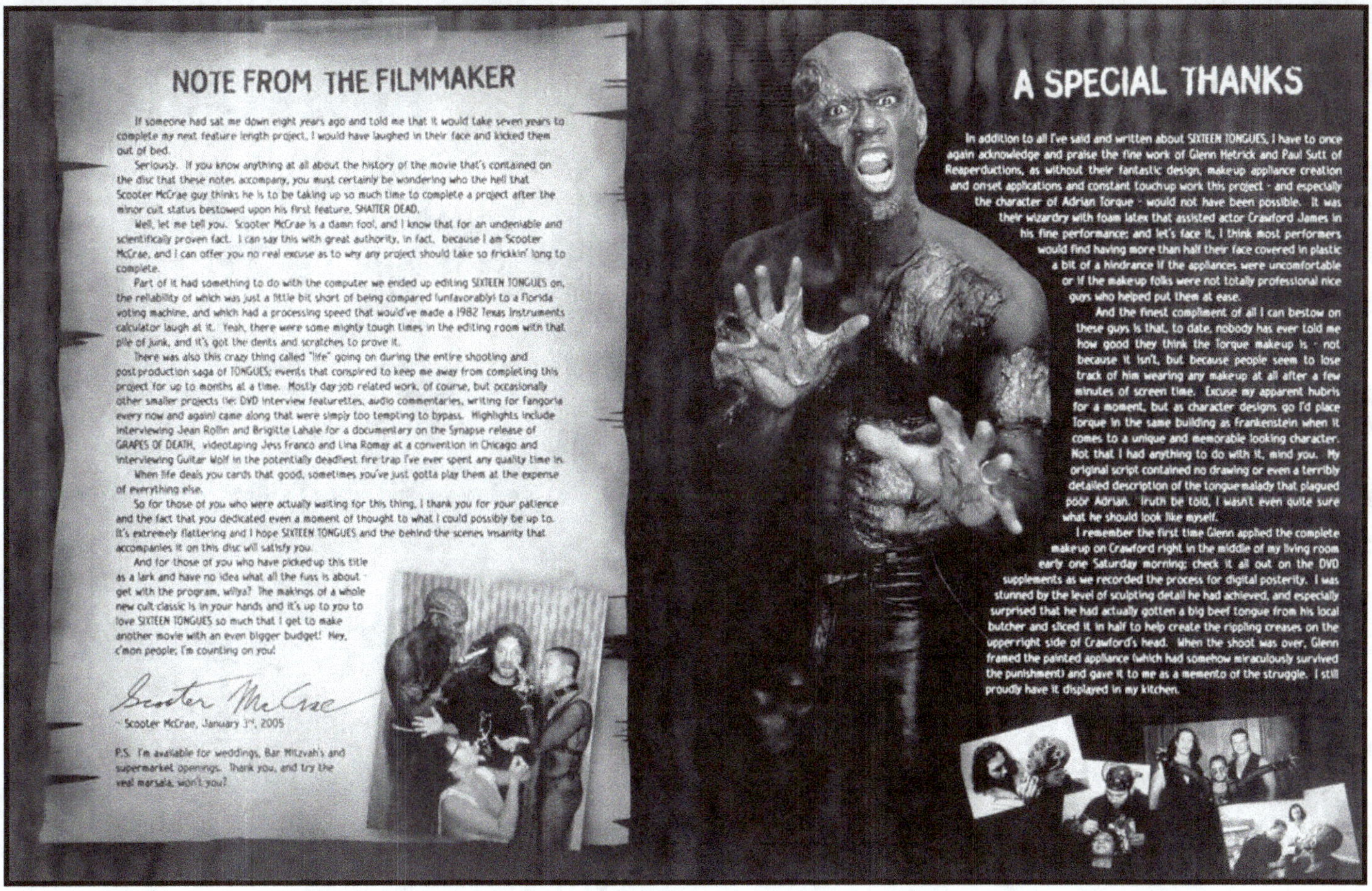

6 74945 11889 4

NOTE FROM THE FILMMAKER

If someone had sat me down eight years ago and told me that it would take seven years to complete my next feature length project, I would have laughed in their face and kicked them out of bed.

Seriously. If you know anything at all about the history of the movie that's contained on the disc that these notes accompany, you must certainly be wondering who the hell that Scooter McCrae guy thinks he is to be taking up so much time to complete a project after the minor cult status bestowed upon his first feature, SHATTER DEAD.

Well, let me tell you. Scooter McCrae is a damn fool, and I know that for an undeniable and scientifically proven fact. I can say this with great authority, in fact, because I am Scooter McCrae, and I can offer you no real excuse as to why any project should take so frickin' long to complete.

Part of it had something to do with the computer we ended up editing SIXTEEN TONGUES on, the reliability of which was just a little bit short of being compared (unfavorably) to a Florida voting machine, and which had a processing speed that would've made a 1982 Texas Instruments calculator laugh at it. Yeah, there were some mighty tough times in the editing room with that pile of junk, and it's got the dents and scratches to prove it.

There was also this crazy thing called "life" going on during the entire shooting and post production saga of TONGUES; events that conspired to keep me away from completing this project for up to months at a time. Mostly day job related work, of course, but occasionally other smaller projects (ie: DVD interview featurettes, audio commentaries, writing for fangoria every now and again) came along that were simply too tempting to bypass. Highlights include interviewing Jean Rollin and Brigitte Lahaie for a documentary on the Synapse release of GRAPES OF DEATH, videotaping Jess Franco and Lina Romay at a convention in Chicago and interviewing Guitar Wolf in the potentially deadliest fire-trap I've ever spent any quality time in.

When life deals you cards that good, sometimes you've just gotta play them at the expense of everything else.

So for those of you who were actually waiting for this thing, I thank you for your patience and the fact that you dedicated even a moment of thought to what I could possibly be up to. It's extremely flattering and I hope SIXTEEN TONGUES and the behind the scenes insanity that accompanies it on this disc will satisfy you.

And for those of you who have picked up this title as a lark and have no idea what all the fuss is about - get with the program, wilya? The makings of a whole new cult classic is in your hands and it's up to you to love SIXTEEN TONGUES so much that I get to make another movie with an even bigger budget! Hey, c'mon people, I'm counting on you!

Scooter McCrae

- Scooter McCrae, January 3rd, 2005

P.S. I'm available for weddings, Bar Mitzvah's and supermarket openings. Thank you, and try the veal marsala, won't you?

A SPECIAL THANKS

In addition to all I've said and written about SIXTEEN TONGUES, I have to once again acknowledge and praise the fine work of Glenn Hetrick and Paul Sutt of Reaperductions, as without their fantastic design, makeup appliance creation and onset applications and constant touchup work this project - and especially the character of Adrian Torque - would not have been possible. It was their wizardry with foam latex that assisted actor Crawford James in his fine performance; and let's face it, I think most performers would find having more than half their face covered in plastic a bit of a hindrance if the appliances were uncomfortable or if the makeup folks were not totally professional nice guys who helped put them at ease.

And the finest compliment of all I can bestow on these guys is that, to date, nobody has ever told me how good they think the torque makeup is - not because it isn't, but because people seem to lose track of him wearing any makeup at all after a few minutes of screen time. Excuse my apparent hubris for a moment, but as character designs go I'd place Torque in the same building as frankenstein when it comes to a unique and memorable looking character. Not that I had anything to do with it, mind you. My original script contained no drawing or even a terribly detailed description of the tongue-malady that plagued poor Adrian. Truth be told, I wasn't even quite sure what he would look like myself.

I remember the first time Glenn applied the complete makeup on Crawford right in the middle of my living room early one Saturday morning; check it all out on the DVD supplements as we recorded the process for digital posterity. I was stunned by the level of sculpting detail he had achieved, and especially surprised that he had actually gotten a big beef tongue from his local butcher and sliced it in half to help create the rippling creases on the upperright side of Crawford's head. When the shoot was over, Glenn framed the painted appliance (which had somehow miraculously survived the punishment) and gave it to me as a memento of the struggle. I still proudly have it displayed in my kitchen.

Reversible cover art for the original Sub Rosa DVD release.

All Light Paintings by Patrick Rochon.

AESTHETIC TERRORISM:
Scooter McCrae And *Sixteen Tongues*
By Mike Watt

In Scooter McCrae's mind, there is only one hope for independent film "aesthetic terrorism." Consider his movie, *Sixteen Tongues*:

Sometime in the future, human beings will be created in laboratories, water comes for a price from machines boasting "92% pure!" and hotel guests have to pay to have their pornography channels turned off. Humans of this world (not too far removed from our own) live in a constant state of sensory overload, to the point of utter desensitization, and the only outlet left is violence.

With hallways plastered floor to ceiling with explicit pornographic posters, the Sappho Motel is a microcosm for the sewer that our technological rampaging world has become. Inside, three very lost and very damaged souls are brought together via karma and circumstance. Renegade cop Adrian Torque (Crawford James), once a model officer protecting and serving, lost over 60% of his skin, burned away in a terrorist attack. In a nihilistic medicinal emergency, his charred flesh and muscle was replaced with the tongue meat of the other sixteen victims. Down the hall lives Ginny Chin-Chin (Jane Chase), a lab-grown assassin searching for the doctor who grafted clitorises beneath her eyelids, every blink keeping her in a state of sensual overload, keeping her from sleep and sanity. Meanwhile her lover, Alik Silens (Alice Liu1), rewires her own body into a living circuit so she can painfully search the "data stream" for her brother's killer. They're living in a world where the only real emotions are grief and rage. Ginny's violent tendencies can only be staved off by the blood of her victims. Alik wants to love Ginny, but is obsessed with her quest for revenge. And Torque, who was once a very good cop, now rapes and tortures suspects in order to drown out the voices of those whose deaths contributed to his skin grafts.

Except for brief forays into Torque's dungeonesque interrogation room—or when accompanying Alik's consciousness into the dizzying digital "data stream" (which feels both retro and prescient of our modern view of "cyberspace")—the viewer never leaves the grim griminess of the Sappho Motel. And save for brief encounters with a handful of the Motel's prostitutes, junkies and other lost souls, the viewer spends the entire running time with Torque, Ginny and Alik. It's their stories and situations we're required to identify with, which is rarely made easy. Our introduction to Torque is during a violent interrogation where he orally rapes a suspect; Ginny and Alik, lovers more out of necessity than affection, meet the viewer exhausted and emotionally bludgeoned, nearly sexless despite their nudity. Gradually, their stories of abuse by the system, by circumstance, by life and by themselves, is shared with, rather than revealed to, us. In spite of Torque's and Ginny's immoral violence, our sympathies are dredged up in spite of ourselves. As the movie progresses, the patient viewers will be rewarded even as they're robbed of the moral high ground. By the time the credits roll, your numbed brain will still realize that you've never seen anything quite like *Sixteen Tongues*—and this is not meant to be ass-kissing hyperbole. It's best to approach this film with an open-mind and an armful of pessimism, because this is not a story that holds your hand and tells you that, in the end, everything will be okay. Like the best literary science fiction, *Sixteen Tongues* casts the future in a dark and oily shadow.

If you need Hollywood shorthand to describe *Sixteen Tongues*, it's *Blade Runner* meets *Salo*; or maybe William Gibson's take on Luchino Visconti's *The Damned* (1969). More appropriately, it's a singularity born in the mind of its writer and director, Scooter McCrae. Shot on digital video over a grueling Brooklyn summer, *Sixteen Tongues* is only McCrae's sophomore film, following his controversial philosophical sex-and-goresoaked zombie movie, *Shatter Dead*. His extremely limited budget required that McCrae and producer Alex Kuciw fulfill nearly every production role. "Unlike *Shatter Dead*, which had no crew to speak of and a relatively tight but manageable shooting schedule, *Sixteen Tongues* needed a much larger crew and was a nightmarish shoot with days lasting a minimum of fourteen hours and stretching out to as long as thirty-six hours during the worst day ever! Thank goodness everybody was not only talented and professional, but patient as well," McCrae said. "Part of the difficulty was that in order to save money, I was my own cameraperson, so that meant I was not only directing the actors but also lighting the sets and operating the camera as well. I don't recommend that to anyone as it just creates more pressure on you, and you have to find the balance in your brain between judgment facilities—that is, balancing the technical matters against the performances

---

1 Punk rocker and a regular on—of all things—*Sesame Street*.

of your actors and which is more important to you during the more complicated shots. What crew was there—Alex and the make-up EFX people and two rotating production assistants—were great and tireless workers, but there just wasn't enough of them. And the weather, July and August at their hottest, made the shooting conditions occasionally horrifying in a small, sealed room with no air conditioning."

While it's tempting to dismiss Hollywood when lauding the independently made movie, *Sixteen Tongues* could never have been made by a major studio with big stars. Not because the moguls would never risk burying Gerard Butler under grotesque prosthetics or keep a shaved-headed Anne Hathaway topless throughout the running time—or cast unglamorous middle-aged woman as her lesbian lover, but because the majors, famished for mainstream American dollars, would never risk telling a story so grim and so intensely personal. A big-budgeted *Tongues* would seek redemption for its damaged trio, shoehorning a happy ending somewhere into the narrative, if only represented by an aspect of Alik's data stream. Worse, Hollywood wouldn't risk the underlying message, that without personal connection and the ability to escape the world you've trapped yourself in, there is no redemption—not for the three anti-heroes, not for any of us. Worst of all: we may not even deserve that redemption.

"I don't consider myself a pessimist," says McCrae, "so I don't like to say that we're doomed as a race; it has a judgmental ring to it. If pollution changes weather patterns, food, water and air quality, and continues to mutate us in tiny ways to the point where what is considered 'human' now might not exist in two hundred years, offering that possibility up for discussion seems healthy and practical to me; not bleak, but realistic. We're simply not the same human beings we used to be, in terms of cognitive and physical abilities, since the worldwide industrial revolution began. I think we live in a fairly bleak world, but we surround ourselves with enough distractions to make it bearable; computers, television, music and sex are great ways to keep ourselves occupied while the planet spins and burns away.

"In the end, if watching one of my movies can help a person realize how numbed to their own moral stupidity they've been made by corporate-owned media or acknowledge how two-thirds of the things they do in the average day are meant to waste their time and energy and keep them occupied by the powers that are in charge, then I'll feel like I've done something right. Not all negative feelings are destructive; I remain creatively productive and try to hurt as few people as possible and I don't need a "god" cushion to fall back on to have a well-adjusted and compassionate moral core."

So, in a nutshell, *Sixteen Tongues* is meant not for the squeamish, the prudish or the impatient. It is, however, readily accessible. It should be noted of the original release, however, that even the physical DVD was controversial, as McCrae and Kuciw decorated the disk face with many explicit images from the Motel's hallways, resulting in a record number of returns from shocked wholesalers and rental houses (remember those?). Which makes one wonder what these places thought they were ordering in the first place.

McCrae's fatalism comes cheerfully, however. He means what he says, but he generally delivers it with the greatest hyperbole known to man. "Overall, the world of indie filmmaking as we've always known it and romanticized it to be, always wanted to be a part of, is dead. Kiss it goodbye, baby. The major studios purchased that poor genre and fucked the cheap whore till it bled and then left it for dead in the back of a dark alley," he said. "Set your goals and ruthlessly follow them, and when I say *ruthlessly* that doesn't mean being reckless or screwing other people to make your way to the top. When a friend does me a favor I do them a favor back; that's the currency that makes the low-budget storytelling industry run. Anyone who breaks that train of trust must be hunted down and killed immediately before that kinda' shit spreads any further. [But] maybe we are doomed or, blessed finally, to shit where we eat; and by that I mean us indies gotta keep on making good stuff for each other to watch if we're gonna survive. And if I may mangle the ending of Ray Bradbury's classic novel "The Martian Chronicles", perhaps we indie-humans have finally seen the indie-Martians and they are us."

I suppose I should ask you to describe the story of 16T in your own words, as I've failed miserably in two attempts to do it in my own.

Listen, I've given up on that sorry task as well. I'll just give you the synopsis we sent out for the screening:

In the future, two very special people are hiding away in a very special place.

Adrian Torque is a police officer who has lost more than half his skin to an explosion that should have killed him. Instead, his destroyed epidermis has been replaced with the tongue meat of all the people who were killed that horrible night. Where once he only felt, he is now being slowly driven mad by a never-ending stream of tastes.

Virginia Chin is a genetically engineered combatrix with a clitoris implanted beneath the epicanthic fold of each eye and a taste for blood. Her uncontrollable murderous impulses keeps her barely one step ahead of the law ... and each blink of her eyes keeps her tightly poised within a state of heightened stimulation that only the blood of her enemies can sate.

And now, in a run down adults-only franchise called the Sappho Motel, where even the most obscure desire of every occupant can be met for a price, they are about to collide...

So there you have it; screams "commercial", don't it? Alex and I wrote that, so I can't take all the credit, but I think it's an accurate summation of what people will be seeing on-screen when the damn thing finally arrives.

You mentioned before that the title was inspired by the song "Sixteen Tons". How did the idea develop beyond the title?

Hard to say. I think it started as a joke I told at parties (which I'm sorry I don't remember) and kind of grew into an idea that tickled me enough to try and figure out what kind of a plot could contain two characters this extreme. It wasn't easy and I'll have to let others decide if I was successful, though I personally have very mixed feelings about it. I'm not saying the project isn't successful, of course, but I don't know that I exactly achieved what I set out to accomplish and that always disappoints me. I feel the same way about SHATTER DEAD.

Funny how my mind works, but when you ask me how the idea developed beyond the title I can only add that quite often the title comes first and helps drive the idea to completion for me. TONGUES is a great example of what happens when you're listening to music and hear the lyrics wrong. You just never know what the heck is gonna inspire you. I mean, shit; what would The Platters think if they knew their recording of the song lit a fire in me that's kept me hard at work for the last seven years and I didn't even hear what they were singing correctly? So many ideas I get are from mishearing what someone says or only seeing half an image; it's like one of Dario Argento's tortured artist protagonists trying to reconstruct a crime with only a half-clue and a whole lot of imagination.

As SHATTER DEAD is less about zombies and more about the idea of religion, government, depression, love and sex, what are the underlying themes explored in "16 Tongues"?

Most important to me was mortality and the taboos and barriers people are willing to trample to maintain their own existence. Machines are fascinating because they are an idealization of how the human body should work; all the parts fit together perfectly, function in a complimentary style, and if there's a problem or disharmony, that's what spare parts are for. It's funny that machines and our bodies use the term "parts" interchangeably, as bodies have parts but technically machines have pieces. Part of it is that we as human beings are projecting our own fears and wishes onto the machineries we create. It's rather hopeful in a misguided way. Optimism has always seemed much more liberal and forgiving in its outlook to me than the conservative pessimism that currently drives our countries foreign policy.

It's also got a hint of environment vs. hereditary traits in it; one character's been born bad (through artificial means) and the other one has been made bad by circumstances beyond their control. Is one kind of 'evil' more forgivable, more sympathetic (if you will) than another? Although it was written and shot seven years ago, that's a very 9/11 kinda' question for me that time and the circumstances we live in have made more relevant. This is a project I made during the Clinton years that is finally coming out to play in the Bush II Monarchy. The project itself had no overt political stance or point-of-view while we were making it, but the era in which we are releasing it begs some kind of political introspection if for no other reason than the fact that we are experiencing a very conservative administration at the moment. The images in this project would always be considered troublesome and explicit no matter who was in charge of the system, but I think they seem even more transgressive right now.

Betrayal and trust are the other themes that wind their way through the various intricacies of TONGUES. In that sense it's a much messier project than SHATTER DEAD, which had one strong main thematic motif and a bunch of various secondary themes that flowed from it. I prefer working that way, but with TONGUES I just kinda' gave up and decided to emotionally pursue what it was about the story that interested me instead of trying to invest it with additional meaning first. It's a lot sloppier on a structural level, but I think it's what the project needed in order for it to express itself fully and most honestly. You can't shoehorn a story into an idea or vice-versa and expect perfection. At least I can't.

There are things in "16T" that make the "gun-barrel copulation" scene in SHATTER DEAD seem tame. How do you convince your actors to do these things? What makes capturing these images important to the film?

I've never had to convince any of my actors to do anything. If I'm interested in working with a performer, I give them the script to read and then let them tell me if it's too far outside their window of possibility. If they say it's just too much for them and they wouldn't be comfortable doing what the role requires, I thank them for their honesty and move on to the next possible performer. I've been very lucky so far and I guess a good judge of character as I haven't had any major changes-of-mind from a performer in the middle of a shoot.

When we were filming the sex scene, which is quite explicit even though it doesn't quite (technically) cross over into hardcore territory, my actress objected to a specific moment that the script called for in which the other character was going to ejaculate on her face. She asked me if there was some other way of showing it; like having him cum on her breasts or maybe even her ass instead. I thought about it and realized she was right. Having him cum on her face was just too much to challenge the audience with; having him shoot his load on her breasts was probably a much more interesting and exciting image and turned out to better accomplish the script's original objective.

I just finished telling you that I didn't shoot a hardcore scene and now I'm talking about the cum shot! Let me be clear; it's a fake ejaculation. And when you see it in the finished project, you'll understand exactly why we had to fake it. It always gets the most visceral reaction I've ever seen in a theatre for one of my projects. At the Fantasia screening the guy seated in front of me yelped out loud and turned away from the screen. As you could imagine, it was one of the most satisfying moments of my brief career.

There are numerous themes running throughout—and this was back in 1999!—interconnectivity of virtual strangers, the dangers of technology, how loneliness can lead to madness, etc. What was your original intention as to the "Themes" of 16T?

I'm so new to computers that I'm sure part of my intention was to examine my own curiosity and discomfort with the technology; the awkwardness and the dislocation of electronic communications. I try not to write themes, but characters who are confused and trying to come to terms with a change in their life; that may well be the common thread that connects all of my work. The changes may be extreme, whether it be zombies or radical body modifications, but all good genre stories begin with some kind of grotesque transformation or interruption of the ordinary world.

Technology isn't necessarily dangerous, but its application certainly can be. That's why Oppenheimer was a fucking idiot. What good did he expect to come from nuclear weaponry? He's the kind of scientist who should have been beaten to death and had his ashes scattered all over Hiroshima. I couldn't even write a story about someone so stupid. I'll stick to writing stories about people covered in tongues and clits. These people I can relate to.

I wish I could be more specific about my intentions, but if I knew exactly what I was writing and why I was writing it I probably wouldn't even waste my time. For me, the journey of writing is its own revelation and its own reward. If I know exactly how a story is going to end, I usually can't write it, or when the ending that inspired me to write the story in the first place does arrive it doesn't work anymore. Writing is like a map that's never laid out the same way twice; even if all the landmarks remain the same, they're always in a different location.

Both movies have one thing in common beyond the bleak tone - throughout the storyline, the audience develops sympathy for the unsympathetic characters. Ginny, Torque, even Alix and Stark's character in S.D. - they're not particularly likeable people, but their situations are enough to invoke sympathy. Is this a conscious choice of yours, or did tonal lightning strike twice?

I'm glad to hear you found Torque sympathetic, because I did everything in my power to stack the deck against him when I was writing the script, but when the time finally came time to cast the part, I did everything I could to subvert what had been written and find a performer who a viewer would feel some empathy towards. As both the writer and the director, I find this to be the most productive way to work as contradictions make for interesting characters.

SHATTER DEAD was slightly different in that the lead character, Susan, while she had some eccentricities and was quick to violence, was meant to be a bit more of an audience identification figure in the writing, but on-set I had Stark play the scenes like she was Clint Eastwood; very cold, playing her emotional cards close to her chest. People don't realize how hard it is to do that kind of acting. When you watch the SD blooper reel you see what a zany, vibrant dame she is in real life.

The question in dime-store-psychology genre literature is always: why do ugly people do ugly things? I'm more interested in seeing how "ugly" people, who might never do a bad thing, are bent by society's hatred of ugliness to do terrible things. There's a Victor Hugo quote that I'm fond of, maybe because it appeals to my liberal guilt: "The guilty one is not he who commits the sin, but the one who causes the darkness". SIXTEEN TONGUES is dark. Hit "play" on the disc and activate the guilt, kiddies.

Why would anyone stay at the Sappho Motel? With the porn covering every surface - do you feel that, in that world, that has contributed to sensory-overload, leaving violence as the only outlet?

The design of the Sappho Motel, to me, looks to me like the interior of your average 42nd Street porn shop taken to the next level. The advertisements certainly are blazingly in-your-face, but that's the nature of selling people essential things that are normally free in the first place; sex, water, cable television. I mean, c'mon -- paying money for cable TV is like being charged money for shit that was free the first time when you're watching a GILLIGAN'S ISLAND re-run, right? What a scam. So you've gotta jazz things up, distract people from the fact that there's no reason for them to be paying for certain goods or services that nature provides for free.

I can't say it's a motel I'd like to stay at, but when I see an S & M club like the recently relocated Hellfire, there's a lot of the same cheesy, candy-colored decorations there and the inhabitants don't even think twice about it. You'd think people who dress up in cool leather outfits on the weekend would have better interior decorating tastes. But the location and the way it looks are secondary to the needs of their lifestyle. I'm sure if it was designed to look like a Norman Rockwell painting the inhabitants would still be fucking and pissing on each other in the hallways.

People give in to the temptation of allowing their senses to become overloaded far too easily. Every morning on the train to work, I see people wearing headphones while reading a newspaper and sipping hot coffee, and I'm amazed at how they coordinate all that. I can't do any of these things while traveling because the train provides me with valuable thinking time to work out problems with life or writing; I can't fill my every waking moment with some kind of pleasurable distraction and I don't know how other people do it. Also, I'm a bit of a klutz.

What was your reaction to some companies returning your DVD due to the disk art? I was pretty surprised by it. I don't think that's a movie you're likely to order by accident.

Honestly, I'm not too surprised by the returns; I warned Alex (my producer) that we'd probably get a reaction like that. The label artwork was pretty extreme but didn't show anything that wasn't displayed quite prominently on the walls of the Sappho Motel at ten times the size. When it happened, Ron at Sub Rosa sent me an e-mail wondering: "What the hell did they think they were ordering? BAMBI?!?" Maybe Bambi is the name of the woman with the spread-eagled three-chambered vagina. Most porno discs that I've seen don't even have artwork that explicit on them, but I thought that what had been designed here was quite appropriate for the project. I tried to make sure everything about the disc, even the menu screens, supported a worldview that would be consistent with the movie viewing experience.

But since the returns seem to be boosting sales with word-of-mouth, I'd like to take a moment to thank the narrow-minded, censoring, pin-headed idiots who returned the discs in the first place. You've gotten me far more sales and attention than I would have gotten if you hadn't been such self-righteous moral guardians to begin with. Sleep well.

P.10: "The Rick Trembles cartoon was published locally the week we screened at Fantasia in a free newspaper called The Montreal Mirror. It was printed in black-and-white in that paper, so this color version was provided exclusively to me by the artist. Rick has had two books of his Motion Picture Purgatory reviews published by FAB Press so far and they are all excellent reads -- great art and great criticism. - Scooter"

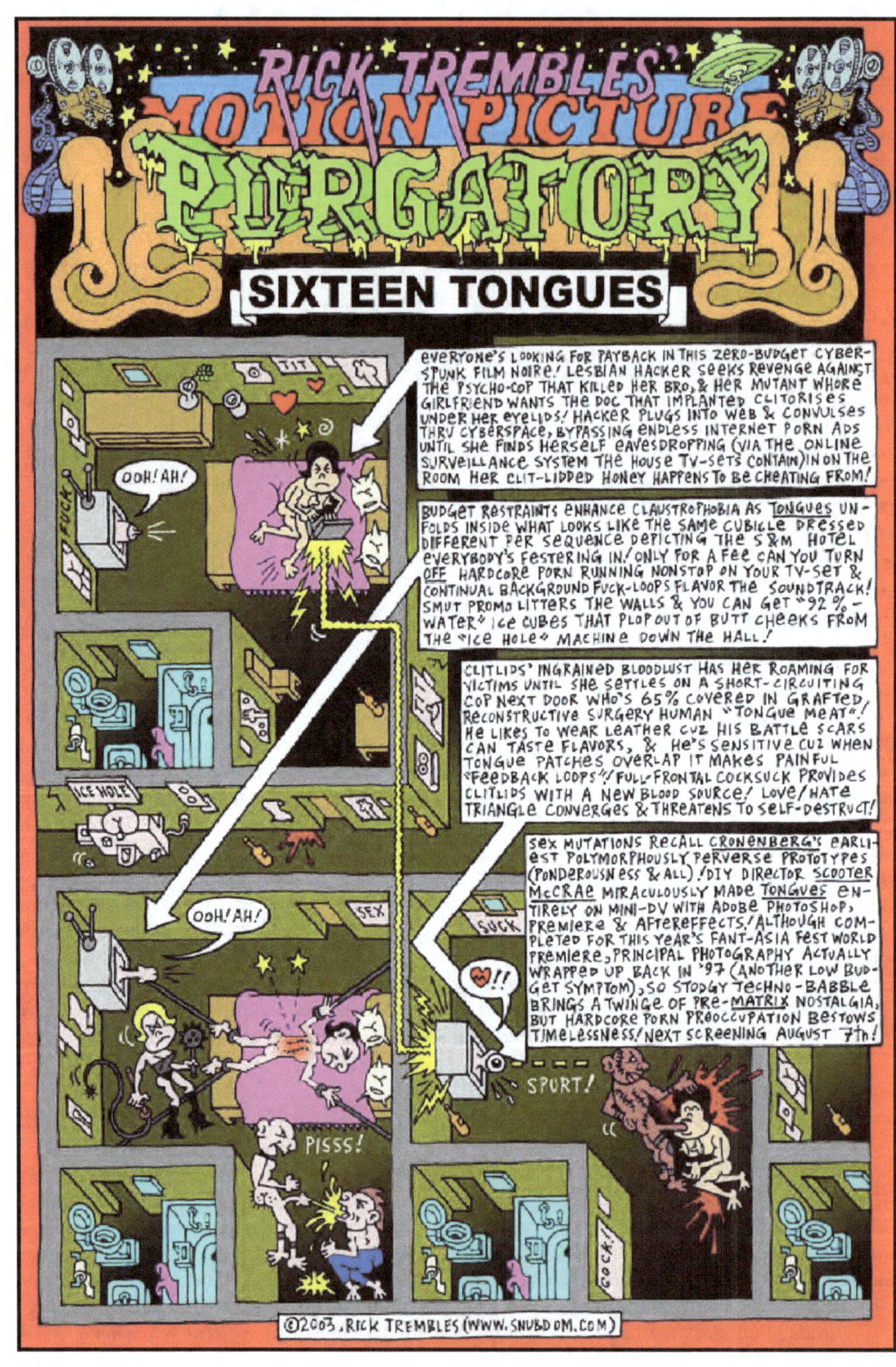

SIXTEEN TONGUES

"They Owe Their Souls to The Company Store..."

A Screenplay

by

Scooter McCrae

Final Draft
July 4th, 1997

SIXTEEN TONGUES Screenplay Notes

PAGE 1:

The first thing that is immediately apparent from the screenplay title page is that this script —unlike the one for SHATTER DEAD, which was composed on a typewriter—was completed on a computer and then printed out. Final draft date is July 4th, 1997 and we began shooting a little over a month later on August 15th. I'm not sure how many drafts it took me to reach this official version, but I'm sure I started out (as was my habit at the time) doing a handwritten first draft that I then input into the little Mac laptop I had at the time. Wanna know how old that laptop was? At the time, it had an LCD screen that was perfect for typing up documents, but there was no way to watch movies or look at photographic images on it. In fact, it's the ancient laptop that you see in the movie itself being used by the Alik character as she sits in bed typing away at one point. But now perhaps I'm getting ahead of myself....

Note that while most of the dialogue in this scene is what we shot, the costumes are quite different and the room itself is not the cell we ended up using. We lucked out getting the prison cell set because it was one of the 'scenario rooms' at the S&M dungeon that we ended up shooting at, and it was a lucky stroke for us as it added some production value and was more fun to shoot in than the bland interrogation room sketchily described in the screenplay.

The description of Torque's physical condition is rather vague and non-committal as I was unsure just how extreme we'd be able to go with the make-up EFX due to budgetary constraints. Thankfully, Glenn Hetrick and Paul Sutt did an excellent job with the design and execution of the make-up and I left the look of it to their combined imaginations as I trusted them and wasn't quite sure myself what would look best on-camera.

L: Producer Alex Kicew send writer/director Scooter McCrae; R: Jane Chase (as Ginny Chin-Chin) and Scooter.
Photographer currently unknown.

1.) INTERIOR POLICE CAGE - NIGHT

The room is dark except for the pool of light created by a single
low-watt light bulb capped by a dark tin lampshade. A Prisoner is
sitting beneath the light, back to the camera, with a leather mask
loosely slipped over their head.

The Sound of metal sliding against itself, and the door to the
room folds open. A Police Officer wearing a frightening uniform
which looks like a bullet-proof cardinal's robe enters; his face
is hidden beneath a hardened face-plate which he zips open and
slides back as he steps forward and loudly closes the door.

                    TORQUE
          "Tah-dah. No surprise for you, right
          scumbag?"

The Officer is Adrian Torque, a damaged looking man of around 35
with strange pink patches placed strategically and cleanly within
the maze of his dark and otherwise awful looking skin.

                    TORQUE
          "Wondering what took me so long, huh?"

The Prisoner in the chair does not move, as hand and foot straps
keep any movement restricted. They are the only two people in
this tiny room. Adrian leans in and grabs the loose ends of
string from the Prisoner's mask and roughly draws them tight.

                    TORQUE
          "There. You happy now? I told you
          I was gonna' do this to you if you
          didn't talk and you didn't talk. So
          now here we are."

Torque finishes the lacing-up process with a good tight knot. The
Prisoner in the mask breathes heavily with fright. Adrian unzips
some squeaky flaps, revealing the eye and mouth holes in the mask.
It's impossible to tell if the masked person is male or female;
just blue eyes, lips and teeth.

                    TORQUE
          "Look at you sitting there; one-hundred
          percent grade-A wet stink shit. Show
          me your smile now, scumbag. Let's see
          those Jolson pearly-whites flashing while
          I have you sing 'Mammy' for me. That
          you're so smart with that pretty little
          mouth of yours is what I've been hearing
          about all over the block."

SIXTEEN TONGUES Screenplay Notes

PAGE 2:

Crawford James, the actor who portrays Torque, was actually our second choice to play the role (it's okay for me to write this now—we told him so at the time). He did a great read, but I was concerned he was almost too sympathetic and our first-choice actor was a much more traditionally 'manly' tough guy who possessed a stonier visage.

The first actor was ready to go but he brought to our attention one change that needed to made to the script in order for him to accept the role: it needed to be made clear to the audience that the prisoner getting beaten up in the opening scene was a woman and not a man.

Producer Alex Kuciw and I didn't even flinch; the answer to that request was a firm NO. My intention was for the sex of the prisoner to be indeterminate, but I was not going to go out of my way to indicate that they were female. I don't think we were even sure at that point who was going to play this part, so it probably could have gone either way. But we found the request distasteful and not a good indicator of other possible roadblocks we might hit along the way as production continued. I didn't want someone who wasn't 100% comfortable doing the role as written.

So we jettisoned that performer and went with Crawford, who was wonderful to work with and pretty fearless about doing everything we asked. The world needs more performers like the gems I ended up working with on this movie.

The actor who ended up playing the prisoner was Johnny Tingle, who was a fixture in the S&M community at the time and he was really looking forward to getting pushed about and 'beaten up' in this scene. His zest helped push Crawford into the manic energy zone he needed for the character at this juncture. It was a fun scene to shoot, but also exhausting for everyone involved.

The Prisoner says nothing, but begins to shake noticeably, head hanging low in shame and fear.

> TORQUE
> "Sure you are. But don't you worry;
> it's just you and me, and the sound-
> proof walls here tonight."

Torque stretches out his arm and solidly slaps the leather head. The Prisoner writhes in silent agony.

> TORQUE
> "OH YEAH! Are you likin' that yet?!
> There's more where that came from!"

Slap! Adrian delivers another solid shock to the Prisoner's head. The Prisoner moans loudly in pain.

> TORQUE
> "You can stop that shit right now;
> you're not in pain yet."

Wham! Torque pulls back and punches the Prisoner squarely between the eyes, breaking the nose of the bouncy leather-head which bobs loosely back and forth. From the mask's mouth hole, dark blood dribbles.

> TORQUE
> "Okay; that hurt, you little fuck.
> You'd better soften up that head of
> yours now before I have to do it
> for you."

The Prisoner looks up at Adrian Torque, eyes burning with pain and rage. Coughing, the Prisoner brings up and spits out a wad of blood.

> PRISONER
> (Hoarse Whisper)
> "Please... stop..."

Torque looks down at the mess on the floor while nursing his punching hand.

> TORQUE
> "Don't go making a mess in here,
> asshole. Now open up your pretty
> little fucking mouth..."

The Prisoner's mouth, frozen with terror, opens up just a crack; more blood mixed with saliva trickles out and down the chin.

PAGE 3:

Looking back on how this scene was written, I'm surprised that I didn't indicate in the description that we were not going to dwell on the more explicit sexual aspects since the actions as described are pretty graphic. In all of the screenplays I have written since, I always make a note early on that no matter how graphically the actions are described, we are not making a pornographic movie and a graphic description of an action does not guarantee that the shoot itself will involve performing said acts for real.

So yeah, while technically SIXTEEN TONGUES would have to rated NC-17 for all of the explicitness, this violent stuff was not meant to be titillating and showing an erect cock was a story detail and not just prurient tomfoolery.

I'll probably be typing this a lot in the book, but I once again thank these actors for trusting me and my instincts when it came to what we shot and how we shot it. I think the on-set vibe was good and everyone felt like we were working on something unusual and unique.

When we submitted this advert to Variety, we tried to be careful how we worded it so we didn't set off any alarms in the editorial department, because once you have the word NUDITY in your description they put you under a microscope to make sure you're not some horrible porno person trolling the acting community for future victims. Sure enough, they asked to see a copy of the screenplay before they would publish the ad (talk about soft censorship going on under the hood!), so of course we complied. And also of course, I chopped out the big sex scene and did some additional rewrites to soften all of the nudity and sexual content before handing it over to them. So a hale and hearty FUCK YOU to Variety for sticking their nose into places it doesn't belong. I'm sorry I didn't save a copy of the 'Disney version' of the script as I'm sure it must have been hilarious. You can also see that at this point Alik was Allen, as we hadn't experienced Alice's great audition yet.

                         TORQUE
            "Yeah, right; you call that 'open'?
            I'm about to make a cunt out of your
            stupid face, and I'm gonna' need a
            whole lot more room than that for what
            I'm gonna' be jammin' in there. Now if
            you make it so I have to ask twice, I'll
            just crowbar your whole fuckin' jawbone
            right off at the hinge."

The mouth of the Prisoner stiffly opens a little bit more.

                         TORQUE
            "Now show me the worm inside that
            rotten-apple head of yours, scumbag."

The tongue of the Prisoner slides forward invitingly, the mouth
opening wider. Torque unzips his leather pants and slides his
hand inside, fumbling around for his cock.

                         TORQUE
            "Here's some good, solid advice for
            you; loosen up your throat and you
            might even enjoy yourself. And I'm
            warning you right now, that the first
            pinch of tooth I feel bearing down on
            me and I'll pull out, spray your face
            and then crack your skull wide open
            and fuck that next."

Torque belts the Prisoner once more across the side of the head
for good measure.

                         TORQUE
            "You heard me; loosen that shit up!
            Now get ready for a long, hot load..."

Torque steps forward and slides his hard cock in the Prisoner's
mask mouth-hole, entering slow and solid, placing his hands on the
flaps of the mask and pulling it down onto his stiff member.

                         TORQUE
            "Yeah, that's it. Fuck it; I don't
            want to hear what you have to say
            anyway. Come on - relax; I know
            you've got some more room in that
            sweet little punk mouth of yours."

Torque forces slow up-and-down movement in the leathery head which
struggles in his tight grasp.

SIXTEEN TONGUES Screenplay Notes

PAGE 4:

Whew! Looks like I was in quite the mood that day when I wrote the climax to this scene…! Thankfully, what we ended up shooting was a bit less extreme than what's written here, although it was certainly extreme enough. I'm sure during rehearsal we streamlined things a little bit to keep the flow of the scene going without having to add yet one more punch and puke to cap it all off.

One detail I enjoyed was that after Torque ejaculates in the prisoner's mouth and blood comes dribbling out, the audience has no idea that this is actually Torque's bloody cum and not the prisoner's blood. This was obviously not the scene to go into an explanation of that plot point, but as a writer it was something I was happy to have planted in plain sight early on for discriminating viewers to enjoy on their umpteenth screening of the movie (because how many people haven't watched TONGUES hundreds of times by now…?!?).

In the movie, the squib effect that the make-up gents provided for this moment is one of my favorite shots in the movie. It was my first time doing a shot like this and they totally nailed the spray on the wall behind the head. We dissolve out of the scene from the withering bloody head to the pornography on a TV screen and the transition is perfect in my mind.

                        TORQUE
            "Oh yeah; there you go, kiddo. You
            keep up that tongue and tonsil action
            and I'll give you just what you want
            you little cunt mouth. You hungry
            little cunt mouth. Uh huh..."

His pumping action becomes more furious as Torque gets ready to
ejaculate. The Prisoner groans loudly and gasps for air; the
request is loudly ignored.

                        TORQUE
            "You're gonna' hold out for air
            just a little bit longer, fuck
            mouth. I'm almost there. I just
            wanna' squirt my shit down the back
            of your throat, hot and sweet, and
            then you'll get all the air you want.
            Oh yeah - I'm almost there, you
            little scumbag..."

Torque pulls the leather-clad Prisoner head down quick and hard on
his cock and ejaculates with a loud grunt that seems to squeak out
of every pore of his stiff body. When he has finished, Torque
pulls the Prisoner's head off of his cock and staggers back with
exhaustion. The Prisoner coughs, bringing up a mouthful of bloody
cum which splats onto the floor with a wet slapping sound.

                        TORQUE
            "What the fuck is this? Didn't I
            tell you not to make a mess in here?
            Who do you think has to do the cleaning
            up after hours in this brick hellhole?!
            You're fucked now, asshole. And I
            mean truly fucked..."

Torque steps forward and unleashes a powerful punch into the
Prisoner's stomach. The Prisoner leans forward and vomits.

                        TORQUE
            "Shit; now that's it; the end. Say
            goodnight, fucker..."

Torque pulls the gun out of his shoulder holster and fires point-
blank into the face of the Prisoner a few times; the leather mask
airs itself out like a dark leather zit with each loud discharge.

Putting the gun away, Torque pulls a handkerchief out of his
pocket and wipes the mess off his biomechanical penis; it's a
nightmarish concoction of flesh and plastic. When he's done, he
deposits the rag in the Prisoner's dead leather mouth.

SIXTEEN TONGUES Screenplay Notes

PAGE 5:

At this point, I had no idea that we would end up creating a fairly elaborate title sequence to start the movie, so I had originally imagined the movie would have a cold open and just the title would briefly show-up at this point. It was a nice idea, but I think what we ended up doing instead was a much better choice. I love the opening credits with our tiny highquality 3CCD medical camera zipping over naked bodies both before and after some evocative charred flesh make-up was applied to our beautiful models. I always thought of it as being our version of one of the classic James Bond opening credits scenes created by Maurice Binder, but with graphic nudity.

Gads, how I wish we had the time and resources to do some Pussy Cola and Cock Juice adverts! In the end, I think the non-stop stream of reverse-censored porno footage (the faces are covered, but not the genitals) was the best and most mind-numbing choice. I can tell you that just being on-set with that tape loop playing constantly while shooting was almost enough to drive anybody and everybody mad after a while. Anonymous bodies constantly fucking non-stop is the equivalent of watching industrial machinery clattering back-and-forth endlessly with no real build-up or climax; a particularly spiritually draining level of Hell.

The enormous amount of voice-over begins on this page and rarely lets up for the rest of the script. It was a conscious decision to try and provide backstory and live commentary to what was happening on-screen. I was definitely inspired by the often dead-pan voice-overs of the characters in David Lynch's DUNE, some of which are hilarious (intentional or not is arguable at a few key moments). I wanted a similar effect here, with the commentary sometimes intertwining with the dialogue to create disorienting results. Sometimes it works and sometimes it doesn't. Oh well. I tried to do something different for whatever that's worth.

5

Closing up his pants, Torque spits on the Prisoner's dead body.
He slips his leather outfit back on like a second skin, zipping it
up until he is completely covered from head to toe. He reaches up
and crunches the overhead lightbulb in his bloodstained hand.

FADE TO BLACK.

CREDIT FADES UP FROM BLACK:

                        SIXTEEN TONGUES

FADE TO BLACK.

2.)   INTERIOR TORQUE'S MOTEL BEDROOM - NIGHT

The only light illuminating the room comes from a television set
that receives scrambled commercials for Pussy Cola and Cock Juice.
Adrian, fully dressed to his gloves, untangles himself from the
blanket as he sits up in bed with a dazed look.

                         TORQUE (V.O.)
               "Two days. I've been asleep in my
               clothes for the past two days. At
               least, I think it's sleep. I don't
               really remember any of it, so I guess
               it must be sleep..."

Adrian unbuckles his belt, tossing it and the gun holstered into
it on the bed as he shakily rises. He stumbles towards the dark
bathroom.

                         TORQUE (V.O.)
               "My name is Adrian Torque. I'm a
               police officer in the light of day.
               Justice is a delicate thing, but it's
               servants must not be...so...delicate..."

3.)   INTERIOR TORQUE'S MOTEL BATHROOM - NIGHT

The overhead light blooms to life as Adrian enters. He pulls out
his wallet and removes a card, running it through a slot next to
the sink, activating an infrared water sensor. Leaning forward,
he activates a spurt of hot water.

                         TORQUE (V.O.)
               "I was damaged in the big one back in
               oh-seven, when the Kiwanis raided the
               Jersey border and poked a Bingo clatch.
               Seventeen dead, including me, but being
               a cop has it's privileges in war time,
               and now I'm a special fella'..."

SIXTEEN TONGUES Screenplay Notes

PAGE 6:

On both this and the previous page Torque's voice-over uses familiar words in unfamiliar ways to create some audience confusion. Is this meant to be slang? Or has the Kiwanis Club really evolved into a terrorist organization? Wait, was there really some kind of melee inside an actual convent? And of course, I had to name check one of my favorite movies, THE BIG SLEEP. I enjoyed the idea of creating a science fiction future world (approximately 2025) where viewers would get the feeling of almost understanding what's going on, but not quite. This was probably a big mistake on my part, but an interesting experiment and I'm glad I gave it a try. Wish me better luck next time!

The bottom of the page introduces us to Ginny Chin-Chin (portrayed as lean, mean, and energetic by the wonderful Jane Chase). In the screenplay, I had her cutting and burning herself in order to try and keep her murderous rampage urges under control, but we abandoned that during the shoot as we already had enough make-up EFX to worry about and adding more work (and having to worry about continuity for that as well) was not something we could handle with our very tiny crew. If we had more time and money, I would have liked to have kept this little detail as I thought it helped make the character more sympathetic and showed that she was really trying to do what she could to not hurt other people.

6

Adrian removes his shirt, revealing the patches of pink, spongy flesh that dots his naturally darker complexion. When the sink is full, the water stops and an L.E.D. readout displays a total of $2.50 being charged.

                    TORQUE (V.O.)
          "They woke me up from that big sleep,
          because they couldn't afford to lose
          the best."

Adrian removes his gloves, careful to make sure that the bare skin of either of them doesn't touch the other one. He dips them one at a time into the hot water, brining up water that he flecks on his chest with his fingers.

                    TORQUE (V.O.)
          "They covered what was left of me with
          a new layer of skin that could stretch
          and feel, made out of the tongue meat of
          the other sixteen nobodies who had been
          made wet against the convent walls that
          awful night. Just goes to show you that
          out on this battlefield, the explosion
          you *hear* is never the one that *kills* you..."

Putting his gloves back on, he rubs the water into his chest and neck and then grabs a towel off the rack. He Exits.

4.) INTERIOR TORQUE'S MOTEL BEDROOM - NIGHT

Adrian sits down on the edge of the bed and dries himself. He coughs and lies back on the bed in pain, spreading out his arms and legs and spasming.

                    TORQUE (V.O.)
          "Fuck! Shit! Goddammit! I need ice!
          Christ! Water is turning into a habit
          I can barely afford anymore."

DISSOLVE TO:

5.) INTERIOR SILENS' MOTEL ROOM - NIGHT

Silhouetted in the darkness, Ginny Chin-Chin sits up in bed and scratches at the series of burn marks and knife scars on her bare arm as her lover, Alik, lies quietly asleep beside her. Ginny is twenty years old and Asian with short, dark hair.

                    GINNY (V.O.)
          "I dreamt I had to give a speech in

SIXTEEN TONGUES Screenplay Notes

PAGE 7:

I'm impressed it took all of seven pages until I finally started scribbling notes in the margins of the script. Usually those start on page 1. In this case, I'm sure it was a late addition and I didn't want to upset the page layout and mess up everything that came afterwards. It was probably added so the actress wouldn't think she'd be walking out into the hallway stark naked.

It also acts as a correction, since later on the page she's described as wearing 'transparent latex underwear that is sticky with sweat'—which doesn't sound too flattering, does it? The shower curtain dress that our costume designer created was a much more elegant solution to the problem of what she should wear.

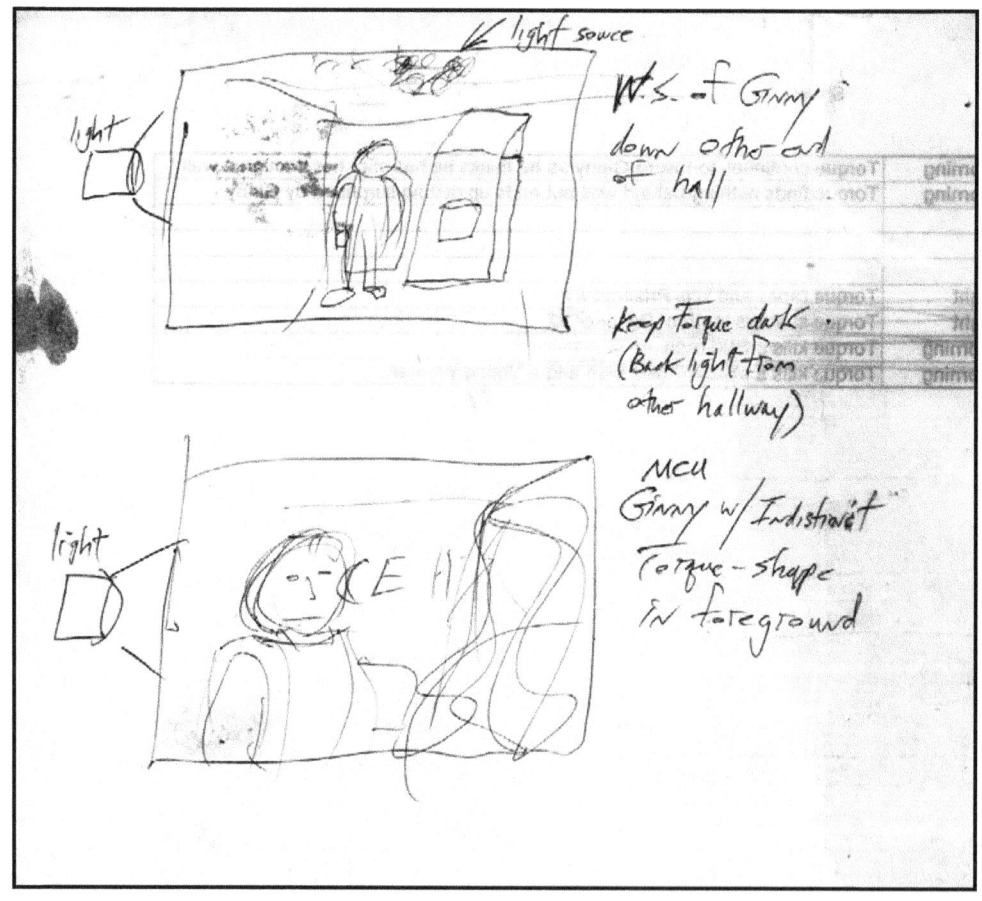

Storyboard for the first meeting between Torque and Ginny by Scooter McCrae.

Note that this hastily drawn scrawl was done on the back of the shooting schedule, which is what you are seeing bleeding through through the image. With our budget, no sheet of paper ever got wasted when it could be used at least two or three times.

24

front of a huge audience of strangers.
And I was so nervous about what I was
gonna' do with my hands ~~while speaking~~,
that I went to a doctor and had my arms
surgically removed. I felt so much
less awkward and spoke to them clearly
as I could, but I don't remember a word
I said."

Ginny sighs and brings her legs out over the side of the bed.

                    GINNY (V.O.)
          "Doctors; I'll bet they were all doctors.
          Now wouldn't that make a lot of sense?
          A thousand mute medicine men wanting to
          hear their creation speak. I hope I told
          them all to fuck off and die."

She balls her hand into a fist that shakes with anger.

*She picks up her
shower curtain dress
from the floor*

DISSOLVE TO:

6.)   INTERIOR MOTEL HALLWAY - NIGHT

Adrian is dressed just enough to cover the pink patches all over
his body, and stiffly wanders down the hall. At the other end of
the hall is an Ice Machine kept under surveillance by a security
camera system and a woman making use of the machinery.

Here we get out first good look at Ginny Chin-Chin; she is a young
woman with powder-white skin and vaguely Asian features. Dressed
in transparent latex underwear that is sticky with sweat, she is
using her credit card to fill-up a tiny bucket with ice.

Adrian and Ginny look at each other suspiciously for a moment from
opposite ends of the hallway as they continue what they are doing.

Adrian is standing behind her now, waiting to use the machine; she
turns to face him, looking him up and down.

                    GINNY
          "Haven't I seen you somewhere before?"

                    TORQUE
          "Are you done with that?"

                    GINNY
          "Yeah; sure."

She moves out of his way. Adrian runs his card through the slider
and positions his bucket under the ice spigot. She continues

PAGE 8:
Although we shot this scene as written, when in the editing room I chopped out this entire page of dialogue as the scene played better and a little bit more tense with the two characters just checking each other out silently while they retrieve their coolant from the Ice Hole dispenser.

Sometimes these things happen and you don't know for sure why. It played fine, but it seemed to be eating up too much time without adding much to the overall story. I do miss it as these exchanges introduced the first time that dialogue and voice-over will be jockeying back-and-forth during conversations, while also giving the characters a few grace notes that reinforce their personality types.

looking at him suspiciously.

> GINNY
> "Yeah, definitely. We must've met at
> a party or something. I never forget
> a face."

> TORQUE
> "I'm sure. This one's a little tougher
> than average to get out of the mind."

> GINNY
> "Nothing a dermatologist couldn't fund
> a new home with."

Adrian stiffens a finger and taps her wet, latex draped shoulder.

> TORQUE
> "Isn't it a little dangerous running
> around the hallways dressed like that?"

> GINNY
> "When I can't afford water, I save up
> sweat. Besides I won't hurt anyone."

> TORQUE (V.O.)
> "This whore's got nice tits."

Adrian snorts and shakes his head.

> TORQUE
> "What'd you say your name was?"

Ginny's attitude becomes more playful, almost seductive; her tone
seems to annoy Adrian.

> GINNY
> "I didn't."

> TORQUE
> "Enlighten me."

> GINNY
> "Ginny. Ginny Chin-Chin."

> TORQUE
> "Uuuh. A real live rock star."

> GINNY
> "Sorry, pal. Now you've got *me* mixed
> up with someone else."

SIXTEEN TONGUES Screenplay Notes

PAGE 9:

More jettisoned dialogue. I was very sorry to lose the line "drug wars, corporate wars and water embargoes" as I thought it gave a brief look into the terrible world outside of this hotel that these people are living in.

Which reminds me that one choice we made that the screenplay backs up was that I didn't want to show any exterior shots of this future world; not even of the hotel itself. Is it in the middle of a big city or on the outskirts of the Las Vegas desert? Does it look like a classy joint or some rundown Podunk hellhole in major need of renovations? I wanted a singularly insular world that had a claustrophobic feel to it, so limiting the production to two hotel rooms, a hallway and a couple of already existing fetish rooms felt just right— even if sticking to our guns might have proven a bit too alienating for most viewers who wanted a little bit more context to understand this world.

Science fiction is a tough genre to judge sometimes. You want to give just enough information for the audience to be able to function in your created world. The danger of providing too much or too little information is that viewers might start asking too many questions while watching and become distracted from the story you are trying to tell. Overall, I'm pleased with what we accomplished, especially given time and budget, but you're always going to second guess yourself once the comments start coming in and you discover what audiences glommed onto and what confused them. It's a tough genre to do innovative work in.

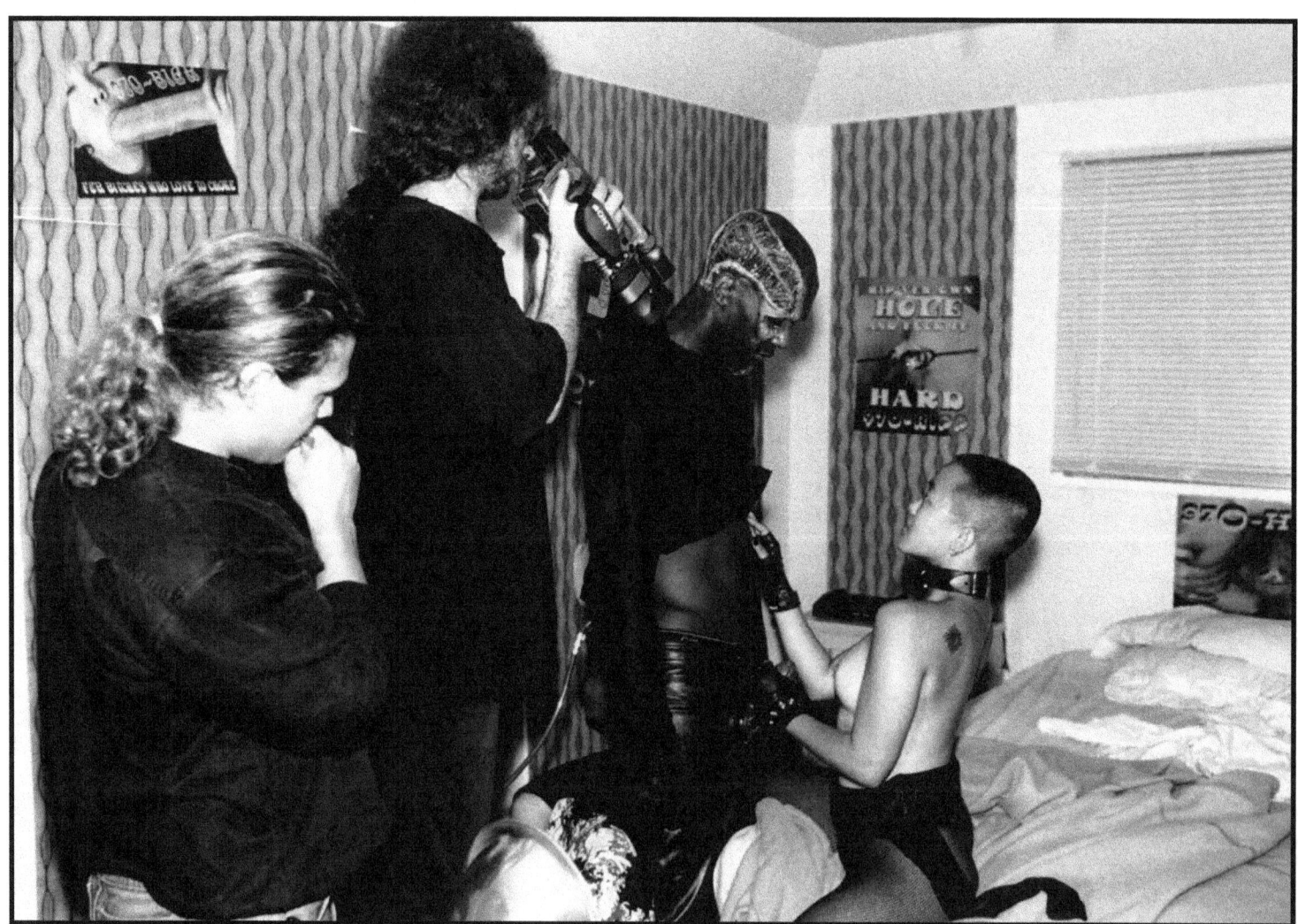

9

> TORQUE (V.O.)
> "Wouldn't be the first time..."

> TORQUE
> "Whatever..."

Torque turns, his ice bucket filled, and begins to walk away; she
follows him down the hallway.

> GINNY
> "Drug wars, corporate wars, and water
> embargoes. What leaves a man looking
> like *that* in this day and age of while-
> you-wait fix 'em ups?"

> TORQUE
> "You really feelin' that lonely girl,
> or are you just hurtin' for some spare
> change tonight?"

> GINNY
> "Not used to all the attention, huh?"

> TORQUE
> "Not without paying for it."

> GINNY
> "Oh no, mister. I feel like the one
> who should be paying you."

Adrian stops walking and Ginny practically bumps into him,

> TORQUE
> "Listen; give me a break tonight, will
> ya'? If you're still in the mood to
> come knockin' after you're done making
> the rounds, you know where I'll be..."

Adrian puts his hand on her shoulder, firmly planting her where
she stands. He turns and walks away, entering his room as she
watches him.

7.) INTERIOR TORQUE'S MOTEL ROOM - NIGHT

Adrian has wrapped his ice up in a wet towel which he applies one
at a time to each of the pink patches of flesh that envelops him.

> TORQUE (V.O.)
> "Ouch. After forty-eight hours of
> being dry, this shit really begins

SIXTEEN TONGUES Screenplay Notes

PAGE 10:

In the early drafts of the script, Alik Silens (the indefatigable Alice Liu, who is just fantastic in a thanklessly difficult role), was a Caucasian male character whom I wanted to be played by Larry "smalls" Johnson from SHATTER DEAD. That changed when Alice showed up to audition for the Ginny Chin-Chin role. She did a great job, but I felt she was wrong for that character. However, I liked her so much that I rewrote the Alik part just for her. Overall, I think this was better for the story as it created more fluidity in the sexuality of the characters and also made the scarcity of white folks an interesting part of the story dynamics, since almost all of them are seen either living like trash on the dirty floors of the facility or sex workers in the hallways of the hotel.

All good science fiction isn't just about predicting the hardware upgrades, it's about analyzing the sociological changes and class structures of the future, which are harder to predict than the inevitable technological advances. The one thing in this script that I never thought would come to pass by 2025 is creating a race of Ginny soldiers, but I went with it anyway as it was helpful in supporting all of the other issues and concerns I wanted to examine. So sometimes you have to give a ridiculous idea a pass in order to get to the good stuff. Did anyone think we'd really have BLADE RUNNER Replicants running around by November 2019? I sincerely doubt even the writers thought so, but they had bigger ideological fish to fry so they went for it.

You can tell this is my personal copy of the shooting script when I have prop reminder notes written on it....

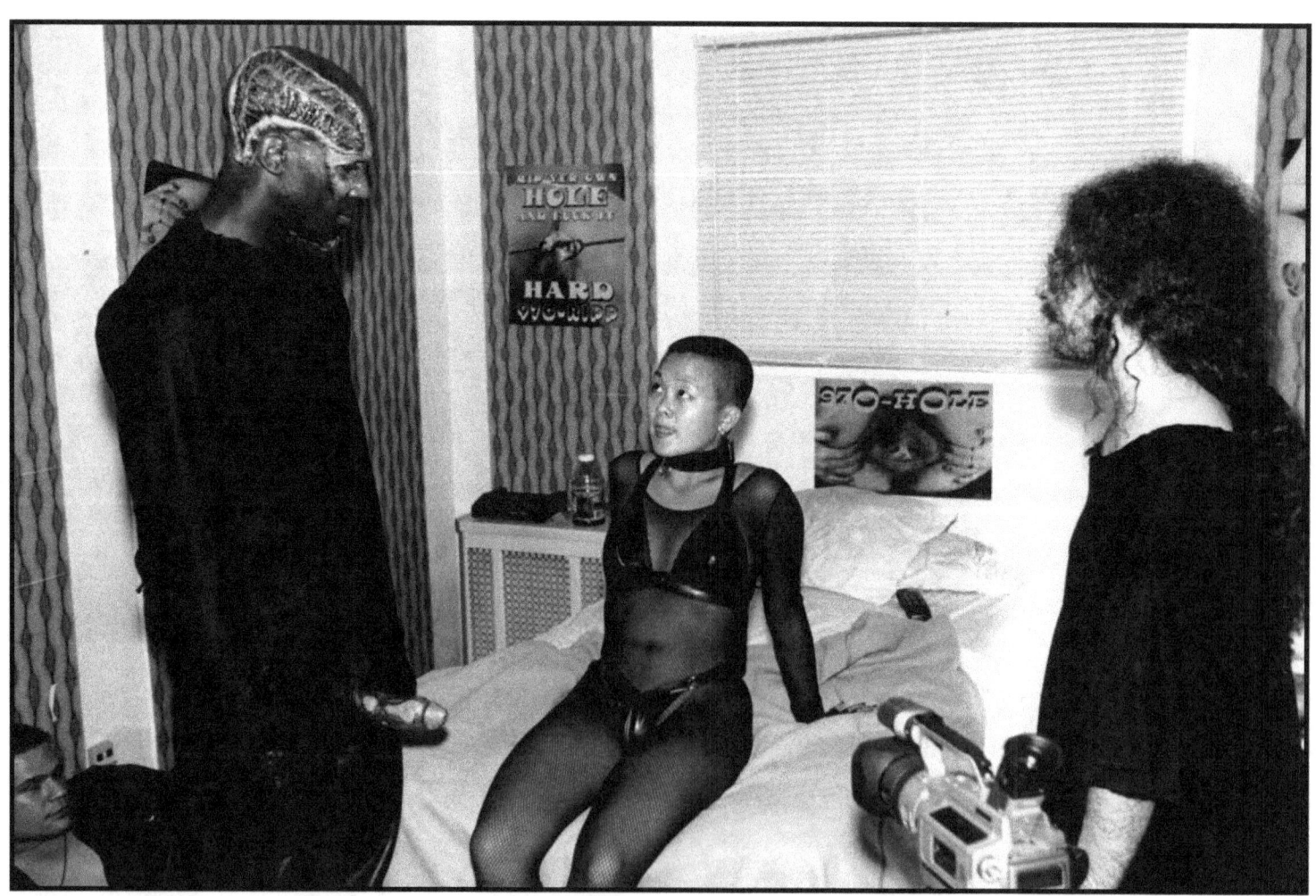

> to hurt; I would've filled the tub
> and slept in it if I could've afforded
> to. But a man's gotta' make do when
> he's on the run..."

Adrian breathes a sigh of relief and rises, stretching himself as he walks around the room. He pours the rest of the ice in his bucket on the bed. He undresses and lays down on top of the cool cubes, closing his eyes and breathing deeply...

8.) INTERIOR SILENS' MOTEL ROOM - NIGHT

Alik Silens is a small-framed woman who looks older than her thirty years; she finishes connecting a credit card with a loose cable dangling from it into a numeric punch-pad device.

                    ALIK
          "There we go; finally got it right."

She sits down in front of the television, runs the card through it's slot, and then turns the T.V. off.

                    ALIK
          "It's about time. I'm sick and tired
          of all this shit..."

The door to the room opens and Ginny enters, placing her full ice bucket down on the edge of her night-table. They acknowledge each other and she begins to unpeel her moist garments.

                    ALIK
          "So how you feelin' now?"

                    GINNY
          "Shitty."

                    ALIK
          "Sorry, honey; I'm workin' on it.
          This thing's been giving me trouble
          the whole ~~damn~~ day."
                      fuckin'
Alik rises with her equipment and walks ~~by her~~ into the bathroom.

8A.) INTERIOR SILENS' MOTEL BATHROOM - NIGHT

Punching some new numbers into her keypad, she runs the card through the sink slot. She waves her hand into the sink infra-red sensing area and a stream of hot water comes pouring out; she splashes some onto her face.

SIXTEEN TONGUES Screenplay Notes

PAGE 11:
Weird that I have written a bunch of performance notes all over this page, but I guess in the heat of production sometimes you need to reiterate the obvious to yourself for those on-set moments when your brain is starting to collapse after 12 hours of shooting.

In my notes I see that I changed the blocking so Ginny is already in the bathroom when Alik enters. I must have made that note during a rehearsal as that change speeded things up a bit, but I'm still surprised I wrote it down here.

Production Designer Dan Ouellette did a great job putting together the prop device that Alik uses to recode the debit card for the payment slots. It always looked real and practical to me. It was one of the things we picked up on Canal Street in New York City back when that block was one electronics store after another that sold used, broken and oddball gear for pretty cheap. I remember making the rounds there a few times when I was a prop department production assistant on BASKET CASE 2. Good times....

 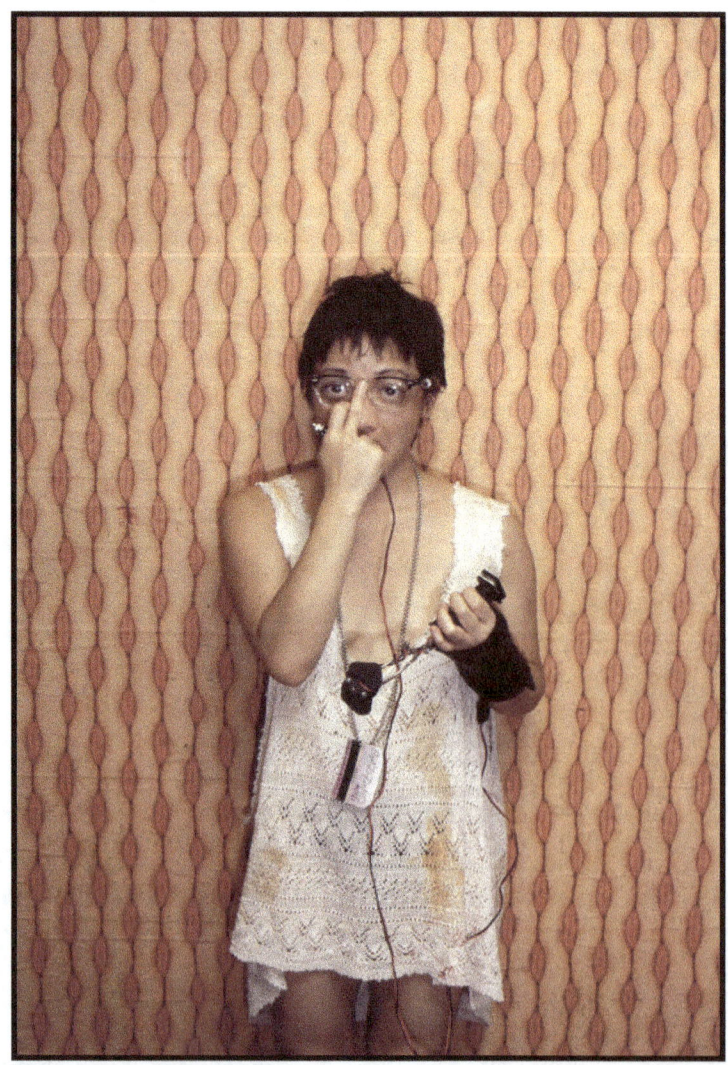

>   ALIK
>   "Oh yeah; that's much more like it."

Alik enters the bathroom - Ginny is already there, waiting.

Behind Alik, Ginny tiredly enters the bathroom. She is naked now,
with a towel slung over her shoulder, revealing an unusually white
powdery look to her flesh. Her bright skin makes the dark circles
under her eyes even more apparent.

>   GINNY
>   "Save ~~a little of that~~ *Some* hot water for
>   me, okay?"

>   ALIK
>   "Sure thing, kiddo."

Alik slides her card through the shower slot. Ginny steps inside
of it, activating a stream of water that she adjusts with a built-
into-the-wall rheostat panel. As the hot water streams off of her
face and into her eyes, she rubs at her eyelids and moans with
pleasure.

>   GINNY
>   "Jeezus, Alik... Thank you..."

8B.) INTERIOR SILENS' MOTEL ROOM - NIGHT

Alik turns off the lights and sits on the edge of the bed as the
sounds of Ginny in the shower continue in the background.

She reaches under the bed, Pulls out a pile of junk she adjusts into some kind of order -

Screwdriver + circuit board fiddling

>   ALIK (V.O.)
>   "I'm running out of tricks - running
>   out of time; I never thought it would
>   take so long to accomplish so much
>   absolute *nothing*..."

8C.) INTERIOR SILENS' MOTEL BATHROOM - NIGHT

Ginny is in the shower, orgasmically sliding her fingers over her
face and eyelids in the stream of hot water.

>   GINNY
>   "Oh yeah... that's it..."

8D.) INTERIOR SILENS' MOTEL ROOM - NIGHT

Alik shakes her head as he places it in her spread palm.

>   ALIK (V.O.)
>   "Almost there, baby. But I can feel
>   it in the air; the quality of feeling
>   that something is *too late*. It's the

SIXTEEN TONGUES Screenplay Notes

PAGE 12:
Another page where the dialogue and voice-over are pretty much fully intact in the final cut. That's a lot of verbiage to have to hack your way through.

And again, similar prop notes. I'm sure that in my mind I was reminding myself that these props actually were part of our 'production value', so I should not lose sight of highlighting them on-camera whenever possible.

I remember when we were interviewing actresses that I warned them upfront that there was a good chance they would be spending a good deal of the shooting schedule naked, and these next couple of pages bears me out. As we had scheduled all of these hotel room scenes between them together in a two-day shooting block in an apartment without air conditioning on August 20th and 21st of 1997, those of us who had to keep our clothes on while working were envious of the actresses who seemed much more comfortable than we were.

Note also that these scenes were shot during what we infamously referred to amongst ourselves as 'the 36 hour day', as we went so late one evening and started so early in the other that I just lay down in the set on the on-camera bed once everyone left after the full day of shooting, closed my eyes for about 3 or 4 hours at most, and greeted everyone as they arrived early the next morning to continue shooting from where we left off. Incredible how professional and enthusiastic everybody was about the production. We could not have completed this project without that level of commitment.

                    'lateness' that has color, a smell, a
                    look even. It's dark and smoky; it
                    stinks of ammonia in the morning and
                    used beer at night. It bores into the
                    back of my head when I try to sleep,
                    and it spits in my face everytime I try
                    to look it in the eyes..."

8E.) INTERIOR SILENS' MOTEL BATHROOM - NIGHT

Ginny rubs her eyes and shivers as an earth-shattering orgasm rips
its way through her body. After the pleasure has passed through
her she leans against the wall for support.

                          GINNY
                    "Did you hear that one, Alik? I
                    was thinking about you. Thanks for
                    the hot water..."

8F.) INTERIOR SILENS' MOTEL ROOM - NIGHT

                          ALIK
                    "Atta' girl, Ginny; you're my sweetheart."

Alik sighs and lies back in bed, spreading herself out on it.

                          ALIK (V.O.)
                    "And so here I am, losing everything
                    I've ever gained with each breath I
                    take, all over again. Revenge is no
                    way for normal people to live their
                    lives. Gods and kings, maybe, but
                    not a poor ol' hacker like me. I'm
                    just a simple little pothole in the
                    information superhighway, and I intend
                    to keep it that way."

Ginny enters the room, dripping wet and drying herself off with a
towel. She falls into bed next to Alik and they breathe in the
silence together for a moment.

                          GINNY
                    "That was pretty intense. Maybe now
                    I'll be able to get more than a few
                    hours of sleep tonight."

                          ALIK
                    "I hope so for your sake, honey."

Alik moves her pile of junk off the bed and pats her hand on it, making a place for Ginny to sit.

SIXTEEN TONGUES Screenplay Notes

PAGE 13:
The second scene in which Torque tortures a prisoner is technically also a dream scene— only this time it's someone else's dream, and not his.

This prisoner is portrayed by make-up EFX artist Glenn Hetrick, who we discovered was also interested in doing acting. He looked the part, was great and a natural on-camera, so it was an easy choice to cast him for real and not just use him because he was also already doing our EFX work.

Note that we did not end up using the tattoo that the screenplay suggested. Glenn already had The Lament Configuration boxes from HELLRAISER inked on his upper arms, so we made sure the costume didn't cover them up as they were so cool looking.

                              GINNY
                "Trust me, Alik. It's ~~just~~ as much
                for your safety as well..."

                              ALIK
                "Really? It's been that bad?"

                              GINNY
                "Yeah, really. But it's not your fault,
                or mine. It's just the way it is."

Alik runs her fingers over Ginny's hair and, grabbing the towel,
helps her dry off her back.

                              ALIK (V.O.)
                "This must be the end of the world;
                the same thing happening over and over
                again because whoever's in charge has
                run out of new ideas and new things to
                have happen. Watching natural disasters
                and the same old conversations spiraling
                around each other in a moron waltz into
                the great big nothing. Never thought
                that I'd be around to see it happen...
                I guess nobody does."

Ginny reaches over and grabs the bucket full of ice. She sits up
on the bed and moves away from Alik.

                              GINNY
                "Okay; let's give it a try and see..."

                              ALIK
                "Good luck, baby."

Alik watches Ginny prepare her ice-packs as she herself lies back
in bed and begins to drift off into sleep.

DISSOLVE TO:

9.) INTERIOR POLICE CAGE - NIGHT

The room is lit from above by a single bulb capped by a dark tin
lampshade. Towering over the Prisoner strapped to the chair is
Adrian Torque in full leather uniform.

The Prisoner has cropped stubble spread out on the back of his
head; on his forehead are tattooed the words: "Abandon All Hope Ye
Who Enter."

PAGE 14:
Once we realized we were not going to create the tattoo in the script, I scratched out the dialogue that referred to it. Looks very professional, doesn't it?

Admittedly, I'm sorry we lost the "subtle stuff" and "I'm an artist" verbal exchanges as I think they would have been funny and a nice change of pace before all of the nastiness explodes on the next page.

Torque leans in close to the Prisoner and runs his finger across the tattooed words while slowly moving his lips to read them; he makes the moment feel dangerous.

>   PRISONER
>   "You know, you're not supposed to
>   touch me, officer."

>   TORQUE
>   "No room left for 'here'?"

>   PRISONER
>   "It's implied. That's enough."

>   TORQUE
>   "Most people don't expect that kind
>   of subtle stuff from a serial rapist
>   with a taste for blood."

>   PRISONER
>   "I'm an artist."

>   TORQUE
>   "Who isn't, asshole? And now howzabout
>   answering some questions before I pull
>   all your fucking teeth out with a pair
>   of pliers?"

>   PRISONER
>   "I've gotten a lot of people passing
>   through here and asking me questions.
>   Your approach is the most unique, so
>   far."

>   TORQUE
>   "That's cause I wanna' know what it
>   was about Tabby Phillips that made
>   you see the words 'next victim' come
>   steaming out of her poor living body
>   before you snuffed her with a bolt
>   cutter. And I've got all night in
>   this Cage booked solid with you until
>   I find out."

>   PRISONER
>   "I'll have to go to the bathroom at
>   some point. I hope you've figured
>   that into your busy schedule."

>   TORQUE
>   "You like women, mister fuck-up?"

PAGE 15:

There's an amusing improvisation Glenn did that made it into the movie. Instead of admonishing Torque to "lay out your thirty bucks like everyone else and get the hardcover edition" as written, Glenn said "you can pick it up on CD-ROM." Twenty-five years later, this is especially amusing, as—yes—the CD-ROM back in 1997 seemed like the wave of the future when it came to where book reading was headed towards. But now here we are in 2022 and brand-new hardcover books are thirty bucks on average and probably nobody remembers what the fuck a CD-ROM is. Which points back to my earlier comment that it's not about predicting the technology of the future but analyzing the sociological changes to come. And I'm pleased to say that despite all the possible digital options, people still seem to enjoy the tactile feel of the pages of a book in their hands.

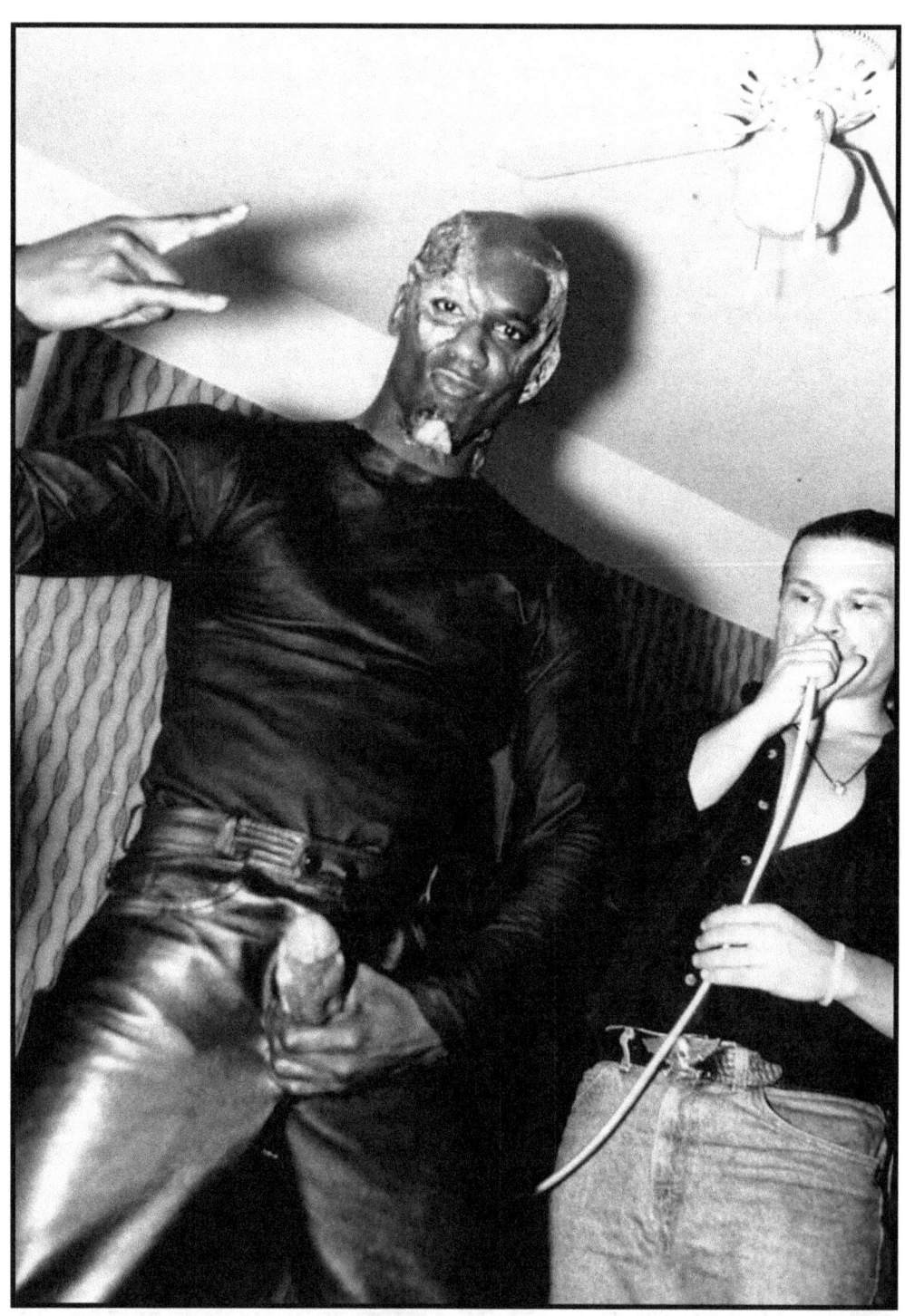

                    PRISONER
        "I have a name, officer."

                    TORQUE (V.O.)
        "*Officer*; just hearing that word out
        of your sick mouth makes me cringe..."

                    TORQUE
        "Maybe it all stems from some child-
        hood psycho shit; is that it? Did your
        mamma touch you funny while you were a
        baby? Or maybe daddy made you suck his
        dick one time too many? Is that what's
        made you the thing I'm about to kick the
        shit out of?"

                    PRISONER
        "Look; I am sick and tired of being
        treated this way. Just untie me and
        toss me back in the can. If you want
        to know what I've done, how I did it
        and what makes me tick, you can lay
        out your thirty bucks like everyone
        else and get the hardcover edition."

                    TORQUE
        "I guess that'll make you a mighty rich
        man when they set you free in about
        twenty-five years?"

                    PRISONER
        "And young enough to enjoy it. Gotta'
        start the killing while you're still
        young, Officer Torque, or the benefits
        run out too soon."

Torque leans forward and puts the full weight of his body behind
the punch he delivers to the Prisoner's face, nearly knocking both
of them over. Recoiling in shock and pain, blood comes pouring
out of the Prisoner's mouth and nose.

                    PRISONER
        "I'll have your badge and your ass
        for this one, you sick, brutal fuck!"

Kicking over the Prisoner's chair, Torque tips him flat on his
back and sits on his chest to hold him down. Torque pulls an odd
looking pair of long silver pliers with tapered tips from his belt
and pries open the Prisoner's mouth with the bottom of his shoe.

PAGE 16:

I have always found the idea of having ones exposed tooth point crushed while leaving the root of the broken tooth intact to the gum to be a horrifying fate. Glad I found a way to incorporate it into the screenplay. It was challenging to shoot on-set, especially with such a tight schedule. This scene was done on the night we shot at the S&M dungeon, so we had a lot of footage to get over the course of a single evening and there were quite a number of special effects involving blood-filled squibs and the fake tooth-and-gums appliance for this scene. It was an all-night shoot and the final night of shooting for the production; August 31st, 1997.

All Light Paintings by Patrick Rochon.

PRISONER
"What the fuck are you doing to me?!"

Inserting the pliers into the Prisoner's mouth, Torque tightens the pinchers around a select tooth.

TORQUE
"When I picked this up and decided to come down here, I really did have every intention of pulling out all of your fuckin' teeth one by one. I was gonna' do that, but then I thought maybe you'ld enjoy that just a little bit too much..."

Adrian's hands shake with exertion as his fingers tighten hard around the handle of the pliers. The Prisoner squeals with pain; there is a loud snap, and Adrian is suddenly showered with tiny bits of calcium and enamal as a tooth shatters.

TORQUE
"The time for talking is over, asshole. It's time for you to suffer and scream out loud in pain."

Skrunch! Torque turns his attentions to the next tooth he will be crushing into dusty pieces.

TORQUE
"I'm looking forward to reading about this in the last chapter..."

The Prisoner's tortured gurgling continues on the Soundtrack as we

DISSOLVE TO:

10.) INTERIOR SILENS' MOTEL ROOM - NIGHT

Alik is restlessly flaying around in bed next to sleeping Ginny, suffering from some kind of nightmare. She awakens with a start and sits up as Ginny continues to sleep.

ALIK (V.O.)
"Killed like he was some kinda fuckin' animal, but he wasn't. He was sick and he needed help. Sure as fuck was no way to lose your brother..."

Silens moves off the bed without disturbing Ginny, who has a large pack of ice resting on her eyes. Alik's hands are wrapped in plastic bags filled with ice, which she unties and removes as she begins to crawl across the floor towards a pile of burnt-out junk.

PAGE 17:

It was fun in the shower scene and this page to sprinkle little hints about the clitoris' that Ginny had implanted under her eyelids. I liked the idea of there being something obvious about what she was doing but not quite understanding how it worked or what was going on until is outright explained in full later in the script. Although I can't say I was directly inspired by DEEP THROAT, I do think that in my subconscious a riddle had been planted by that movie; after the throat, where might be another interesting spot to misplace the female ground zero pleasure point? The eyes seemed like a moist and natural spot for the relocation, especially to a voyeur like myself.

                    ALIK (V.O.)
          "Every night it's the same nightmare.
          I'm sick and tired of it. Makin' me
          dead and lazy inside. Making me
          accept all their sick lies as facts.
          Sometimes they try to trick me into
          thinking that bad things only happen
          in your *mind* every night and not out
          there where it counts. But they do.
          All the time."

                                    the glove & tightens the hinge
She picks up ~~pieces of the wiry construct~~ and examines it between
her blackened fingertips, fitting some parts together and tossing
others away.

                    ALIK (V.O.)
          "Jeezus, look at this shit; looks like
          what I feel like inside. Gotta' fix
          all this stuff up and take another shot
          at it. Sure, it's a dangerous game,
          the truth; but peace of mind is always
          worth it in the end; to me..."
                              at least
Alik coughs and Ginny slowly rolls over, slowly sliding back into
consciousness.

                    GINNY
          "Alik...?"

She sighs and puts down the wires in her hands.

                    ALIK
          "Why don't you go back to sleep."

                    GINNY
          "I can't. I'm tired of trying."

                    ALIK
          "Want something to drink?"

                    GINNY
          "I want you..."

                    ALIK
          "I'm falling apart after my last spin
          in the Web, babe. Look, I know you're
          feeling antsy, so try rubbing your
          eyes for a while and..."

                    GINNY
          "Fucking bitch; stop messing with me!"

SIXTEEN TONGUES Screenplay Notes

PAGE 18:

Towards the bottom of the page, the description of Ginny's outfit is far different than the one we ended up using in the movie—and for that, I'm glad! I love her look in this movie so much that it seemed to me she should have had many more movie adventures based just on looks alone. Every generation needs its BARBARELLA, dammit! And the smarter the better for such a character.

It may seem like a fine point, but I also wanted in the dialogue to point out that I didn't think any of these unusual characters were 'freaks', and that the use of the word 'different' was a more accurate and sympathetic summation of them and the odd situations they found themselves trapped in. It also makes me happier to hear people speak of 'Frankenstein's creature' over 'Frankenstein's monster', which removes the judgment from the description and offers many more interesting possibilities for interpreting the character.

She throws her packet of ice at Alik, and it shatters against the
wall just behind her head.

                         ALIK
             "I've had enough pain for one night,
             thank you."

Ginny begins to blink her eyes uncontrollably and her body spasms
as she tries to speak. She slaps herself across the face a few
times to bring herself under control. Alik watches like she's
seen this a dozen times before, but not without pain.

                         GINNY
             "Oh god, I can't take this anymore.
             I'm starting to get the feeling back
             in them already..."

                         ALIK
             "You know, that whole thing really moved
             me the first time I saw it, but now it's
             just kind of..."

                         GINNY
             "Shut-up, Alik! You're barely worth
             half-a-wink to a girl like me after
             all the wall current you've taken up
             your sorry ass. You're even beginning
             to smell like wet wires..."

                         ALIK
             "Listen, if this is just some kind of
             excuse and you're looking for new meat,
             go air it out in the hallway until you
             find someone who's willing to..."

                         GINNY
             "You really mean that, don't you?
             After all this time, you still see me
             as some kind of fucking *freak*, right?"

Alik sighs and looks down at the floor as Ginny sits up and gets
dressed on the edge of the bed. She slides on thigh-high leather
boots, arm-length leather gloves, and drapes an unbuttoned leather
skirt around her abdomen as they continue talking..

                         ALIK
             "*Freak* is your word... I never called
             you that. I like *different*..."

SIXTEEN TONGUES Screenplay Notes

PAGE 19:

I much prefer that in the movie Ginny holsters her gun to her boot instead of having a skirt to pull it out from. One look at Jane in full costume for the first time and it was obvious that this was NOT a character who would be wearing a leather skirt while hunting in the hotel hallways.

In retrospect, there's probably way too much dialogue between them in this scene, but I was trying to establish the relationship between their characters while also making sure that the dots connecting their story to Torque's was starting to take shape in the mind of the audience. It's inelegant, but I did the best I could at the time.

19

>   GINNY
>   "Yeah, I know how different. You know,
>   I'd settle for *special*, in a crunch."

>   ALIK
>   "Ginny, I'm really just not up to
>   speed on this kinda' word-game stuff
>   right now."

>   GINNY
>   "Fine. I mean, what the fuck have
>   you done for me lately? Everytime
>   you get on the Web you just end up
>   in a smoking heap on the floor with-
>   out a third of the shit you hoped to
>   get in the first place."

>   ALIK
>   "Security is hot-tight with that crazy
>   asshole on the loose right now. You
>   think I can just waltz into the Police
>   Web without trying to figure out about
>   twenty different kinds of friggin'
>   security codes?"

>   GINNY
>   "I've had it up to about *here* with ~~what~~ your
>   needs; give me a shout when you think
>   it's about time you did *me* some favors..."

Ginny, putting on a latex shirt and a leather neck collar, rises
'fully dressed' and moves towards the door.

>   ALIK
>   "Stupid fucking whore..."

In one quick motion, Ginny pulls out a gun from her skirt and
pushes it into Alik's face as she stands over her.

>   GINNY
>   "I didn't make me like this, Alik!
>   You think this is the way I want to
>   live my life?! That's why I came to
>   you in the first place!"

Alik quakes in fear as she stares at the gun muzzle shaking in her
face with anger.

>   SILENS
>   "Shit, Ginny... please don't..."

SIXTEEN TONGUES Screenplay Notes

PAGE 20:
When we shot the bullet through the head bit on-set it didn't end up working and we didn't have the time or resources to do a second take. Unfortunately, the misfire ended up spraying the ceiling and the other walls with blood and other gooey stuff, completely bypassing the place on-camera it was all supposed to hit, right behind Alik's head. We ended up getting the shot we needed a couple of months later in my apartment bathtub, using one of the fleshy-looking wall panels we saved from the set behind the actress. Nobody has ever noticed the switcheroo, as there's no discernable difference between the footage (thanks also to Alice's performance continuity). A small triumph for our lowbudget shoot!

Speaking of those wall panels, in addition to them being designed by Dan Ouellette, he also had the task of physically creating them as well. The production ended up purchasing a thousand dollar printer that output larger than normal sheets of paper, which was a pretty big deal at the time. In the end, it turned out to be cheaper doing it this way as it would have been a lot more expensive if we had to have all of the various posters and wall panels professionally printed instead. Also, can you imagine that we could have found a place that would have printed out even a quarter of the obscene images we plastered the walls with? I don't think so. As an added perk, Dan got to keep the printer when we were done and he got a lot of use out of it for other gigs over the years.

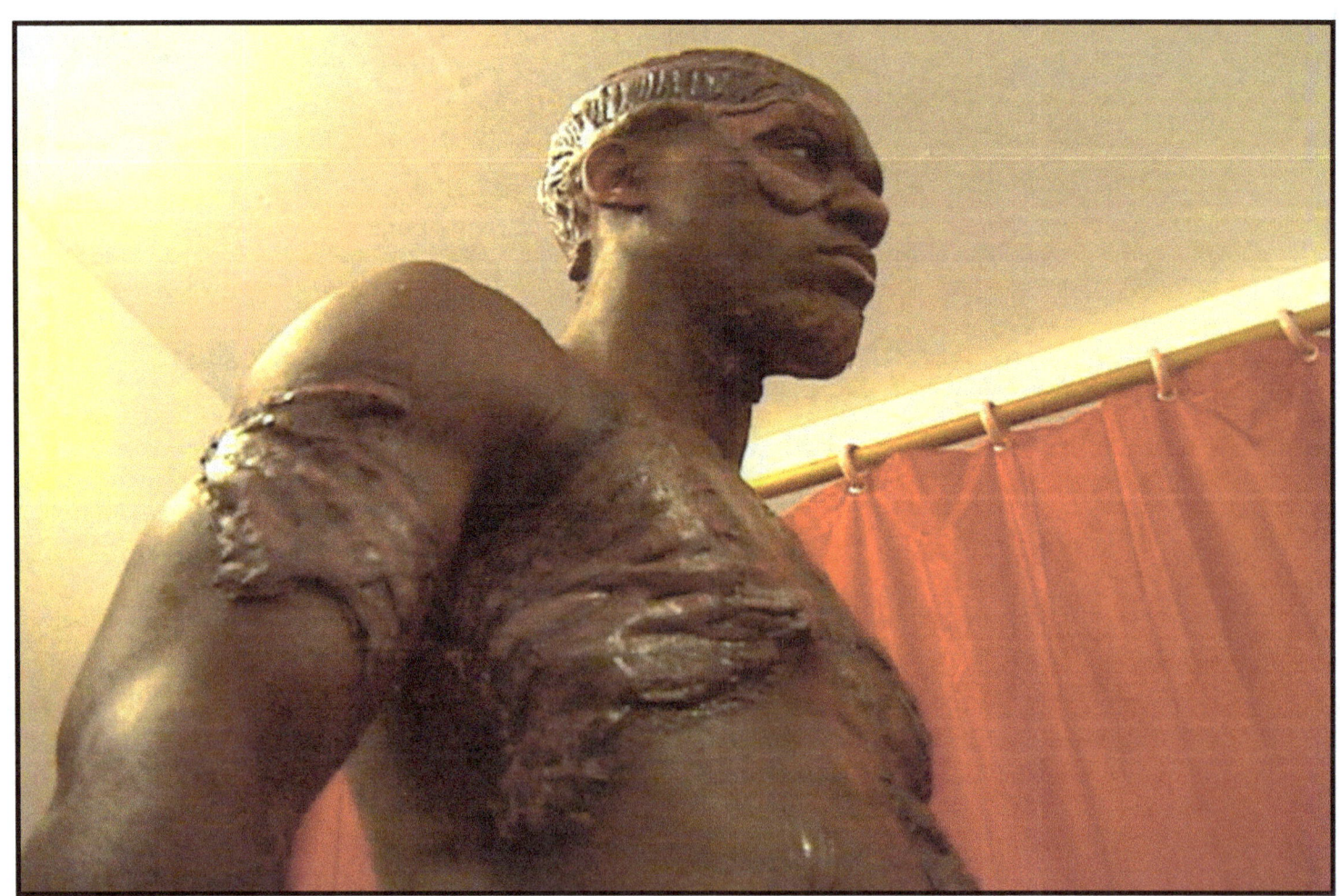

Ginny steps back from Alik, her face ignited with anger. She brings one hand sharply on top of the other with a slap and fires her gun, emptying all the cartridges into Alik's head.

Alik's head is sprayed all over the wall as Ginny's insane rage is finally satisfied. She roars like a triumphant animal.

In SLOW MOTION, the Camera sees the gun's full bullet cartridge falling to the floor, it bounces noiselessly on the carpet, as if we are within a dream...

...and we are. Alik removes her hands from her eyes and sees Ginny staring wide-eyed and unblinkingly. Without turning her gaze from Alik, she kneels to pick-up the fallen bullet cartridge.

> ALIK
> "For chrissakes, that was way too close
> for my tastes..."

> GINNY
> "It's not *me*, Alik, but the *instinct*.
> I'm programmed to pull the trigger, but
> *not* to render the gun harmless first.
> That's a ~~pretty~~ special modification
> I've been able to make because of the
> way I feel about you. I'd think a
> brainy gal like you would appreciate
> something like that."

> ALIK (V.O.)
> "I know, and *I do*, my broken Venus..."

> ALIK
> "I promise you one day we're gonna' find
> the scumbag who ashcanned you."

> GINNY
> "You keep working on that, why don't
> you? Look, I know that you know better
> than to pull that kinda' stuff on me;
> you must be one tired little hacker
> tonight, Alik..."

> ALIK
> "Yeah, I am..."

Ginny lowers her gun and gets on her knees, nuzzling at Alik's exposed abdomen and sniffing at all her parts.

PAGE 21:
How amazing are these two actresses? Nearly half a page of dramatic dialogue that Jane delivers to Alice's exposed crotch while at close range. That's serious dedication on both of their parts, and I will always love them both for putting their trust in me that you could shoot such a thing in a serious manner without embarrassing either of them as people or performers. Taking a risk every now and again is at least half the fun of making a movie.

                    GINNY
     "I can smell the blood inside you,
     but it's not out here yet, is it?"

                    ALIK
     No, not yet. But soon. Probably in
     about two more days.

                    GINNY
     "I don't think I can wait. Not the
     way I'm feeling right now. *Too Weak...*

                    ALIK
     "I understand... I really do."

Ginny rises and steps out of Alik's face with an expression of
longing. Alik exhales deeply and crawls back to the bed as Ginny
Exits the room without even looking back at her.

                    SILENS (V.O.)
     "You poor ~~thing, I hope~~ tonight you can
     find a way to do what needs to be done
     without anyone getting hurt..."

11.) INTERIOR MOTEL BASEMENT HALLWAY - NIGHT

Ginny is slowly walking along in the darkened hallways of the
Motel Basement, stepping over the fallen bodies of derelicts
asleep in garbage and their own sour piss.

                    GINNY (V.O.)
     "Jeezus, my eyes are wet and hungry
     tonight; just smelling all the hard
     man-meat in this place is making my
     lids go fuckin' crazy..."

Ginny sits down on the floor across from one of the sleeping bums
on the hallway floor. She brings her legs up under her chin and
rests her head, examining the face of an unconscious Derelict.

                    GINNY (V.O.)
     "What are you doing here? You, who
     must have started out with a home,
     and family and friends who loved you.
     Why are you lying here on the floor
     while some escapee from a petri dish
     like me can afford a room? Is that the
     cruel trick life's played on you? Or
     did I kill everyone who could have
     helped you without realizing it?"

PAGE 22:
The actor playing the derelict was the oldest performer in the entire cast. It's always nice to have someone older— like Robert Welles as The Preacher Man in SHATTER DEAD—who brings a bit of gravitas to the proceedings so it doesn't look like it was made by just a bunch of twenty-something year old's running around with a camcorder. Okay, maybe we dirtied him up a bit and had him lying in hallway filth, but it's a nice moment and I like Jane's disgusted reaction to him "tooling around" inside her headspace.

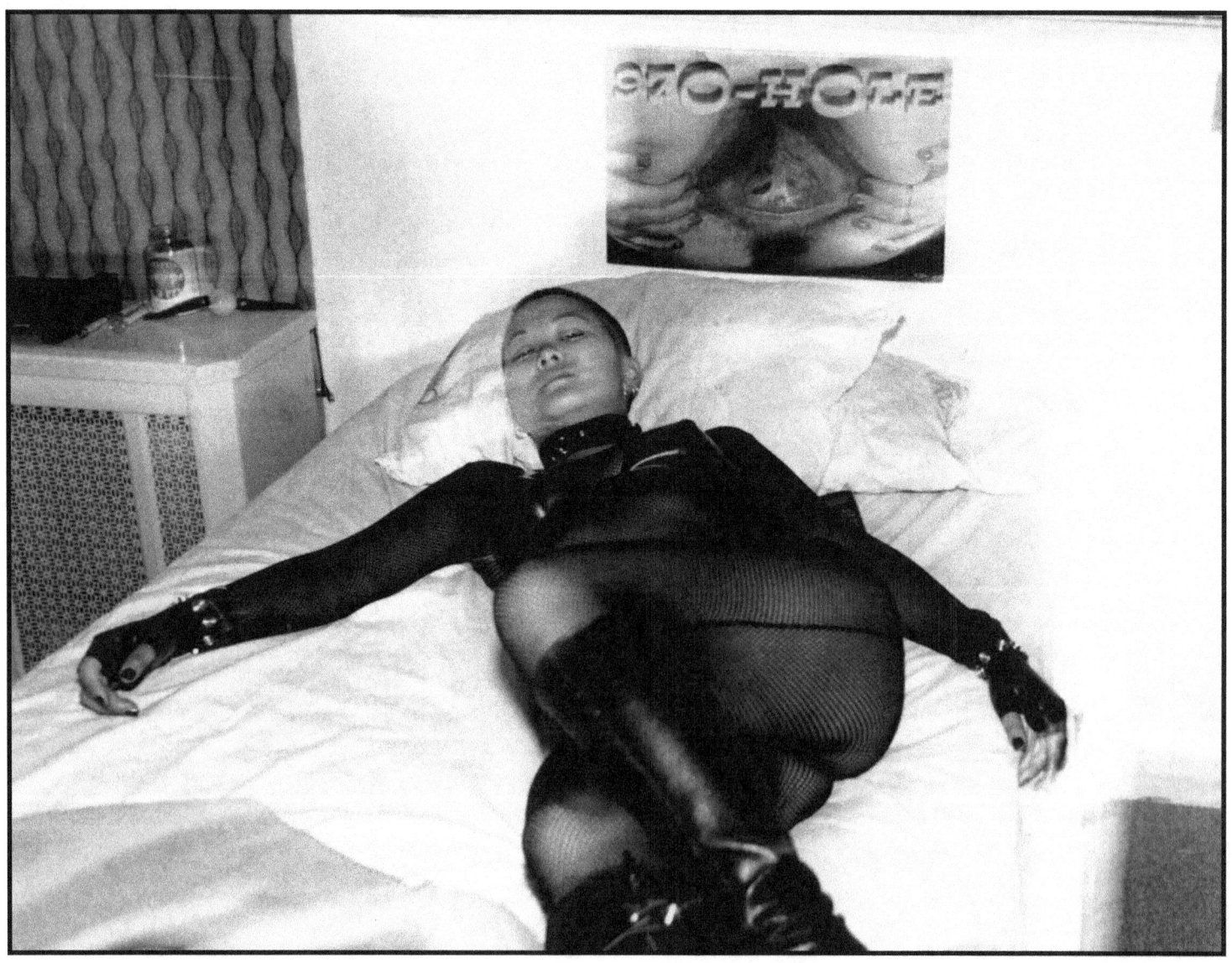

She reaches out to the sleeping Derelict and pats his greasy hair
as she whispers to herself.

                    GINNY
          "Whatever I've done to you, I'm sorry."

The Derelict awakens, sees Ginny and sighs. His eyes wander from
her face to her legs and whatever else as he scans her body with
his hungry eyes.

                    DERELICT
          "Hey there, young lady... I'm... uh..."

                    GINNY
          "Shhh, old man. I know what you want,
          but you can't afford it. Your wallet
          or your body; I could shatter them both
          with a sneeze, I think."

                    DERELICT
          "Howzabout a ciggie for a peek, honey?"

She presents a tone of disapointment, but expectation.

                    GINNY
          "Lotta' good that does me."

                    DERELICT
          "I'd offer you a drink, but..."

                    GINNY
          "Now you've got my interest. What have
          you got burning a hole in your pocket
          besides your half-a-cock?"

The Derelict reaches into his jacket and pulls out a bottle of
Southern Comfort.

                    DERELICT
          "Got the devil's cough polish."

Ginny holds out her hand and the Derelict passes her the bottle.
She takes a hearty drink, and gives it back to him.

                    GINNY
          "So what's in it for you, grandpa?"

                    DERELICT
          "Can I touch you?"

SIXTEEN TONGUES Screenplay Notes

PAGE 23:

Jeezus, enough with the non-stop dialogue and voice-over already, eh? I think this may be the wordiest script I've ever written, especially compared to the on-screen action ratio (ie: people are yammering while standing in place a lot more than anything else they could be doing instead). At the time, that was kind of the intention, but in retrospect there really is too much talking and at a certain point it just become noise. Too much information for the audience leads to overload, a loss of interest in what is being said and, finally, viewer apathy. I say this despite the fact—as you'll see reading through the screenplay—that we ended up cutting out whole swathes of dialogue and voice-over in the edit room. I'm sure at the time I was also concerned with ending up with a movie that ran full feature-length. We made our 82 minutes with plenty to spare on the cutting room floor.

                    GINNY
        "Sure; be naughty, but polite about it."

The Derelict touches Ginny's lower leg, working his way up the
knee and thigh with gentle, but sloppy, squeezes.

                    GINNY (V.O.)
        "Just like everyone I've ever met; a
        price tag with a half-off sale printed
        on the other side if you take the time
        to flip it over. Just like the last
        punk who thought they could help me as
        long as I stayed naked and flat on my
        back. God damn, just like..."

                    DERELICT
        "Just like my little girl..."

                    GINNY
        "Sure; whatever. Keep on rubbing it,
        daddy. That feels real nice..."

The Derelict's eager hand is moving up-and-down between Ginny's
legs, shakily stroking near her crotch as she closes her eyes and
opens her mouth in mock enjoyment.

                    GINNY (V.O.)
        "Sick little fucker. What is it about
        daddies and their little girls? Does
        every one of us know what it's like to
        have daddy steal-a-feel when nobody is
        looking? I know I woulda' killed my
        old man if I'd a had one..."

                    DERELICT
        "It wasn't like that..."

                    GINNY
        "Huh? What's that, old man?"

                    DERELICT
        "I woulda' never touched my little girl."

Opening her eyes and falling out of her false ecstacy, Ginny leans
forward angrily.

                    GINNY
        "What the fuck?!"

                    DERELICT
        "Nothing."

PAGE 24:
Note to myself to shoot what should probably should have gotten its own scene number— or at least an 11B status since it continues directly from the derelict scene. We must have shot these two bits on different days for some reason, even though they shared the same location. It might have had to do with a make-up EFX reason, since blood was involved for the scene where Ginny is pounding the walls of the hotel. I've always been fond of this moment for the camerawork, Jane's performance and the music that accompanies it.

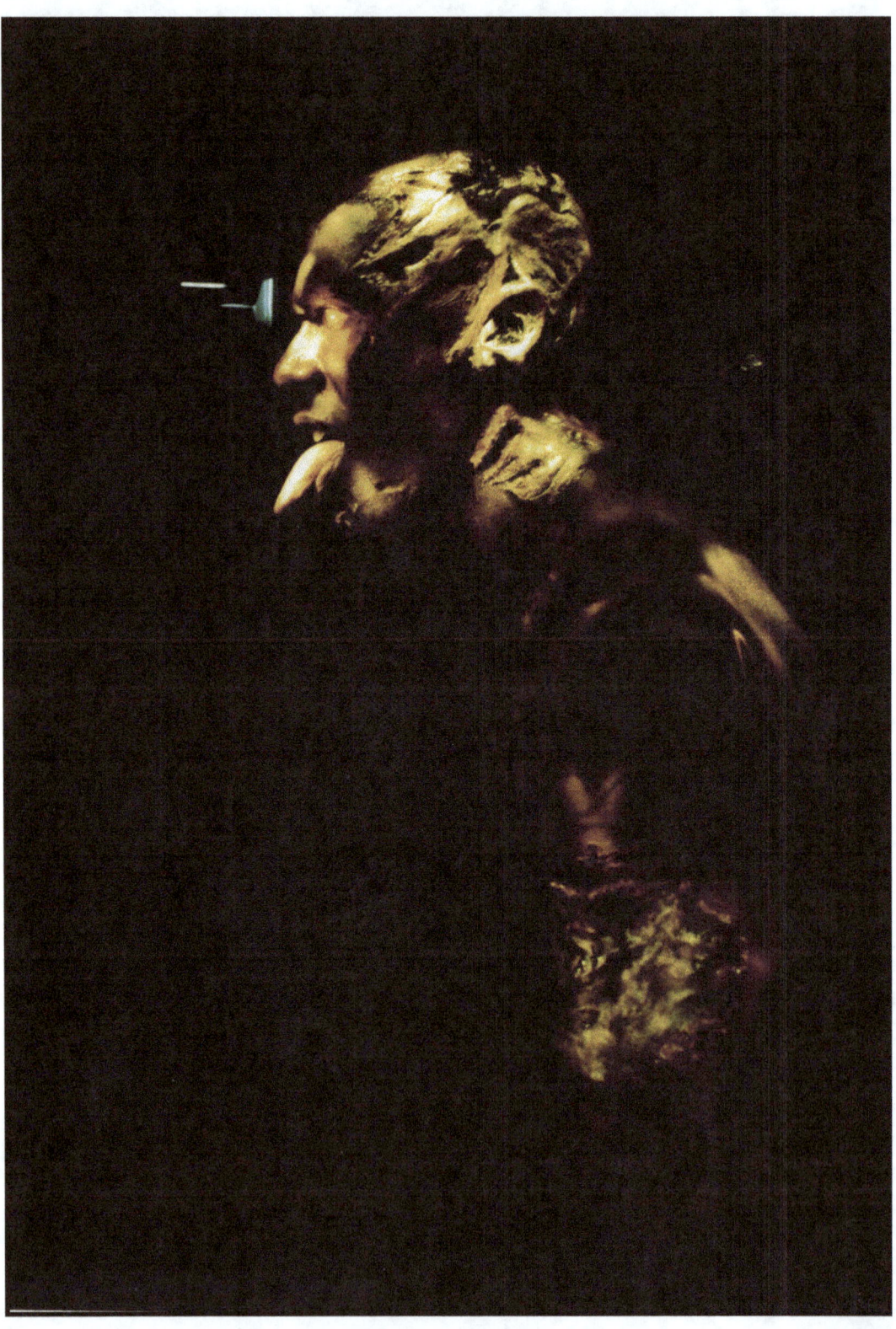

Ginny pulls her leg back and kicks his hand away from her as the
Derelict recoils, upset.

> GINNY
> "You've been tooling around in my head,
> haven't you? You 'paths are all a bunch
> of scumbags. My shit isn't any of your
> fuckin' business. No wonder they left
> you for dead on the floor."

Ginny wipes off her leg and rises. She walks towards the other
end of the hallway, keeping her fury barely in check.

> DERELICT
> "I'm sorry! It's not my fault! I can't
> turn it off!"

> GINNY
> "It's one thing to be born a fuck-up,
> old man. It's another thing to let the
> whole world know about it. Think about
> *that* while you're jerking off into sleep..."

The old Derelict has tears streaming out of his eyes as Ginny
disapears around the corner.

> DERELICT
> "Please don't leave me... I didn't
> choose to be like this; nobody wants
> to be a freak... It was an accident..."

pounding walls w/ fists

SLOW DISSOLVE: Ginny's Voice-Over begins as she wanders down this
Hallway and into another Hallway.

> GINNY (V.O.)
> "Christ, it figures; I think I was
> beginning to like the way he was touching
> me. Now *that's* a weird feeling..."

Ginny bangs her head along the wall as she walks, causing her nose
to bleed as she continues walking.

> GINNY
> "No kill. Not to kill. Don't kill.
> Must keep control. No kill..."

12.) INTERIOR SILEN'S MOTEL ROOM - NIGHT

Alik is sitting in front of her laptop computer, tooling around on
the World Wide Web.

Sitting in Bed

SIXTEEN TONGUES Screenplay Notes

PAGE 25:

In the movie, this scene ends before anything involving the ring that Alik examines or the pierced vagina body double. We never shot either of these. I'm not sure at what point we decided to drop these shots, but I don't miss them as we had enough going on without introducing any additional body modification subplots to an already over-complicated storyline. I suspect that Jane was probably relieved as well that we didn't have an explicit insert shot of someone else's vagina that would have been meant to represent hers. It was a pretty extreme choice to have made, and yes—I will admit to missing the 'Olympics' comment that Alik makes on the next page.

Revisiting the script now, one thing that pleases me is that I'm glad to see I gave absolutely zero fucks about what might be considered impolite material being casually mixed into this science fiction world. Images that many would consider pornographic are integrated into the story without passing judgment on them. Just another detail to help build up more layers in the world building.

                    ALIK (V.O.)
          "She's right, as usual, and now I can't
          sleep. Still too much work that needs
          to be done. Gotta' slide me some late
          Triple-U's and dust the Web with Snatch..."

Alik types in a command:

              "INITIATE SNATCH PROGRAM"

The Computer Screen darkens with a page of binary information.

                    ALIK (V.O.)
          "Snatch is all I have left now. The
          only thing left in my repertoire that's
          gonna' get me the passwords I need."

Alik continues clumsily typing.

                    ALIK (V.O.)
          "Typing; slowest way to work the
          interface. I'll probably spend the
          rest of the night doing this with
          all the flags I'll be slappin' in
          the ether along the way. What a
          total waste of my time..."

Alik stops typing and rubs at her tired eyes.

                    ALIK (V.O.)
          "Next, I've gotta' figure out a way to
          make this work without all this keyboard
          jockeying. Get this whole operation a
          lot more like 'one-stop-shopping' for me."

Momentarily distracted, Alik sits back and pulls out a golden hoop
earring from her laptop set-up which she rolls around in her
fingertips, examining it in the light from the computer screen.

                    ALIK (V.O.)
          "As soon as the time's right, baby,
          I've got a little something here that
          will cheer you up..."

DISSOLVE TO:

14A.) DAYDREAM CLOSE-UP - NIGHT

Close-Up of Ginny's pubic mound as she runs her fingers delicately
over it, spreading her vaginal lips to reveal about a half-dozen
rings dangling from her pink flesh. (A PIERCED BODY DOUBLE)

SIXTEEN TONGUES Screenplay Notes

PAGE 26:

I'm not sure what inspired me to write the 'almost-happy scene' comment in the margin, but it is funny and kind of true. This scene went on forever and got trimmed to deliver the bare essentials of understanding exactly what Alik was trying to accomplish when she jacked her brain into this early version of the internet.

The blocking also got changed to keep them both just lying in bed and eating the whole time as it was easier and saved us from having to do any additional set-ups. Which was a good idea, as this shoot was also part of the 36 hour day I mentioned earlier and we needed to move as fast and furious as possible from one scene to the next. The entire shooting schedule was only 10 days to shoot 77 pages of script (not including the opening title footage which we shot months later over the course of an afternoon), and every day had some kind of action set piece or special make-up EFX that needed to get done. It was the tightest and craziest shooting schedule I've ever had to deal with.

26

> GINNY (V.O.)
> "It's beautiful, Alik. Thanks."

> ALIK (V.O.)
> "Look at you; now you've got more
> rings than the olympics down there."

> GINNY (V.O.)
> "I love you so much..."

Alik's hand comes into Frame and she brushes her fingertips over
Ginny's exposed pubic region and the display of rings.

DISSOLVE TO:

15.) INTERIOR SILEN'S MOTEL ROOM - DAYTIME

FLASHBACK: Bright red light is pouring in through the room's half-
parted venetian slits as Alik stands naked at the window, holding
up a pair of thick sunglasses to her eyes.

> ALIK
> "Jeezus, that is one bad U.V. day
> out there..."

> GINNY
> "Oh no, you're not gonna' try to
> change the subject again, are you?"

Alik puts down the glasses and turns to face Ginny; she is also
lounging around naked, lying in bed and eating some leftover food
from a carton with a fork.

> GINNY
> "I still don't understand why you
> have to do it two different ways
> like that; typing and scrambling
> is a fuckin' waste of time!"

> ALIK
> "Ginny, you've just gotta' trust me
> on this one. The only way I can
> slide into a system without setting
> off all the security flags is to not
> trigger or change anything as I go
> along with the electrical flow; you
> understand that much, right?"

> GINNY
> "Are you patronizing me, Alik?"

Wow, an almost-happy scene in this flick---

SIXTEEN TONGUES Screenplay Notes

PAGE 27:

At some point in an earlier draft, there was yet ANOTHER flashback within this flashback (hat tip to another favorite movie, OUT OF THE PAST), but it got dropped when we realized that there was no way we'd be able to get it done with the schedule and budget we had.

In the missing scene, Alik demonstrates to her colleagues exactly how the SNATCH program works. Basically, it was a computer program that mimicked the look of whatever sign-in page it was sent to attack, so that when a person received this faux replica of the page they thought they were signing into, they were actually giving away their valuable information to this program—hence the term 'snatch'. You see? It wasn't just a dirty sex joke!

I was sorry to lose the scene as the SNATCH program now makes zero sense to viewers, even though it's not essential to the plot. I thought it was pretty cool. Keep in mind that at this point, in 1997, Google didn't even exist yet and people were surfing the internet with dial-up connections. It really was a very different technological world back then, so the idea of breaking into something resembling the internet by jacking in your own nervous system seemed like a pretty neat thing to be able to do and much faster than normal internet speeds at that time. Demonstrating yet again (sorry for repeating myself) that tech predictions are often the weakest link in most science fiction movies.

27

She smiles and sits down in front of her on the edge of the bed;
Alik really is trying to make her understand a difficult concept.

>   ALIK
>   "Listen up, babe; this is some pretty
>   tough stuff I'm trying to make you
>   understand. Bear with me and I promise
>   you'll get it."

>   GINNY
>   "Okay; make your point, geekette."

Alik picks up a forkful of food from Ginny's tray, eating it and
then using the fork to demonstrate her description.

>   GINNY
>   "Oh yeah, nice..."

>   ALIK
>   "Here we are; see how the fork is
>   one long section that breaks off
>   into four smaller ones at this end?
>   When I'm inside the system as an
>   electrical impulse, I'm traveling
>   along the broad section until I
>   reach these four choices."

>   GINNY
>   "Each of which is a different program?"

>   ALIK
>   "No, not quite. All the same program
>   in the end, but different sections of
>   it. I need to go down the right path-
>   way, but I can't determine which is the
>   corrct one on a molecular level. I need
>   to figure all that out on my computer
>   beforehand."

>   GINNY
>   "Or you might go down the wrong strand."

>   ALIK
>   "Exactly. And trigger security systems
>   or alert users of a foreign presence.
>   Don't want any of that now, do we?"

>   GINNY
>   "Wow, that's so smart. I can't believe
>   they kicked you out of school for coming
>   up with this kind of stuff."

SIXTEEN TONGUES Screenplay Notes

PAGE 28:
The laptop that Alik uses throughout these scenes was the one I wrote SIXTEEN TONGUES (and a number of other screenplays) on. It was a Macintosh PowerBook 140, with an LCD screen that was great for text but not so great for images. It was completely out of date by the time we were shooting, so I thought it would be amusing to use it as a retrofitted piece of junk. For what it had to do, it was perfect for the part. There is a shot or two where you actually get to see the working LCD screen in action. I have mostly fond memories of the machine as it allowed me to more easily collaborate with other people on writing projects since we could share our work back-and-forth via floppy discs. Does any of this make any sense to someone under 25 years old…?

                    ALIK
        "Nobody listens to the science geek..."

                    GINNY
        "Geekette."

Ginny leans forward and gives Alik a long, deep kiss on the lips.
Alik responds with a soft caress and they begin to make love.

                    GINNY
        "Hey?"

                    ALIK
        "Yeah?"

                    GINNY
        "How come you didn't use your program
        to change your grades? Why'd you let
        those assholes kick you out of school?"

                    ALIK
        "I guess I'm honest. I guess I'm just
        a really sweet gal; don't you think?"

DISSOLVE TO:

16.) INTERIOR SILEN'S MOTEL ROOM - NIGHT

THE PRESENT: Alik looking at her Computer viewscreen, tapping her
fingers on it uncomfortably, unable to concentrate on anything.

                    ALIK
        "Shit; sweet gal my ass. I'm turning
        into some kind of fucking asshole, babe.
        What the hell am I doin' blowin' out my
        fuse and letting you run around in this
        toilet all by yourself?"

                    ALIK (V.O.)
        "That's not the only reason, is it?
        Feeling a little horny all of a sudden?"

                    ALIK
        "Dammit, I can't stand not knowing."

Alik rises and puts the Web Gear on her hands and forehead as she
plugs it all into a nearby electrical outlet.

                    ALIK (V.O.)
        "This place is too big and dangerous

Gets out of bed onto the floor)

SIXTEEN TONGUES Screenplay Notes

PAGE 29:

Even people who hate this movie—and they are legion—find the dialogue exchange and the concept on this page about having to pay to turn the TV off pretty damned funny. It's my favorite gag in the movie, and I hope that it's in no way prescient as sometimes I really do think that this might be a smart way for a business to generate revenue in our completely overstimulated future.

Although the voice on the other end of the phone was supposed to be a woman, I ended up dubbing the part myself as it was the quickest and easiest way to do it, and as I found the dialogue amusing I think I just wanted to gift the moment to myself after a long and arduous shoot. It's my first cameo in the movie. More about my second cameo when it arrives later on...

Crawford totally nails the fine line between annoyance and disbelief in his tone of voice and helps fully sell the joke. It's probably the only perfect moment in the entire movie, and not every movie gets a perfect moment.

to go through for a tiny thing like
me. I'll start by checking out the
security cameras and all the electronic
monitoring devices in the building."

17.) INTERIOR TORQUE'S MOTEL ROOM - NIGHT

Adrian is sitting on the floor in front of the television with a
portable phone in one hand as he tries to turn off the video image
with the other.

> TORQUE
> "Hello? Yeah, I'm calling in from
> room #173. It's about the television.
> It's been on since I got here, and now
> I can't turn the damn thing off."

> WOMAN (V.O.)
> "Of course, sir. All you have to
> do is run your credit card along
> the slot by the volume knob; then
> you'll be able to turn it off."

> TORQUE
> "Huh? But if I do, won't that put
> some kind of charge on my account?"

The Woman at the other end of the line sounds surprised, and just
a tiny bit annoyed.

> WOMAN (V.O.)
> "Yes, sir. That's the point."

> TORQUE
> "Well, that's kind of crazy, isn't
> it? I mean, I've never been to a
> place that charges you to have the
> T.V. turned off."

> WOMAN (V.O.)
> "It's a fairly new policy since the
> merger, sir. I'm sorry you weren't
> made properly aware of it..."

Click! Adrian turns off the phone and tosses it on the bed.

> TORQUE
> "Jeezus christ; I can't even afford
> to shut this fuckin' thing off..."

PAGE 30:

August 30th sure was a heavy workload shoot day, wasn't it? The reason I wrote this note was to remind myself to grab that footage during the hallway shoots because both performers were on entirely different locations at least a hundred miles apart. The bedroom set was a location on the outskirts of New York City and the hallways were shot at a college in Nassau County (Long Island, New York).

And yes—that bedroom when re-lit and re-dressed served as both bedrooms for our three main characters. Because BUDGET.

Adrian stares at the pornographic advertisements for a moment, sighs, and grabs a towel off the edge of the bed which he tosses over the screen.

He runs his fingers over the flickering fabric and the barely concealed images beneath.

>   TORQUE
>   "Look at all that useless cunt...
>   I swear to fuckin' god I'm gonna'
>   bust a nut looking at this shit..."

There is a knock at the door; Adrian rises and opens it, finding tired Ginny standing there looking at him, her eyes fluttering erratically.

CU Him
CU Her

>   TORQUE
>   "You again? What the hell's wrong
>   with your eyes, kid?"

yeah?

>   GINNY
>   "Please let me in?"

Adrian thinks about it for a moment, not quite sure how to handle this as he taps his fingers on the side of the door.

>   TORQUE (V.O.)
>   "This bitch has got some pretty hot
>   pussy up for grabs tonight..."

>   GINNY
>   "I promise I'll make it worth your
>   while if you do."

>   TORQUE (V.O.)
>   "Like a fucking book; easy to read
>   and impossible to put down."

>   TORQUE
>   "Playing me for a sucker would be
>   the biggest mistake you'd ever make;
>   and the last one..."

>   GINNY
>   "Look at me, man. Isn't it obvious
>   that I need a little bit of help
>   right now?"

He opens the door

Adrian steps back out of the doorway and lets her inside. She quickly moves towards the bed and Adrian closes the door, locking it and turning to face her.

SIXTEEN TONGUES Screenplay Notes

PAGE 31:
From the moment Ginny enters Torque's bedroom, this was the very first scene we shot with these actors together on the second day of shooting. I remember at the time that the reason we did this was to get the most extreme and graphic sex scene on the schedule out of the way, because if anyone was going to quit, this was the scene that would probably be the cause of it.

Thank goodness, everything went smoothly and professionally and no animals were harmed, etc.

I once again cannot say enough good things about these actors. In addition to the sexual content it is also a very long scene that goes on for nine solid pages with a ton of dialogue and interior monologue intertwined throughout. Between the make-up EFX, the lighting and the blocking, it was a difficult scene to pull off in a single day, but we got it done and everyone was exhausted by the time we finished shooting. And thankfully, we got good footage as well.

                    TORQUE (V.O.)
          "Make her beg for it; she needs it
          real bad."

                    TORQUE
          "I'm a little tired so lets make
          this quick. I'm not a doctor..."

                    GINNY
          "A doctor's not what I need."

Ginny sits down on the edge of the bed, tenderly rubbing at her
eyes and moaning loudly. She pauses, and notices the police badge
sitting on the night table next to the bed.

                    GINNY
          "You're a cop?"

Adrian shrugs and snorts as he answers.

                    TORQUE
          "Sure, if that's what you're lookin'
          for."

                    GINNY
          "No, really. I wanna' know."

                    TORQUE
          "Okay, yeah; so what's it to you? I'm
          not about to slap the cuffs on you; not
          unless that's the kind of thing you're
          into."

                    GINNY
          "No; that's pretty mundane stuff for
          a fancy girl like me."

                    TORQUE (V.O.)
          "Slutty little cockteaser."

                    TORQUE
          "Fancy, huh?"

Adrian moves over to stand directly in front of her, towering over
her as they talk.

                    GINNY
          "I'm not like any other girl you've
          ever met. I've got some very special
          modifications..."

SIXTEEN TONGUES Screenplay Notes

PAGE 32:

As you can see by the scratched-out dialogue, there was a certain point at which I decided to not have any of the characters refer to each other's ethnicity, which I felt was a component of what made this future world slightly different from our own. Although it's nowhere explicitly stated in the script, in my own mind I had posited that the African American and Asian population were now the majority wherever this story was taking place, and Caucasians were now not only the minority, but the so-called 'lower class', as they are the ones living in squalor and trying to eke out an existence in the hotel hallways as sex workers. Our lead characters can afford their rooms or are at least smart enough to recharge their credit card by whatever means necessary when needed.

It's important to me as a writer to have this kind of information in my head during the creative process in order to envision a world that has some kind of consistency of thought that links everything together and creates a kind of continuity—even if it's not forthrightly stated out loud.

My favorite line of dialogue on this page is "Nobody talks to a cop unless they need some kind of help." I don't envy anybody the job. It's hard, thankless work.

                    TORQUE
          "You don't look plastic."

Ginny smiles wryly as she suffers.

                    GINNY
          "No, I'm out of a tube, not out of
          a box, big daddy. I'm a pleasure
          model with her happy button in a
          funny place."

                    TORQUE
          "Do tell."

                    GINNY
          "You see, the reason I'm such a
          naughty little girl is that I've
          got a clitoris implanted under the
          epicanthic fold of each eyelid.
          Everytime I blink, I come. I'm a
          little bit maxxed out about now."

                    TORQUE
          "I'm not surprised, you don't look
          Asian, even with the eyejob. I'd say
          the guy who designed you had a weird
          sense of humor."

                    GINNY
          "Oh, yeah. We'll see how hard that
          sick mother-fucker laughs once I catch
          up to him."

                    TORQUE (V.O.)
          "Not as *hard* as my cock is right now."

                    TORQUE
          "None of which tells me what you're
          doing here and why you're telling me
          all this crap or what kind of help it
          is you need."

                    GINNY
          "What makes you think that I need any
          kind of help?"

                    TORQUE
          "Who are you kidding? Nobody talks
          to a cop unless they need some kind
          of help."

33

Ginny nods and gives him a sincere look of understanding.

> GINNY
> "I'm looking at you thinking that
> you've probably got a bottle full
> of hate worked up for the doctor
> botch who did you wrong, just like
> I do. Revenge makes some people
> lonely, but hate can bring people
> together. So what do you think of
> all that?"

> TORQUE (V.O.)
> "I think it's time for you to shut-up
> and start spreading your legs."

Ginny reaches forward and strokes the bulge that is beginning to
form in Adrian's pants.

> TORQUE (V.O.)
> "That's it, girl. Go for it!"

> TORQUE
> "I'm beginning to think you're a
> combat unit that's been modified in
> the tube. That's the only practical
> reason I could see for you're being
> the way you are."

She leans forward and kisses the bulge. Adrian is appreciative,
but unmoved by her actions.

> GINNY
> "That's not a very nice thing to say."

> TORQUE
> "You want polite? Go suck on a fucking
> doorknob. You're a combat mod, and I'll
> bet you've got the numbers to prove it."

> GINNY
> "So what's the big deal if I do?"

Adrian lowers himself onto one knee, bringing himself face-to-face
with her.

> TORQUE
> "I don't need you going spastic
> and snapping me in half while I'm
> givin' it to you, so lift up your
> arm and let's have a look."

SIXTEEN TONGUES Screenplay Notes

PAGE 34:

Hey, this Torque guy has a wireless device inside his head that helps him get onto the internet without having to plug into a physical outlet. That's science fiction, ain't it?

How times have changed. In 1997, such a thing seemed like more of a big deal, and while even smart lightbulbs have Bluetooth connections in them in 2022, we still haven't found a way to jack our body's nervous system directly into the internet yet, but I have a feeling it's something we could possibly see in what's left of our lifetimes.

34

Ginny sighs and slowly lifts up her arm. Adrian leans in close to
get a better look her tattooed numbers.

> TORQUE (V.O.)
> "Nice; this one's gonna' taste sweet."

> GINNY
> "Need something to write those on?"

> TORQUE
> "Shhhh. Quiet, I'm getting a Link."

Silence. A blank expression briefly crosses Adrian's face.

> TORQUE (V.O.)
> "She's a killer. I can smell it."

> GINNY
> "Wow. How are you doing that with-
> out some kind of hardware?"

> TORQUE
> "I'm special, okay?"

> TORQUE (V.O.)
> "Arrest her. She must be arrested."

Adrian leans in and gives Ginny a deep, responsive kiss. Standing
up, he towers over her again and undoes his belt.

> TORQUE (V.O.)
> "Oh my god; what the hell am I doing?"

> GINNY
> "So what did the link-up tell you?
> That I'm gonna' suck your cock?"

> TORQUE
> "Pretty much. But there wasn't a
> price list, so I'll leave that part
> up to you."

> GINNY
> "I'll be getting as much out of this
> as you will, so we'll call it even."

> TORQUE
> "You couldn't afford me anyway."

PAGE 35:

We never did get the biomechanical penis I wanted on-camera for this scene. There was so much going on and the penis that was created didn't really look much different from a typical cock, although it was built to pulsate (which it did just fine). When the shoot was over, Glenn gave me a fantastic biomech dick he created for us to do insert shots with after the fact, but we never did get around to it as trying to match the set background and the lighting proved too difficult, and then finding a hand/mouth double to play with it was another issue as well.

Also, except for a kiss, we never see Ginny actively fellate the cock, which I was fine with. Jane did not feel comfortable going that far with the scene on-camera and I agreed that it was unnecessary because the audience knew what was going on and there was no need to dwell on the explicitness of it. Her performance here is great without having to ask her to do something well outside her comfort zone.

I guess if we were shooting this in 2022, we'd have to have an 'intimacy coordinator' on-set. We had no such thing back in 1997, so we choreographed it as we went along between the actors and where I—as the cameraperson—would be shooting from, so we knew which angles would work best to let the viewer know what was going on without showing them exactly what was going on. It was an interesting 'dance' to partake in.

                         TORQUE (V.O.)
              "This is a bad idea! Dangerous!"

Zip. Ginny starts opening the zipper of Adrian's pants.

                         TORQUE
              "Do you enjoy all that killing, or
              is it just a job to you?"

                         GINNY
              "I could be asking you the same
              question, officer whatever-the-fuck
              your name is."

                         TORQUE
              "Call me Adrian."

                         GINNY
              "That's a girls name, isn't it?"

Adrian reaches into his pants and slides out his biomechanical
penis. It is 'erect', the plastic tubes and flesh pulsating.

                         TORQUE (V.O.)
              "Stupid bitch..."

                         TORQUE
              "Honey, does this look like a girl's
              cock to you?"

                         GINNY
              "Looks like a chess-pole with all
              those little squares."

                         TORQUE
              "Check-mate."

She strokes his cock a few times and then begins sucking on it as
they continue their conversation.

                         TORQUE (V.O.)
              "Holy shit; I'm in love!"

                         TORQUE
              "Hmmm. That feels pretty good."

                         GINNY
              "What were you expecting?"

                         TORQUE
              "Something stranger."

SIXTEEN TONGUES Screenplay Notes

PAGE 36:
More than once on this page the script describes Torque grabbing Ginny's hair. When I originally wrote this, I had no idea we'd be casting someone who had a mostly shaved head. In addition to her natural beauty, I remember being thunderstruck by Jane's overall appearance when we first met her and saw her lack of hair for the first time (she had a full, lustrous head of hair in the headshot she sent us, with a Post-It note attached that informed us she now had a shaved head). She probably might have gotten the part based on looks alone but thank goodness she was also an excellent actress.

In retrospect, I'm not sure why I would have imagined this character who has multiple vaginal piercings and cuts and burns herself to have had a traditional head of hair, but having things change and come into focus as a project develops is part of the fun of it all. We really lucked out with Jane.

                         GINNY
              "Give it time."

                         TORQUE (V.O.)
              "Shut-up and suck!"

Adrian brings one his gloved hands around to grab a handful of
Ginny's hair and control her pace. She pauses occasionally to
make a sarcastic comment.

                         GINNY
              "Why don't you take off the gloves,
              mister romance?"

                         TORQUE
              "Gotta' keep them on."

                         GINNY
              "Oh yeah, you sure don't look like
              one of *those*..."

Adrian pulls her off of his cock and leans down to face her.

                         GINNY
              "Ouch! Let go, asshole!"

                         TORQUE
              "There's a couple of personal notes
              about me you should know, babe, before
              this goes any further. I'm not some
              kind of fuckin' freak like *that*, okay?"

                         GINNY
              "Yeah; so why the fuck do you look like
              Frankenstein, fellow freak?"

                         TORQUE
              "Accident. Lost 65 percent of my skin
              in a blast, and had it all replaced with
              volunteer tongue meat. I'm a little
              bit sensitive about it..."

                         GINNY
              "Well then, you got it; I sure won't go
              bringing that up again."

Adrian smiles and loosens his grip on her hair; he sits down on
the edge of the bed and Ginny moves back from him.

SIXTEEN TONGUES Screenplay Notes

PAGE 37:

Does anyone remember mad cow disease? What an odd reference, even from me! I suspect that part of why I referenced it is that it's a progressive neurological disease that affects the brain and eventually results in dementia (and death). The mental deterioration aspect was appealing to me since Alik hypothesizes later in the script that tongue cells have been surreptitiously replacing Torque's brain cells in an attempt to take over his body. Which is kind of like a biological version of her SNATCH program. There are no coincidences in a screenplay, dammit!

The one thing I'm really sorry we didn't shoot on this page is Torque licking his leather jacket from the shoulder to the wrist. I'm not sure why it got lost in the rehearsal process. Maybe it broke the flow of the dialogue too much? Or perhaps it simply got lost along the way amidst the enormous amount of dialogue and exposition that gets exchanged in this scene. Either way, it would have been a great image and a nifty grace note for the sybaritic side of Torque's character.

Sheet1

Scene #	Location	Context/Time	Brief Description
Friday, August 15th / Saturday, August 16th			
Scene 2	Torque's Motel Bedroom	interior/night	Torque wakes up
Scene 3	Torque's Motel Bathroom	interior/night	Torque fills sink and rinses himself
Scene 4	Torque's Motel Bedroom	interior/night	Torque in frustrated discomfort
Scene 7	Torque's Motel Bedroom	interior/night	Torque relieves himself with ice
Scene 24	Torque's Motel Bedroom	interior/night	Torque argues with himself
Scene 26	Torque's Motel Bedroom	interior/night	Torque continues to argues with himself
Scene 17	Torque's Motel Bedroom	interior/night	Torque can't shut off his t.v.
Scene 17A	Torque's Motel Bedroom	interior/night	Ginny talks to Torque while giving him head
Scene 17B	Torque's Motel Bedroom	interior/night	Ginny continues to go down on Torque
Scene 17C	Torque's Motel Bedroom	interior/night	Torque comes on Ginny's eyelids
Scene 17D	Torque's Motel Bedroom	interior/night	Ginny realizes that she has blood on herself
Scene 18A	Silens' Point Of View	virtual reality	Alik ends up looking at Ginny and Torque
Scene 18C	Silens' Point Of View	virtual reality	Alik still watching Ginny and Torque
Sunday, August 17th / Monday, August 18th			
Scene 21	Motel Hallway	interior/night	Ginny contemplates while strolling
Scene 21A	Motel Hallway	interior/night	Ginny leans against Silens' door
Scene 25A	Adjacent Motel Hallway	interior/night	Tori and Maki yell at Ginny
Scene 25B	Motel Hallway	interior/night	Ginny runs into Terry pissing on a Man
Scene 38	Motel Hallway	interior/morning	Ginny rambles down the hall
Scene 12	Motel Basement Hallway	interior/night	Ginny stops and talks with Derelict
Scene 13	Another Motel Basement Hallway	interior/night	Ginny bangs her head on the walls
Monday, August 18th			
Scene 14	Silens' Motel Bedroom	interior/night	Alik opens Snatch Program on his laptop
Scene 16	Silens' Motel Bedroom	interior/night	Alik thinks fondly of Ginny
Scene 16C	Silens' Motel Bedroom	interior/night	Alik plugs in his WebGear to go looking for Ginny
Scene 18	Silens' Motel Bedroom	interior/night	Alik is sitting on the floor engrossed in his WebGear
Scene 18B	Silens' Motel Bedroom	interior/night	Alik masterbates
Scene 18D	Silens' Point Of View	virtual reality	Alik's eyes flutter in the nothingness of static
Scene 18E	Silens' Motel Bedroom	interior/night	Alik takes off WebGear and crawls into bed

Page 1

Production Schedule for SIXTEEN TONGUES.

                         TORQUE
          "No, I don't mean like *that* kind of
          sensitive. I mean I can't have one
          tongue patch touch another one or I'll
          get a feedback loop. And feedback is
          the worst kind of pain there is when
          you're a guy like me. That's the kind
          of sensitive I mean."

Curious, Ginny reaches out and touches one of the exposed patches
of flesh on Adrian's arm.

                         TORQUE
          "These patches let me feel, but what
          I'm experiencing is a variation on
          taste sensations. It took me some
          time, but I discovered the hard way
          that I don't like the taste of
          synthetics on my skin. So I wear
          leather, because of it's flavor."

                         GINNY
          "Lucky for you that mad-cow shit took
          out two-thirds of the bovines. I sure
          never saw the price of skin so cheap."

                         ADRIAN
          "Yeah; I guess the only unfortunate
          by-product of this little discovery
          is that I've developed a bit of a
          habit..."

                         GINNY
          "A taste..."

                         TORQUE (V.O.)
          "A fetish."

Adrian takes his arm away from Ginny, bringing it up and lovingly
licking the leather from the shoulder to the wrist.

                         GINNY
          "That's why you don't wear any kind of
          make-up to cover that up?"

                         TORQUE
          "Try gargling with mascara or chowing
          down on lipstick sometime and you'll
          you'll see what I mean. Looking good
          tastes like shit all over..."

SIXTEEN TONGUES Screenplay Notes

PAGE 38:

This is the page where an awful lot of story arcs finally come together. Ginny craves blood to calm her shattered nerves, Torque ejaculates blood in order to get a real-deal orgasmic jolt when he cums and Alik is a voyeur who takes some pleasure in watching Ginny cheating on her. Yep, there's a lot to unpack here.

In the past, I've referred to the SIXTEEN TONGUES story as a "what if THE GOOD, THE BAD AND THE UGLY took place inside two future hotel rooms instead of the Civil War era West?" exercise in writing. To be clear, I am no way trying to compare the result of what we tried to do here with one of the greatest of cinematic masterpieces, but I was intrigued to try and use Leone's storytelling template and shifting character alliances as a springboard for a completely different story that—nonetheless—took its inspiration from what he had wrought.

And while things might feel a bit contrived because of the attempt to connect everything together, I really did try my best. Hopefully after 25 years I'm a slightly better writer now.

Sheet1

Scene 8A	Silens' Motel Bedroom	interior/night	Alik sits on bed and thinks
Scene 8B	Silens' Motel Bedroom	interior/night	Alik still thinking to himself
Wednesday, August 20th			
Scene 5	Silens' Motel Bedroom	interior/night	Ginny wakes from sleep
Scene 8	Silens' Motel Bedroom	interior/night	Alik talks briefly with Ginny
Scene 8C	Silens' Motel Bedroom	interior/night	Alik watches Ginny go to sleep
Scene 9	Silens' Motel Bathroom	interior/night	Alik washes and turns on shower for Ginny
Scene 9A	Silens' Motel Bathroom	interior/night	Alik fingers her eyelids in shower
Scene 9B	Silens' Motel Bathroom	interior/night	Alik orgasms
Scene 11	Silens' Motel Bedroom	interior/night	Alik argues with Ginny
Scene 11B	Silens' Motel Bedroom	interior/night	Ginny exits leaving Alik behind
Scene 16B	Silens' Motel Bedroom	interior/day/flashba	Alik explains his hacking to Ginny
Scene 23	Silens' Motel Bedroom	interior/night	Ginny argues with Alik then puts him to bed
Thursday, August 21st			
Scene 37	Torque's Motel Bedroom	interior/morning	Ginny wakes and arms herself
Scene 33	Silens' Motel Bedroom	interior/morning	Torque talks to Alik who's stuck inside Torque's mind
Scene 35	Silens' Motel Bathroom	interior/morning	Torque stops up the sink and runs the water
Scene 36	Silens' Motel Bedroom	interior/morning	Torque talks to Alik as the water flows towards him and his demise
Scene 19	Torque's Motel Bedroom	interior/night	Torque and Ginny wake up
Scene 19A	Torque's Motel Bedroom	interior/night	Ginny dresses herself and says goodbye
Scene 20	Torque's Motel Bathroom	interior/night	Ginny talks to Torque while in the bathroom
Scene 11A	Silens' Motel Bedroom	interior/night/daydre	Ginny shoots Alik in the head
Scene 26A	Torque's Motel Bedroom	interior/night	Ginny confronts Torque who knocks her out
Scene 28	Torque's Motel Bedroom	interior/night	Alik plugs directly into Torque who then cuts Ginny
Sunday, August 24th / Monday, August 25th			
Scene 6	Motel Hallway	interior/night	Torque meets Ginny by the ice machine
Scene 29	Motel Hallway	interior/morning	Torque storms out and down the hall
Scene 29A	Motel Hallway	interior/morning	Torque walks down to the next room
Scene 32	Motel Hallway	interior/morning	Torque moves down to Alik's door
Scene 34	Motel Hallway	interior/morning	Torque shoots a Motel Guest
Scene 39	Adjacent Motel Hallway	interior/morning	Torque hears Ginny and starts to talk to her

Page 2

                        GINNY
        "Wow. I never thought I'd meet
        someone as fucked-up as I am..."

                        TORQUE
        "Oh yeah; we're a real lucky pair."

Ginny leans forward into Adrian's lap and continues sucking on his
cock. Adrian swallows hard, trying to maintain his control as he
brings his hands up onto the back of her head. Shakily, he
caresses her hair.

                        TORQUE
        "Let me stand up..."

Adrian rises without Ginny's mouth losing it's grip on his patchy
pole of muscle. Finally, as stiff as it can be, Ginny pulls his
cock out of her mouth and begins rubbing it into her eyes as she
continues stroking it.

                        GINNY
        "All those tubes and shit, and this
        still tastes like the real thing..."

                        TORQUE
        "That must be the blood, baby. It's
        in there doing all the work it should."

                        GINNY
        "Wow. I can smell the blood..."

                        TORQUE
        "Yeah. You'll see."

                        GINNY
        "But you can feel all of this and you
        like it, right?"

                        TORQUE
        "Oh yeah; you won't have any trouble
        squeezing the ball-juice outta' me..."

                        GINNY
        "Not yet; save it for me, baby..."

18.) INTERIOR SILEN'S MOTEL ROOM - NIGHT

Alik is sitting on the floor, covered in sparkly sweat and her Web
Gear, plugged into a wall outlet as she spasms and drools her way
through the electrical web of the motel.

SIXTEEN TONGUES Screenplay Notes

PAGE 39:

I ended up cutting Alik's voice-over for the moment where she worships at the altar of being Ginny's cuckold. I don't remember if we actually recorded the line or not during the looping sessions, so not sure when it was abandoned. Looking back, it might have been better to keep it in. Maybe not quite as it's written here, since the prose is a bit more florid than is in-character for Alik, but something more to indicate her illicit joy of watching (even though her masturbating to it might be enough to sell the moment). I like how she goes back and forth between feeling aroused or feeling guilty about the pleasure she derives. Her character is a ball of confusion lost in a world ripe with overstimulated ennui.

Sheet1

Scene 38A	Motel Hallway	interior/morning	Torque continues to talk to Ginny as he thinks he has shot her through a wall
Scene 40	Another Adjacent Motel Hallway	interior/morning	Torque finds nothing behind wall but ends up getting surprised by Ginny
Sunday, August 31st / Monday, September 1st			
Scene 1	Police Cage	interior/night	Torque rapes and kills Prisoner #1
Scene 10	Police Cage	interior/night	Torque shatters teeth of Prisoner #2
Scene 30	Motel Room #A	interior/morning	Torque kills an old man
Scene 31	Motel Room #B	interior/morning	Torque kills a Middle-Aged Man and a Young Woman

39

18A.) ALIK'S P.O.V.: Scuttling through various electrical pathways and security monitors, hallways, etc. Eventually, she ends up inside of a television set, looking out through fabric at two indistinct shapes, one standing and the other on their knees as they are having sex in their room (The silhouettes of Adrian and Ginny).

Back in the room, looking down at Alik, she uses her free hand to reach down and begin masturbating.

19.) INTERIOR TORQUE'S MOTEL ROOM - NIGHT

The Camera is looking through the fabric covering the Television screen and sees a pair of wide-open eyes watching amidst the storm of brightly flickering pixels.

> ALIK (V.O.)
> "Look at you go, you beautiful thing, performing a miracle with your soft mouth, converting a total stranger over to the mystery of your tireless ways. Worship my Venus! Anoint her with your oil, stranger!"

19A.) ALIK'S P.O.V.: The indistinct shape of Ginny about to bring the silhouette of Adrian to a climax.

> GINNY
> "I can feel it pulsing, like you're ready to burst."

> TORQUE
> "Rocket science, girl; you're the Einstein of head..."

> TORQUE (V.O.)
> "Baseball, income tax, Republicans..."

> GINNY
> "Come on baby, give it to me."

> TORQUE
> "Say *please*..."

> GINNY
> "*Please*...?"

> TORQUE
> "Oh yeah; here it fuckin' comes...!"

PAGE 40:
As you might imagine, the top paragraph on this page was the source of a lot of passionate discussion during the shoot.

When the time arrived for this moment, Jane made it clear that she really did not want the fake penis to ejaculate blood all over her face. She felt that the same or a similar effect could be gotten by having the cock cum on her breasts instead.

I totally understood what she was saying and while I sincerely believe that it would have been more interesting if shot as written, if she wasn't into doing it as an actress it would have adversely affected the performance, and what I needed more than anything was an uninhibited reaction of surprise and ecstasy to sell this crazy moment. There was no way she'd be able to give me what I needed if she were feeling discomfort.

We got what we needed on the first and only take as the EFX boys squirted out a copious quantity of blood, splashing her breasts with the stuff as she jerked the hell out of that fake cock and looked up with joyful astonishment. When I saw what she did with her performance, I had no regrets with what we chose to do and we all got cleaned up and ready for the next set-up.

In the end, a bloody facial might have been more alienating to viewers, so in this instance the compromise was probably a very good idea. Thanks, Jane!

40

Adrian moans as Ginny jerks him off on her hungry eyes, his blood
red cum dribbling all over her smiling face; she ecstatically rubs
the hot red cum into her eyes with the tip of his penis.

Adrian exhales loudly; exhausted, he spreads his arms and falls
backwards onto the bed.

DISSOLVE TO:

19B) Television Snow with Alik's wide-open eyes being swallowed
up by the dancing static.

20.) INTERIOR SILENS' MOTEL ROOM - NIGHT

Alik snaps her hand shut, causing sparks to fly as she cracks the
circuit breaker built into her hand mechanism. She falls onto her
side, shivering with electrical pain.

                    ALIK (V.O.)
          "Ginny, sweet Ginny. Why do you make
          me feel this way about you? How am I
          supposed to help you under these condi-
          tions? I wish I could put you on ice
          while I find the way to cure you; why
          do I have to suffer like this? Isn't
          just *your* pain enough for the two of
          us without *me* having to watch the scum
          of this world steal their pleasures
          from you ~~like this~~ every fucking night?"

Alik crawls into bed, still shaking up a storm. She uses the edge
of a blanket to wipe the tears from her eyes.

                    ALIK (V.O.)
          "And why is it that, deep down inside,
          I get off like a rocket on watching
          every single moment of it happening...?"

20.) INTERIOR TORQUE'S MOTEL ROOM - NIGHT

Ginny looks down at her fingers for the first time and finally
sees that they are not covered with cum, but with blood. She is
shocked, but not unpleasantly so; her speech is tentative.

                    GINNY (V.O.)
          "Ohmigod... What have I done now? Am I
          killing him?! Is this how I'm seeing it?"

                    GINNY
          "I think something's wrong. You
          just got blood all over me..."

[handwritten notes in right margin: "already shot", "Move scene to Bathroom / dissolve", "She examines herself in the mirror"]

SIXTEEN TONGUES Screenplay Notes

PAGE 41:

As originally written, Ginny did not leave the bedroom for the bathroom, and I do not remember why we made that change. In a few pages later on, she does finally go into the bathroom, but a good deal of dialogue that we never even shot gets excised between now and then.

I prefer Ginny going into bathroom when she does so in the movie as it gives each of them a private moment and we can also clearly see the blood on her breasts; I was unsure if it would read as blood to the audience in the darkness and the colored lights of Torque's bedroom. This allows Ginny to lick the blood from her fingers without raising any suspicions and gives Torque a moment to remove the bullets from her gun.

One line I miss: "I think I really like this a lot..." Another one I'm not sure we shot or not, but it didn't make the final cut. My guess is we didn't shoot it as there are quite a number of edits and little changes in the following pages.

41

Torque lies back in bed and zips up, rolling around & stretching like a happy cat as they continue talking

                    TORQUE
          "Nope. Nothing wrong, kid. All the
          damage I've had done and you think
    even ~~all~~ the little things are gonna' be
          workin' alright? What's left of me
          doesn't make spunk; blood gets re-
          routed so I get the jolt of having
          a real bang. But it's just blood..."
                          in the mirror
Wide-eyed, Ginny examines the blood covering her hands, massaging
it into her flesh of her fingers, smelling it, etc.

                    GINNY
          "Wow; that's really fuckin' weird..."

                    TORQUE
          "Yeah, it leaves me feeling a little
          extra tired, but I think it's worth it.
          You wouldn't have even noticed it if I
          had come inside of you."

                    GINNY (V.O.)
          "Blood everywhere, but nobody dead.
          How did I do this? I made the blood,
          without anyone getting hurt. How can
          this be?!"

Licking her fingers clean, Ginny looks vibrant and more alive than
we have ever seen her look before.

                    GINNY
          "I think I really like this a lot..."

                    TORQUE
          "Well, there's a lot more where that
          came from..."

They both exhaustedly laugh. Turning away from Torque, Ginny's
facial features twist a little as she struggles to keep herself
under control. He doesn't notice as he continues.

                    TORQUE
          "I've learned to get used to a lot
          of things. You think they want a
          refurbished fuck-up like me having
          kids? Cum's for breedin', girl, but
          for you I'm bleedin'; Jesus couldn't
          have done it any better for you..."

PAGE 42:

I'm assuming that—based on the circled "This scene has been cut"—cutting this out was probably decided on-set at the last minute. Not sure if we were running behind schedule and needed to catch up by jettisoning unnecessary material or if, since I had removed the previous reference to self-scarring and burns, there was no need to bring it up here and confuse the audience. No real loss here as it would have distracted from the more important material that needed to be presented in their dialogue. I'm glad we had the foresight to not waste time shooting something we knew wouldn't be used.

42

Close-Up of Ginny's hand shaking as it balls itself into a fist;
she uses her other hand to bring it under control.

                         GINNY (V.O.)
                "Must not kill... No more blood...
                I no longer need to kill to make
                the blood..."

DISSOLVE TO:

Adrian rolls over with his arm outstretched reaching for Ginny;
his hand finds the naked bottom of her back as she sits on the
edge of the bed facing away from him. He sees the scars that are
all over her body.

                         TORQUE   bruizes
                "Hey; where'd you get all these scars?"

                         GINNY
                "They're mine. I made them."

                         TORQUE
                "Why's that?"

                         GINNY
                "So I don't hurt anybody; it's this
                little hobby I have that helps keep
                me under control. Did anyone ever
                tell you how you wake up like a cop?"
                          that   Just
                         TORQUE
                "And how's that?"

                         GINNY
                "Asking questions while the sheets
                are still wet."

Ginny rises and looks down at Adrian as she self-consciously
covers herself with her hands.

                         TORQUE
                "Where are you going?"

Ginny turns and goes into the bathroom. She turns on the light,
and he squints as the bright light from the open bathroom door
bathes his eyes; revealing Ginny's unholstered gun sitting on his
night table with her gloves. Unseen by her, he picks up the gun
and examines it.

21A.) INTERIOR TORQUE'S MOTEL BATHROOM - NIGHT

This scene has been cut

PAGE 43:

Lost most of the top half of this page as well, although for some reason I didn't cross it out like on the previous page. I know for certain we didn't shoot any of this stuff either. With the tight production schedule, it was nice to lose a full page of dialogue we no longer had to shoot.

In terms of storytelling, this reveal that they might both be looking for "the same person" is a mistake. It works better when Ginny connects Torque as the killer of Alik's brother later in the screenplay. Also, it's a little too early to reveal Torque talking about himself in the third person as it would have created confusion at this point. It's better that he has his full meltdown later and might even make slightly more sense that way to a viewer.

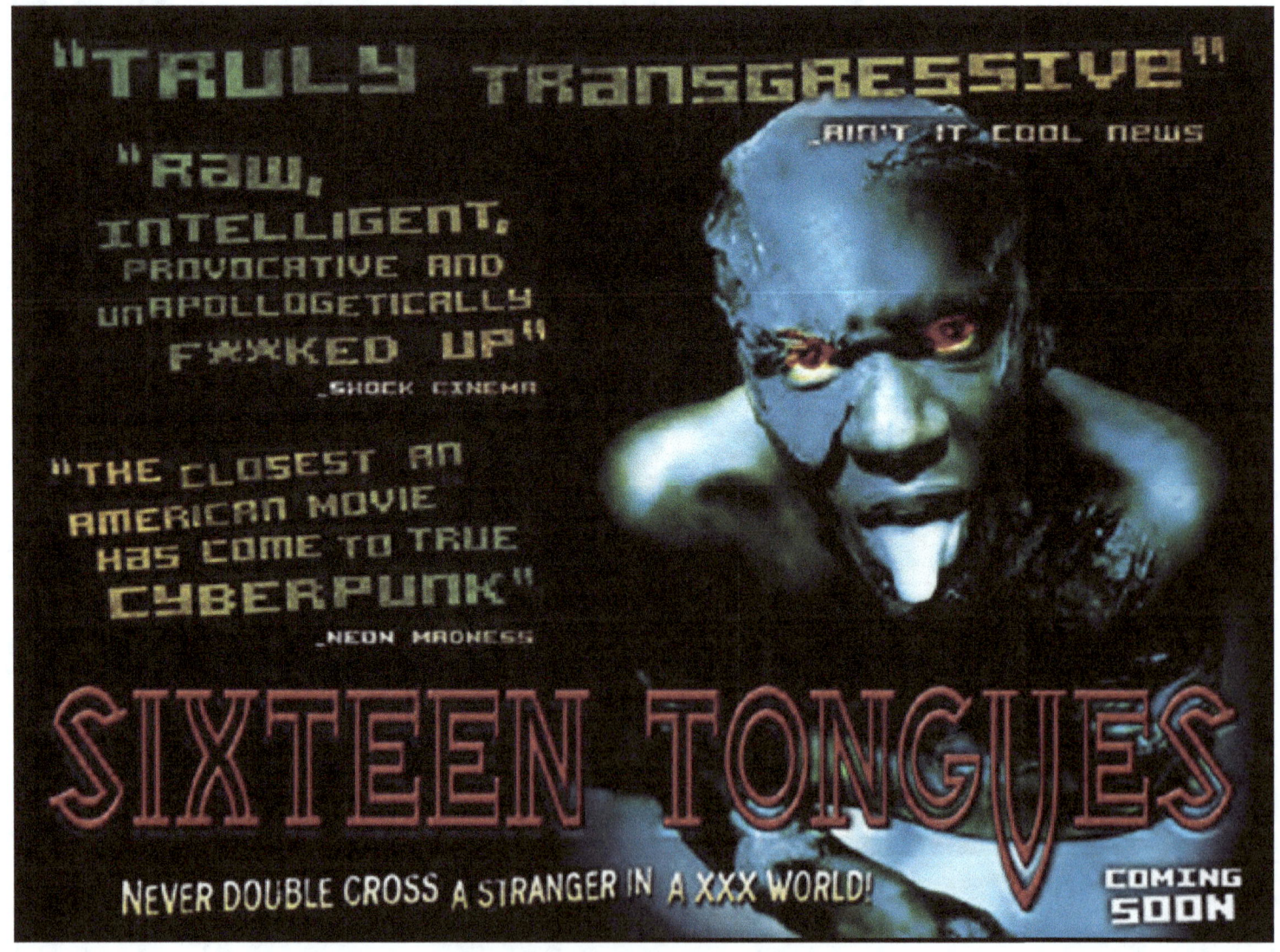

British Quad Style Poster Design.

43

Ginny sits on the toilet seat and wipes her red face clean with a white towel. Her tone is dry and distant.

                              GINNY
                "You can find out things, can't you?"

                              TORQUE
                "Yeah. Maybe."

                              GINNY
                "Maybe I'm really looking for a killer.
                For a friend; you know?"

                              TORQUE
                "Yeah, I know. Maybe so am I."

                              GINNY
                "Some piece of shit who killed a bunch
                of prisoners before he walked away."

                              TORQUE
                "Sounds to me like we both might be
                looking for the same person."

Ginny leans her head out of the bathroom and looks at Adrian.

                              GINNY
                "Yeah, it sure does."

Adrian nods his head and sighs as Ginny walks out of the bathroom fully dressed and picks up her gloves and her replaced gun from the night table.

21B.) INTERIOR ADRIAN'S MOTEL ROOM - NIGHT

                              TORQUE
                "You can stay here for the night, if
                you want. I don't mind."

                              GINNY
                "You must be pretty tired after all of
                that; you just relax and get yourself
                some sleep."

                              TORQUE
                "Really? So that's the way it is, huh?"

                              GINNY
                "Yeah, really. Well, let me know if
                there's anything I can do to help you."

SIXTEEN TONGUES Screenplay Notes

PAGE 44:
The moment where Ginny turns off Torque's television is the only three seconds of silence in the entire movie. No music, no room tone, no sound EFX. It's a precious moment of audio paradise far removed from the constant chatter bombarding the soundtrack the rest of the presentation. Every time this moment arrives, I feel like viewers might have needed just a few more seconds of silence to recover from everything that has come before, so I think I may have misjudged the amount of respite necessary for some audience recovery time. Sorry!

We were never able to shoot the flashback at the bottom of the page. In fact, whose flashback is it? While it might at first appear to be Ginny's, it happens within the context of a computer uplink—so could it be Torque or Alik who is seeing these images online? Later on, we get a very brief shot of a baby with strange eyes as Ginny has a flashback to her own birth at the peak of her fury, just before she kills Torque. Glenn and Paul created the baby make-up for less than a second of on-screen footage.

                    TORQUE
          "Just make sure your permit's in
          order..."

                    GINNY
          "Need to see it?"

                    TORQUE
          "I've seen enough from you tonight."

                    GINNY
          "Must be one of the fringe benefits
          of getting to know a cop."

She blows him a kiss and opens the door, about to exit. Adrian
just lies there and watches her standing silently in the doorway,
looking at him.

                    GINNY
          "Now here's one from knowing a well
          connected girl like me..."

Ginny walks over to the still-glowing television set, whips out
her credit card and runs it through the slot on the box. With one
quick motion she turns off the T.V. and turns to leave.

                    GINNY
          "There; that's better..."

She exits before Adrian has a chance to thank her. He sits up in
bed and rubs at his temples contemplatively.

22.) INTERIOR MOTEL HALLWAY - NIGHT

Need some blood on her shoulder/back

Ginny walks down the hall whistling a tune to herself, stepping
over the sleeping bodies and garbage strewn all over the floors.

                    GINNY (V.O.)
          "Maybe he's the help we need. I wonder
          if I could get him to - no, I won't even
          think about that right now..."

DISSOLVE TO:

GINNY C.U.'s to cut into this montage

**.) FLASHBACK / UP-LINK SEQUENCE

A flurry of computer graphics and video static as we Dissolve to a
series of abstract images which include a doctor's shadow across a
brick wall, a body bag with a pregnant woman inside of it, and the
sound of a baby crying. The voice of a Nurse cries out, and then
speaks...

SIXTEEN TONGUES Screenplay Notes

PAGE 45:

We removed Ginny smoking outside the hotel room door because actors are always using cigarettes as a crutch to look edgy or thoughtful, and I ended up not wanting to add such an overused cliché after avoiding so many others this far into the script. I think she adjusts the straps on her rubber top instead and that feels so much more realistic in this world.

Once again, another faux poetic voice-over for Alik removed. Talk about a hopeless romantic! Just like the other one we removed, it didn't seem like appropriate language for the character we had established. I think it would have been nice to have something more appropriate to replace it, but in the heat of the shoot we just continued marching forward as best we could.

Another point of interest would have been hearing Alik's voice-over while looking at a shot of Ginny waiting to enter the room. I like how that mismatch of voice and image might have been disorienting to the audience.

We ended up blocking the actors in an entirely different way than is written here.

45

NURSE (V.O.)
"Oh my god... Doctor, what are we
supposed to do with *this*...?"

DISSOLVE TO:

22A.) INTERIOR MOTEL HALLWAY - NIGHT

Finally, Ginny is standing near the door to Alik's room. She
stops and ~~lights up a cigarette, lean~~ing against the wall opposite
the door and blowing smoke at it.

*examines some scars
on her arm and straightens up
her look*

ALIK (V.O.)
"Look at her; beautiful like nothing
else I've ever seen. Like a sculpture,
she's a chunk of stone that's learned
to wear it's scars well. And I wish I
had the stoney strength to tell her..."

DISSOLVE TO:

23.) INTERIOR SILEN'S MOTEL ROOM - NIGHT

Ginny enters the room and finds Alik sitting in the corner at the
foot of the bed; her flesh looks slightly singed and she wipes the
tears from her eyes when she sees Ginny.

GINNY
"I've seen you look better; are you
alright?"

*Alik is lying in bed
(continued from her previous
position) -
she sits up and
watches Ginny as
she moves around
her*

ALIK
"He had the T.V. on in his room, and I
slipped inside their Surveillance Web.
You know, the tubes work both ~~both~~
ways for security reasons around here..."

GINNY
"Shit, Alik, that's not fair to you
or to me. You know that..."

ALIK
"Yeah, whatever; so who the hell was
that guy anyway?"

GINNY
"Just somebody else with a whole bunch
of problems; isn't that all I ever seem
to be dealing with these days?"

PAGE 46:
Removed the detail of Alik's period arriving a little bit early as it wasn't dramatically necessary at this point. Better to just keep the conversation moving along as there was a lot for the characters to unpack between themselves already.

> ALIK
> "Once a whore, always a whore..."

> GINNY
> "I can't believe you were watching me
> again with the way it makes you feel?
> Well, don't give me that self-righteous
> bullshit of yours, 'cause I think you
> get-off on seeing that kinda' stuff
> happening to me That's probably why
> you let it keep on happening..."

> ALIK
> "That's not true at all."

> GINNY
> "Oh really? Than why don't you drop
> your drawers and prove it to me? Show
> me your underwear isn't dripping wet
> after my free show."

> ALIK (V.O.)
> "Freak show..."

> ALIK
> "Fuck you..."

> GINNY
> "Yeah; that's what I thought."

Alik reaches a hand into her underpants and brings it out again,
presenting a bloody finger to Ginny.

> ALIK
> "I'm early... So if you need to..."

> GINNY
> "Thanks, but I'm okay now."

Alik turns away from her, embarrassed; she pounds his fist against
~~the wall~~ *the bed* and lowers her head.

> ALIK
> "When I saw what you were doing with
> him it made me mad, but it also got
> me pretty wet..."

Ginny *sits on the bed* ~~comes over to Alik~~ and comforts her; Alik turns around and
they face each other, embracing warmly.

PAGE 47:

This is another pretty long scene that lasts six full pages. I remember when we shot this one, it was during the 36 hour day, so we ended up shooting the first half of the scene and stopped in the middle so everyone could go home and get some sleep. We picked up from where we left off the next day and everything went fine because these were quality, professional actresses, but it certainly wasn't my preferred way of working as it takes a while for everyone to get back into the swing of where things left off. Watching it now, I can't remember exactly where we took the break in shooting, which is a testament to how good a job they did working together.

                         GINNY
          "You know I'm not doing any of this to
          make you angry. I like you too much to
          pull that kinda' shit on you."

                         ALIK
          "Yeah, babe; sure."

Putting her hand on the back of Ginny's neck, Alik discovers some
still-wet blood which is not hers on Ginny. She examines her hand
in horror and presents it to Ginny.

                         ALIK
          "Oh no; you didn't kill him did you?"

                         GINNY
          "I didn't have to. You know I don't
          need ~~too~~ very much to calm down, and he was
          very generous with what he had."

                         ALIK
          "You're scaring me, Ginny. Just what
          did go on in there, because what I saw
          ~~doesn't~~ didn't quite look like..."

Ginny smoothes out Alik's hair and talks in a seductive whisper as
she tries to calm her down.

                         GINNY
          "Forget about it, okay? He's got some
          easy access blood since he got rewired
          after a bad dusting-off."

                         ALIK
          "Lucky guy; must be pretty special."

                         GINNY
          "Yeah, he's a cop. I've been thinking
          maybe he can help us out, or something."

Alik awkwardly pulls away from Ginny and shakes her a little.

                         ALIK
          "Don't fuckin' kid yourself. Oh god;
          you didn't tell him about us, did you?"

                         GINNY
          "Of course not! I'm desperate, but I'm
          not stupid yet."

48

ALIK

"Shit! I just hope you haven't messed
everything up, is all..."

Alik ~~turns~~ gets up and walks away from Ginny; they are both pacing around
the room as they argue loudly.

GINNY

"Stop being such an asshole! I didn't
say anything about you! Jeezus, I'm
probably better off working with him
than with a loser like you, anyway!"

ALIK

"Oh yeah, that's really a sweet thing
to say. Thanks for your undying loyalty
in the face of all this when I really
need you..."

GINNY

"Where were *you*, Alik, when I really
needed you? Why should I need to go out
and find someone who's willing to bust
a nut and put me in gear? You know, the
way I was feeling, he probably ended up
saving a whole lotta lives by letting me
get him off like that."

ALIK

"Oh yeah; sounds like a real fuckin'
hero to me. So what the hell are you
doing crawling back over here for?"

GINNY

"I can't believe the way you're behaving;
like this is the first time I've had to
go out and do this kind of thing!"

ALIK

"Look, just get the fuck out of here
and leave me alone for a little while,
okay?"

GINNY

"Alik, I came back here because of the
way I feel about you. You think it's only
because I need you to find out some stuff
on the Web for me, but I'm sure with my
charms I could find someone else to do that
for me real fast. Even this cop, I'm sure."

49

>   ALIK
> "You're kidding yourself, Ginny. That
> piece of meat isn't a fuckin' cop. What
> the hell would he be doing cooped up in
> a dump like this if he was?"

>   GINNY
> "He must be looking for someone, I guess."

>   ALIK
> "Hiding out undercover, huh? So what was
> his name?"

Ginny thinks for a moment, struggling to remember.

>   GINNY
> "It's a girls name; like Ann, Andrea,
> something like that... Adrian."

>   ALIK
> "Adrian?"

>   GINNY
> "Yeah. That's it."

>   ALIK
> "Did he tell you his last name?"

>   GINNY
> "Got something special planned for this
> guy, Alik?"

>   ALIK
> "Not like that; just wanna' check him
> out and see if he's been sent here to
> find us or something stupid and paranoid
> like that. I don't think I'm leaving a
> big enough footprint for the Feds to
> follow, but I'd rather be careful than
> careless, babe."

>   GINNY
> "I saw his ~~badge~~ dangling sitting on the table; hanging in the bathroom
> all it said on it was Torque. That's
> not really a name, is it?"

Shocked, Alik stops dead in her train of thought; she's heard this
name before

>   ALIK
> "What the fuck...?"

PAGE 50:

I have always loved the way that Jane delivers the line "Yeah; definitely leather", as it's such a silly little joke and I think I'm the only one who laughs at it. I think the joke might have landed better if we had included the moment in an earlier scene where Torque licks his jacket from the shoulder to the cuff. If the audience had that image in their mind, this would have been a more impactful comment.

They both play well off of each other throughout this long scene, and I'm always impressed when performers can memorize huge amounts of dialogue like I provided them with here. I sure don't write the easiest lines, either...

50

GINNY
"Are you alright? You look sick?"

Alik charges towards Ginny, her eyes wide with anger.

ALIK
"He's an ugly mother-fucker, right?
Real tall and covered with bad skin?"

GINNY
"Yeah. Lost a bunch of derma and got
rolled over with a tongue job; never
seen anything like it before."

ALIK
"Holy fucking shit..."

GINNY
"Somebody you know?"

ALIK
"That's the scumbag who tore-up my brother.
But he *can't* be a cop. That's not in any
of the networks I've scanned..."

GINNY
"He's definitely a cop; I saw him do a
Link-Up without a hard interface; ~~never
seen that trick before~~..." *that's a New one...*

ALIK
"Are you sure? I didn't think that was
even possible."

GINNY
"Yeah. I saw him do it."

ALIK
"Wow. Well, this scumbag's a lot more
loaded than I would have ever imagined;
white wall radials and leather bucket
seats to go..."

GINNY
"Yeah; definitely leather."

ALIK
"No wonder this shit is classified so
deep in the system. A fuckin' *psycho
cop*; I had no idea, even after all of
the poking around I've been able to do."

SIXTEEN TONGUES Screenplay Notes

PAGE 51:

As for the nearly empty bottle of grape jam at the bottom of the page, production designer Dan Ouellette once again grabs the bull of his imagination by the horns and provides a quality prop with his "Jammin' Grape Jam" label. You can barely see it in the scene, but it's little details like these that accumulate over the course of a movie and help to create a unique little world.

Dramatically speaking, it's also nice to start a scene with Torque having an argument with his own voice-over.

This scene was part of the first day's shooting schedule. It was the first time we're alone with him after Ginny leaves the room after their sex scene, and I was unsure of how to light it. You might notice that it's the brightest scene in Torque's room, and after we shot it I realized that it was too bright for the look I wanted, so in the edit we darkened it considerably, but the overall 'soft lighting' doesn't match anything else we shot in this space. I would have liked to have been able to go back and reshoot this brief scene, but the schedule was way too tight for the kind of luxury. Overall, it's fine and not too embarrassing, but every time I've seen the movie it pops out from the rest of the visual scheme and nags at me.

51

>   GINNY
>   "Alik, you're killing yourself; you've
>   got to lie down and get some sleep. I
>   don't think you've done anything but
>   worry since I stepped out."
>
>   ALIK
>   "Oh, god, Ginny. I'm so tired of
>   sleeping..."
>
>   GINNY
>   "Now come on and lie down this time"

Ginny takes Alik by the shoulders, leads her to the bed and makes
her lie down on it. She closes his eyes and falls asleep almost
immediately; Ginny runs her fingers through Alik's hair and sighs.

>   GINNY (V.O.)
>   "No way; Alik, you can't be right on
>   this one. He's fucked up, but he's not
>   a killer; they have a smell and a style.
>   They're not like us at all. He's just
>   lonely inside like we are..."

Ginny covers Alik with the loose blanket on the bed and gives her
a kiss on his forehead. She rises and goes to the door.

>   GINNY (V.O.)
>   "I didn't realize just how horrible you
>   could be. You'll say anything to keep
>   me away from him now, won't you?"

DISSOLVE TO:

24.) INTERIOR TORQUE'S MOTEL ROOM - NIGHT

Adrian is sitting up in bed arguing with his voice-over as he
opens up a nearly empty jar of grape jam. Wearing a glove, he
scoops out a glob of the purple goo and spreads it lovingly over a
pink patch of 'flesh' on his wrist.

>   TORQUE (V.O.)
>   "How the hell could you let her go
>   after all the things she's done?"
>
>   TORQUE
>   "I... I don't know... what's come over
>   me... this time..."

SIXTEEN TONGUES Screenplay Notes

PAGE 52:

August 30th really was our workhorse date, wasn't it? That was our last day at the hallway location, so there was no going back if we missed getting whatever pick-ups we needed to get. As you might imagine, it was pretty weird to show up at this beautiful space and then cover up the walls with gigantic posters that spotlighted spread labias and monstrously exaggerated cocks sputtering jizz all over the place. I'm still amazed that we weren't instantly kicked out of the location. As if that wasn't enough, we also had naked performers, blood squibs, fake piss (coming up soon!) and all sorts of other impolite things happening. We were always very careful whenever one of the security guards at the facility was nearby and tried to be as discreet as possible during those moments, but obviously there was no hiding the posters that covered the walls..!

Also note at the bottom of the page that we removed the smoking joint from our beloved Terry character (portrayed by dear friend Terry Postage—so named because we always used to tease him for looking a bit like legendary actor Terrence Stamp). I preferred the audience not knowing what the heck drug he was on at that point so there would be no expectations of what he might do.

>TORQUE (V.O.)
>"Sucking your cock isn't a prison
>sentence, is it? Not even *you* could
>hate yourself that much."

>TORQUE
>"Hasn't she suffered enough? Why do I
>have to add my hands to the punishment?"

>TORQUE (V.O.)
>"You're a bigger whore than she is; I'm
>ashamed to be me, piece of shit..."

>TORQUE
>"And what about me? What about the things
>that I've done? We're just doing what the
>programme tells us to..."

>TORQUE (V.O.)
>"You haven't done a thing except be the
>best cop that you can be..."

>TORQUE
>"I... uhm, I've had lapses..."

>TORQUE (V.O.)
>"Perhaps it's time we examine exactly
>what incidents you're referring to."

>TORQUE
>"There's so... God, I don't even know
>where to begin...

25.) INTERIOR MOTEL HALLWAY #A - NIGHT

Ginny wandering through the corridors towards Adrian's room. She
looks confused, and her steps are tentative as she walks.

>GINNY (V.O.)
>"Alik can't be right. This can't be
>the same person she's thinking of. Not
>here; not now. Not him. I felt his
>pain, and I know the loneliness that
>comes from being different. I can't
>believe that being lonely can create
>monsters. I'm so alone too, but I'm
>not a monster, even after all this..."

Ginny turns the corner and bumps into Terry, a handsome but tired
looking man dressed in black. He's smoking a joint and quietly
focused into his own little world before he is jolted by Ginny.

SIXTEEN TONGUES Screenplay Notes

PAGE 53:
Although the dialogue here is pretty much the same as it appears in the movie, it's also readily apparent that the entire approach to the characters here changed completely by the time we got this scene in front of the camera.

I'm not sure why I wrote the scene with Japanese actresses in mind, but instead we got dear friend and beloved actress Tina Krause and newcomer Maria Pederson for these roles. Both of them had read for the Ginny part during auditions, as I wanted to try out as many different looks as possible for the role since the character could have been realized in any number of fascinating ways.

During our first interview, I remember asking Maria if she was comfortable with nudity. "I'm Swedish!", she replied heartily, as if that was the perfect response to such a question (and it was). I then inquired if she spoke the language, which she did. So when we got on set, I asked her if she could do her lines in Swedish and Tina would do hers in English, but they would both understand each other. Better yet, I didn't choose to have subtitles as the scene plays better and funnier this way.

Once again lucking out, I had two wonderful actresses with great comedic timing who cold deliver the goods while also pretty much completely naked. I also love the bruises that the make-up EFX guys added to them, which I thought would help generate some mystery and sympathy for these hallway sex workers.

                         TERRY
               "Wow, I haven't seen you around here
               in a while and a half."

She looks Terry up and down, but doesn't seem to recognize him.

                         GINNY
               "I've been busy in the South Wing."

                         TERRY
               "That's cool. Got some new tricks
               to try out. You interested?"

                         GINNY
               "Not tonight, thanks."

                         TERRY
               "You sure? I've been saving it up
               for a long time now, and all of that
               time I've been thinking of you."

                         GINNY
               "Maybe later when things aren't so
               crazy for me."

                         TERRY
               "Don't think I'm gonna' be able to
               hold it in that long, babe. Better
               say a prayer for the lucky one who
               bumps into me tonight..."

                         GINNY
               "You got it."

                         TERRY
               "And you don't, babe. It's all put
               out by the same big factory anyway.."

Terry laughs to himself as Ginny quickly moves past him and down
the hallway.

25A.) INTERIOR MOTEL HALLWAY #B - NIGHT

Two Japanese women, Tori and Maki, are sitting on the floor at the
farthest end of the hallway sharing the remains of a cigarette as
they speak to each other in Japanese.

                         TORI
               *"Did you hear that? I thinks someone's
               coming down the hall."*

PAGE 54:

As you might imagine, this was also one of the hallway scenes we were most concerned about security guards at the location walking in on, so whoever wasn't involved with the immediate shooting was posted at opposite ends of the hallway to give us a 'heads-up' if they saw anyone approaching the set. We had robes to quickly throw over the actresses just in case of any intruders, but I don't remember us having any problems during this setup, thank goodness. It would have been terrible for us to be thrown out before we got all our scenes, and there was still plenty to shoot at this point.

Tina Krause as The Bear Trainer, Maria Pederson as The Dancing Bear.

                    MAKI
          "Okay, I'm ready for the next show."

Stubbing out the cigarette in the wall, Tori rises wearing a noisy
leather and chains combo outfit as she unfurls her whip. Maki is
wearing nothing but a tight collar around her neck with a long
chain dangling off of it as she climbs to her feet. Tori grabs
the other end of the chain as Maki folds up her arms, leaving her
arms dangling, and begins to dance a cartoonish little jig. Tori
sings in clipped English as Maki growls.

                    TORI
          "Dancing bear, dancing bare, come and
          see my dancing bear!"

Coming from around the corner, Ginny enters the hallway and stops
suddenly when she sees Maki and her happy dance. An annoyed look
crosses Tori's face as she pulls on the chain and waves Maki to
slow down.

                    TORI
          "That's enough; it's just her."

Maki turns around and sees Ginny; she stops dancing and assumes a
defensive position as she places her hands on her hips.

                    MAKI
          "Yeah, the one who just gives it
          away every night."

Tori and Maki start moving threateningly towards Ginny as they
continue yelling at her in Japanese. Ginny backs away from them.

                    GINNY
          "I don't understand what you're   Just back off, kids.
          saying; please don't do anything
          that might make me hurt you."

                    TORI
          "Hey, why don't you just go away?
          Can't you see we're trying to work
          here?!"

                    MAKI
          "That's right; don't get in the way
          of our business or the big man's
          gonna' come after you!"

                    TORI
          "And so will we! We don't want any
          trouble around here!!"

SIXTEEN TONGUES Screenplay Notes

PAGE 55:

I cannot claim this with complete certainty, but I do feel extremely confident when I say that I don't think that any other director of a movie has ever given themselves an on-screen cameo quite like the one described on this page.

I don't think when I wrote the part that I knew I was going to play the guy who gets pissed on, but as production moved forward and it was getting harder to find performers to do some of the things we were requesting of them, I think it became obvious that it would just be easier if I took the role for the single shot it would entail in the final movie. Also, one less person to transport to the location made logistics easier and helped us stay on-budget.

One important detail I will never forget about this moment was the piss formula that the make-up EFX crew created. I assumed it would just be water with food coloring in it, but as it turned out—unbeknownst to me until after we started rolling the camera—the formula they created incorporated rubbing alcohol for whatever reason (I'm still not sure). I think they said something about providing a more realistic urine-like viscosity to the liquid? I will always love these guys and their attention to detail.

But unfortunately, as I was not aware of the alcohol content, I had my eyes open when the liquid hit my face and boy-oh-boy did that burn. It completely dried out my eyes and it took a couple of minutes for me to open them up and see properly again as I waited for my tear ducts to come back online and properly moisten things up for my poor eyeballs. These are the sacrifices we make for movies. I would do it again now to get the shot we needed.

Shaking, doing everything she can to supress her anger, Ginny turns away from them and quickly goes back down the hallway from which she just came.

25B.) INTERIOR MOTEL HALLWAY #A - NIGHT

Ginny comes back around the corner and faces Terry's back. She looks down and sees a Man sitting on the floor with his mouth wide open as a stream of Terry's hot piss washes over his face. The Man has an ecstatic look on his face as he turns towards Ginny and smiles.

Terry looks over his shoulder at Ginny and grins to see that she's watching them. Ginny lowers her head, ashamed to see the display happening before her troubled eyes.

>   TERRY
>   "You see? All this could've been
>   yours, babe..."

She turns and walks away as Terry continues pissing on the Man and their laughter echoes through the hallways.

>   GINNY (V.O.)
>   "I'm not still one of those, am I?
>   I really have moved beyond where I
>   once was; without even realizing it
>   I've made my decision. There's no
>   turning back now..."

26.) INTERIOR TORQUE'S MOTEL ROOM - NIGHT

Adrian is still sitting on the edge of the bed arguing with himself as the Camera pans up and down his body, admiring him like a well polished motorcycle; Dissolving from one image to another.

>   TORQUE (V.O.)
>   "Wrong again. It *was* her. We've put
>   her number through the system, and time
>   and again we see that all the brutal
>   things that you've attributed to your-
>   self were in fact committed by her."

>   TORQUE
>   "But how is that possible?"

>   TORQUE (V.O.)
>   "She's been following you; not only
>   *sucking* you, but *fucking* with you
>   as well..."

PAGE 56:

I think this scene confuses viewers because it's Torque's mind starting to confuse itself. That's a hard thing to convey in a screenplay and something that would have been far easier to clean up via description in a novel. I tried my best here and went with it. Even now, I'm not quite sure what I would have to do differently to try and make this clearer, so I guess I've learned nothing in the last 25 years.

                    TORQUE
     "But... why would she...?"

                  TORQUE (V.O.)
     "She's working with someone; think of all
     the enemies you've made in your line of
     work. Now how crazy does that seem to you?"

                    TORQUE
     "Not."

                  TORQUE (V.O.)
     "You must find her and arrest her..."

                    TORQUE
     "...For the public good."

                  TORQUE (V.O.)
     "And then you must find out who she's
     working with and why they are doing
     this to you..."

                    TORQUE
     "...For the good of my soul."

                  TORQUE (V.O.)
     "What soul? We're a fucking robot."

                    TORQUE
     "If I don't have a soul, then what's
     this voice inside my head?"

                  TORQUE (V.O.)
     "A ghost."

                    TORQUE
     "I'm not a ghost."

                  TORQUE (V.O.)
     "No, *you're* not, Adrian. But *I* am."

                    TORQUE
     "I don't even know what to do, anymore.
     I don't recognize this voice. Who's
     head is inside of me...?"

                  TORQUE (V.O.)
     "Sixteen extra tongues sewn into your
     hide, pal; how can you expect to be
     hearing *only* one voice above the din
     of the choir inside you?"

SIXTEEN TONGUES Screenplay Notes

PAGE 57:

I'll bet you had no idea I was a talented storyboard artist on top of all my other incredible skill sets? Look at that artwork. Take THAT, Akira Kurosawa!

I did these drawings as a compromise because for this scene, my performers wanted a clearer idea of how we were going to block the scene than I had previously given them for other scenes. I think this was because this dialogue scene was going to become a fight scene, and they were nervous about that. I totally understood and wanted to give them some guidance and reassurance that nobody was going to get hurt while shooting this.

My 'directorial style' for most other scenes involved blocking out movements and positions to some extent, while leaving some room for them to decide how to move in the very limited shooting space. I did it this way as I wanted the shooting style to be more kinetic than anything I had done before, so as my own camera operator I went for a looser, documentary-style look as I moved around and between them as they moved through the space. Overall, I'm very happy with how most of that turned out, and I think they adapted their working style to mine. There were one or two moments where this style led to some collisions with the actors, and I'll talk about one of them later on.

There is a knock at the door; Adrian rises and opens it, revealing
Ginny looking wide-eyed and nervous.

> Torque
> yeah?

                    GINNY
          "Help me?"

                    TORQUE
          "What?"

                    GINNY
          ~~"Before, I asked you to help me find~~
          ~~someone for a friend. But now~~ I want
          you to help find somebody for *me*."

                    TORQUE
          "And who's that?"

                    GINNY
          "I want the doctor who made me. I want
          to know who he is. I want to hold him
          in my hands and make him snap."

Adrian opens the door all the way and leans on it. ~~Ginny steps in~~
a little bit, but remains rigid.

> He opens the door and
> Ginny
> enters

                    TORQUE
          "That's some pretty rough stuff you're
          telling me, girl."

                    GINNY
          "Can you help me? *Will* you help me?"

                    TORQUE
          "Find someone so you can kill them?
          I'm a cop; that's not what I do."

                    GINNY
          "I won't kill him if he can fix me.
          Maybe he could even help you, too.
          God, I'd do anything to ~~make you~~ help
          ~~me out...~~"

                    TORQUE (V.O.)
          "Hmmm. She's back for more."

                    GINNY
          ~~"I just want you to help me find him."~~

> Torque
> profile Medium
>
> Ginny
> profile medium

125

PAGE 58:
The storyboard magic continues with these further gems. I think I really bring those head positions to life with my fine line technique, don't you?

One of the disadvantages of shooting the beginning of this scene with such specificity to the actor blocking and the storyboard positioning is that, when I saw the footage in the editing room, it was relatively lifeless and looked so staged compared to everything else in the movie that had much more frenetic camera energy. Even as we were shooting, I was concerned we might be losing some of the jittery back-and-forth the camera was having with the actors, but I went with it to appease and comfort the performers who craved the safety this way of shooting afforded us—and again, I do not blame them at all as it is the job of the director to make their performers feel safe and comfortable at all times.

If we were shooting this now in high-definition, I suppose I could add some 'camera shake' to the footage in post-production to keep it lively, but adding an effect like that to 25 year old standard-definition video would just further crapify the already pushed-to-the-limits color range of the image.

58

Profile

Torque C.U.

TORQUE
"I'm getting confused, here. I mean,
an hour ago you wanted me to find the
fuck who smoked your buddies. Now
you're back here asking me to rezz up
the Frankenstein who pumped you out.
You gotta' look at that from my point
of view; that's doesn't seem terribly
stable to me."

Profile

Ginny C.U.

GINNY
"I don't know how to make you understand;
I'm tired of living my life like this;
always being just on the edge of snapping
and hurting people. Even friends. When
it hits the fan, nobody's safe. I'm afraid
of myself and the things I'm capable of
doing. Have you ever felt that way?"

TORQUE
"No. But I can't say I'm surprised."

GINNY
"I don't know what you're saying."

turns + walks away

TORQUE (V.O.)
"Are you kidding? I think we all
know the answer to that one."

Adrian grabs Ginny by the arm and pulls her into the room. He
tosses her onto the bed and slams the door shut, locking it, as
Ginny mumbles to herself.

GINNY
"What the fuck is this all about?"

She walks over to
Nighttable + picks up
his badge

TORQUE
"Shut-up, bitch, before I slam your
head inside out."

Ginny stiffens with fear and her eyes open wide.

GINNY
"That's not something I expected to hear
you saying..."

TORQUE (V.O.)
"Kill her now."

127

The real "rarity" in this bunch is the cover of the Cable Guide that is never seen on-screen that our production designer made to be lying around in Torque's room.

> GINNY
> "Maybe I was wrong about you, but I sure hope not."

> GINNY (V.O.)
> "Holy shit; he IS the ~~the~~ one...!"

> TORQUE
> "Wrong about what?"

> GINNY
> "I'm beginning to think that you *do* know what I mean; bloody shoes make squeaky steps, don't they? I know all about it. I'm not proud of my past, but sometimes it comes in handy."

> TORQUE (V.O.)
> "There she goes again with those lies!"

Adrian laughs and moves towards her as Ginny slides herself into a defensive posture on the bed.

> TORQUE
> "Suddenly, I'm not so sure if I like what the hell's pourin' out of your sweet mouth, girl..."

> TORQUE (V.O.)
> "She's been sent here to kill you..."

> GINNY
> "Six innocent men killed..."

> TORQUE (V.O.)
> "...because of a programming error."

Confused, Adrian address his own Voice-Over out loud.

> TORQUE
> "What programme error?"

Ginny is shocked at what she sees happening and works hard to maintain her composure.

> GINNY
> "Look at you malfunctioning even as I try to reason with you..."

> TORQUE (V.O.)
> "Don't let her try to confuse you!"

SIXTEEN TONGUES Screenplay Notes

PAGE 60:

My handwritten note indicates doing swish-pans at this point in the scene, back-and-forth between them in order to try and create some visual dynamism between two people yelling at each other from opposite sides of the bed.

Between that and the note below it for Ginny to flip from one side of the bed to the other indicates to me that I wrote these notes on-set during the blocking session with the actors.

I'm not a big fan of swish-pans, but I do remember thinking that the way Ginny moved from one side of the bed to the other as Torque prowled towards her was well-done by both of them under the fast circumstances. It's a complicated scene due to all the dialogue and working out the physical movements. This is the kind of scene that might take more than a day to choreograph in a larger budgeted production, but we had only a few hours as there was additional stuff to shoot that day as well. The surviving schedule shows we had eight other additional set-ups to do on this very same day. I sincerely still have no idea how we made it through all of these pages in a single day.

                    TORQUE
"I've had enough of your lies, killer.
Have you come here to turn yourself in?
That's the smartest thing you could do."

                    GINNY
"What? What the hell are *you* talkin'
about now?"

                    TORQUE
"You're one of *them* aren't you? One of
the scumbags who tried to kill me?"

                    GINNY
"Oh shit; I know the look in your eye..."

Ginny moves off the bed and stands up; as they talk, she slowly
begins backing away towards the door to the room.

                    TORQUE
"I knew it all along; a renegade combat
model hiding behind a bad set of yellow
flaps. What was I thinking? I should've
smelled the murder in you...?"

                    GINNY
"Fucking piece of shit! *You* killed my
friend's brother! *You're* the one who's
lying, and you're doing it to the wrong
person, cop!"

                    TORQUE (V.O.)
"Little cunt! I can smell it on your
cheap breath."

                    TORQUE
"So who are you working with, whore?
Give me a name. I wanna' know where
to send your pieces."

                    GINNY
"Her name is Silens."

                    TORQUE (V.O)
"And mine is vengeance."

Adrian is momentarily surprised; he recognizes that name and
starts moving threateningly towards her.

                    TORQUE
"Saint Claire Silens?"

131

PAGE 61:

I'm looking at that drawing at the top of the page and I can tell you with authority that—as someone who shot on this set for a couple of very long days—I have no idea what the heck I was trying to show or what the fuck that angle is supposed to demonstrate to anybody involved in the production. But there it is for posterity. I hope at the time it brought somebody some comfort.

During the blocking, we decided that it would be better to have Ginny thrown onto the bed to get punched later instead of slapping her at this point. Overall, I think the way we ended up shooting it plays better than written (which is a lot better than having it be the other way around).

It's an honor just to be nominated...

against this wall

                    GINNY
          "Alik Silens; his sister."

Adrian advances on her suddenly, pinning her against the ~~closed~~ *wall*
door to the room. This doesn't frighten Ginny; it only makes her
angrier and more defensive.

                    TORQUE   *done & start*
          "So that's who you're working for; I
          should have been able to figure that
          out myself. It's all genetics in the
          end. When the violence is that strong
          it must be hereditary; maybe the whole
          line should be destroyed. Maybe this
          nuclear family has finally melted down
          to the core..."

                    GINNY
          "The way you look to be malfunctioning,
          I don't think you'd have much luck with
          spelling your fuckin' name much less..."

                    TORQUE (V.O.)
          "Do it!!"

Wham! Adrian ~~reaches out and slaps her.~~ *throws her onto the bed,*

                    TORQUE
          "You have the right to remain silent."

                    TORQUE (V.O.)
          "This time, make her fuck you!"

                    GINNY
          ~~"You're in big trouble now, mister.~~
          You better back off, 'cause I've got
          a mind to kill you, and what I think
          is generally what happens."

                    TORQUE
          "Be quiet! I'm arresting you!"

Ginny whips out her gun and fires it at Adrian, but it just clicks
emptily as she looks at it in anger.

                    TORQUE
          "I emptied that earlier; I'd a thought
          you would have noticed the difference
          in weight, but I guess you're not as
          good as you think you are..."

SIXTEEN TONGUES Screenplay Notes

PAGE 62:

In a moment that I alluded to a few pages earlier, this is the page where Crawford pulled back his mighty fist to fake-punch Jane and ended up pretty much knocking me on my ass as I was standing right behind him and moving in closer to get the shot 'just right'. I included that moment in the blooper reel on the DVD.

Thankfully, nobody got hurt and we immediately broke into laughter after it happened. It was my fault as I was doing my dancing-around-the-performers shooting style at this point in an attempt to get us back to the tense energy level I wanted from the camera movements.

I got what I wanted on the second take and it was well worth getting my clock cleaned out on the first one.

Also, note the casual racism of the Torque character on this page and also on page 60 with his use of the term "yellow" to insult Ginny's heritage on both occasions. I wanted that aspect to be part of his mental breakdown, and I also wanted it clear that Ginny neither takes the bait of the insult nor sends it back at Torque for being African American. These are the only two times anyone's race is acknowledged in any way by the movie, and I wanted them to stand out.

In that choice, I was thinking specifically of Gene Hackman's character in THE FRENCH CONNECTION. Although he's the hero of the movie, he's also a casual racist who mutters the epithet "nigger" more than once to describe some of the characters he has to deal with. Nonetheless, the movie asks us to accept that about his character as he does his job (or it at least doesn't dwell on him judgmentally for his racist language). I like imperfect characters in stories, and while Torque is no 'Popeye' Doyle when it comes to being a police officer, he's not meant to be evil but an imperfect victim of some bad circumstances beyond his control. I wish things had turned out better for him. He might have been a very good cop before he got his tongue job.

62

With a sweeping motion, Adrian swats the empty gun from her hand *and pushes her*
and grabs her by he arm, but she resists him without flinching. *~~back~~ onto the*
The two of them shake with effort, trying to bring the other one *bed*
under their control.

> TORQUE
> "Bitch, I'm gonna' fuckin' kill you..."

> GINNY
> "Not even close..."

With her other hand, Ginny punches Adrian in the center of his
face; he falls back onto the floor and she jumps on top of him.

> GINNY
> "Not what you had in mind, huh?" *He moves towards her and she*
> *kicks him away*

He rolls over and pins her to the floor, but she kicks him off of
her. As Ginny rises, Adrian grabs her leg, balls up the fist of
his other hand, and smashes her kneecap with it; there is a loud
snapping sound as Ginny's leg joint is shattered.

> TORQUE
> "I don't have time for this shit;
> not while there are lives at stake."

> GINNY
> "Jee-zus...key-rhist..."

As she writhes in agony, Adrian picks up Ginny and tosses her to
the floor. He throws himself onto her back and, while holding her
down, slams his fist repeatedly into her as often as possible.

> TORQUE
> "Tried to trick me into believing I did
> all those terrible things, huh? Well,
> that was your first mistake. I'm not
> taking the fall for anybody, especially
> not for some cheap yellow whore..."

Adrian pulls Ginny's arm behind her as he steps on her back,
wrestling her resistance into submission.

> GINNY
> "Make sure you kill me... or I'll find
> a way to kill you..."

> TORQUE
> "I don't think so, kid. Not the mess
> that I'm making out of you. Now stop

PAGE 63:
As noted in cursive on this page, "Cut rest of scene"—and that is exactly what happened.

Which is good, as I didn't waste time shooting something I wasn't going to use.

I think at this point we realized that on-screen computer graphics created by Robert Morris would get us over this exposition hump and provide visuals that moved the story forward instead. This was relatively early in the history of CGI, and he did great work for us. As we didn't try to do anything to ridiculously showy or state-of-the-art (for that time) dazzling, the simplicity of design and the fine detail of what he did (working with graphics designed by Dan Ouellette) still holds up pretty well and doesn't feel dated—at least in my opinion.

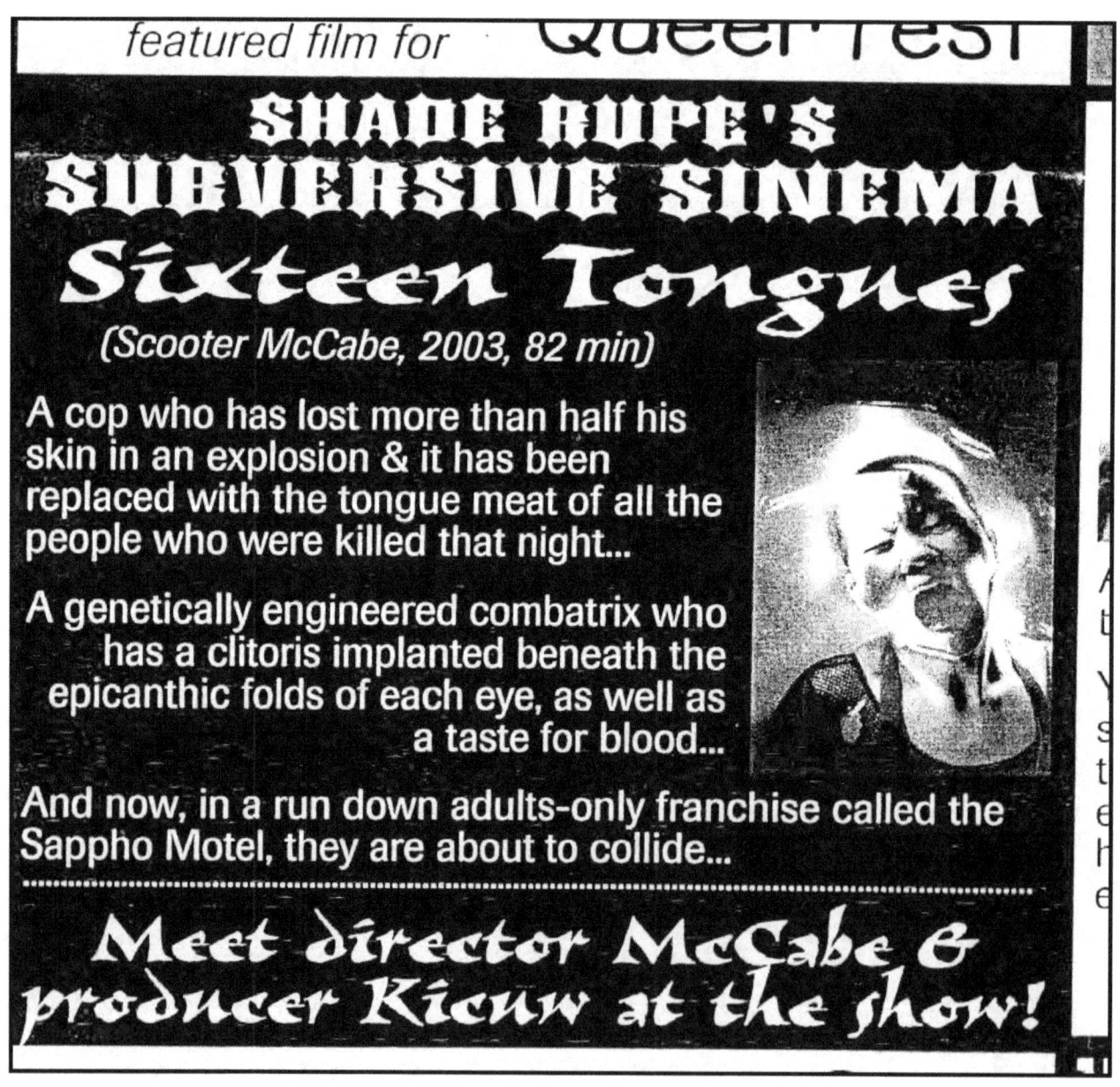

"This was a great screening at the now closed Two Boots Cinema in lower Manhattan. Actors and crew people alike attended and it was a party for us as much as a screening for the brave civilians who showed up. Note that both Alex and I have our names misspelled, although that might have been on purpose in case of a police raid...!"

struggling or I'll pull your fuckin'
arms off!"

                    GINNY
        "Built to kill; that's just the way
        it is. You'll see..."

She stops struggling completely, and Adrian lets her limp arm slap
flat on the floor. He spits on her and steps back from her barely
alive, but still breathing, body.

                    TORQUE (V.O.)
        "It's time to go..."

                    TORQUE
        "You think about that when I toss you
        in the hole, bitch. You think about
        all those people you say I killed..."

                    TORQUE (V.O.)
        "Must let her live. Let her live. Let
        her live so she can suffer some more..."

27.) INTERIOR SILENS MOTEL ROOM - NIGHT

Alik has a laptop computer on the edge of her bed; hunched over it
on her knees, she flips the top open and powers-up the unit.

                    ALIK (V.O.)
        "Alright, asshole. I'm taking a ride
        on the Web and getting inside your
        head. I'm gonna' kick the shit out of
        you from the inside out, and do a
        little fandango on whatever's left of
        your scummy self!"

Alik slides on her headset and flips the tiny microphone under her
lips. She types as he speaks.

                    ALIK
        "Computer, begin your voice activation
        control programme now."

And then she stops typing as she continues to control the computer
with her voice.

                    ALIK
        "Find Sigfried Tango Bravo in the third
        quadrant of Blueboy Zone. Perform hard
        initial resolution. Begin sequence of
        Torque, Adrian, programme file..."

PAGE 64:

Again, all of this low-grade sci-fi gibberish got jettisoned and I don't miss it one bit. The CGI tells the story better and is more fun to look at.

One thing I do remember is that originally I did not want to use any CGI at all. I wanted even the computer world to have a handmade, DIY quality that I thought would be unique to this universe we were creating.

My original intention was to shoot white index cards that would be treated like screens and have images projected onto them in a smoke filled room and we would use the same camera we shot the opening title bodies with, having the camera swoosh by these cards with moving images on them. Then we would digitally stack these various screens one on top of the other and have them whiz by the lens in post production. In fact, I even wanted to have this all done in black-and-white, to further downgrade the look of the digital world that Alik swam through when she entered the electronic world.

Frankly, it just got too complicated and at the end of production, with no time or money left in the budget, it was just easier (for us, anyway) to have Robert work his digital magic, and the results he gave us were beautiful enough that I had no complaints.

I seem to remember part of the inspiration for this was seeing some test footage from TRON on the old laserdisc that was in black-and-white; I loved how it looked and much preferred it to the neon color scheme they ended up using in the final film.

Scooter McCrae with actor Ray Wise at the Fantasia Film Festival. Just because.

64

The computer screen fills up with zeros and ones.

          ALIK (V.O.)
   "Shit; it's a binary password page.
   I won't be able to maneuver like this.
   Gotta' get what I can and plug in."

Shaking her head forlornly, Alik speaks.

          ALIK
   "Enable Snatch Programme."

Alik sits back in her chair, removes her headphones and sighs.

          ALIK (V.O.)
   "Christ, I'm fuckin' exhausted; not
   the best time to be pulling these
   kinds of tricks, idiot..."

Blip! The computer screen responds with a beep.

          ALIK
   "Gotcha'! Too fuckin' easy; would
   have thought of this before if I'd
   known about his Wet-Link and gotten
   some sleep..."

Alik pulls on her Web Gear and plugs herself into the wall.

DISSOLVE TO:

28.) INTERIOR ADRIAN'S MOTEL ROOM - DAWN

An oily swirl of shapes and colors coalescing into shapes that
don't look like anything at all as we hear Alik's voice echoing on
the soundtrack.

          ALIK (V.O.)
   "Can barely see anything... Shapes
   moving through shadows and smoke in
   the pale light of consciousness as a
   lightning bolt cracks open an idea..."

          TORQUE (V.O.)
   "Who the hell are you?!"

          ALIK (V.O.)
   "Where am I...?"

PAGE 65:

Robert Morris did a particularly great effect here, taking us from Crawford's audition photo (yes, we loved using his head shot as it's the only brief moment where we get to see him without the elaborate make-up he wears for the entire movie) to the live-action footage of him looking at himself in the mirror. It still looks pretty damn good, but at the time—25 years ago!—it seemed nothing short of a miracle to have made a movie with such a totally cool EFX shot in it! Hard to believe we were on the cutting edge for all of about five minutes.

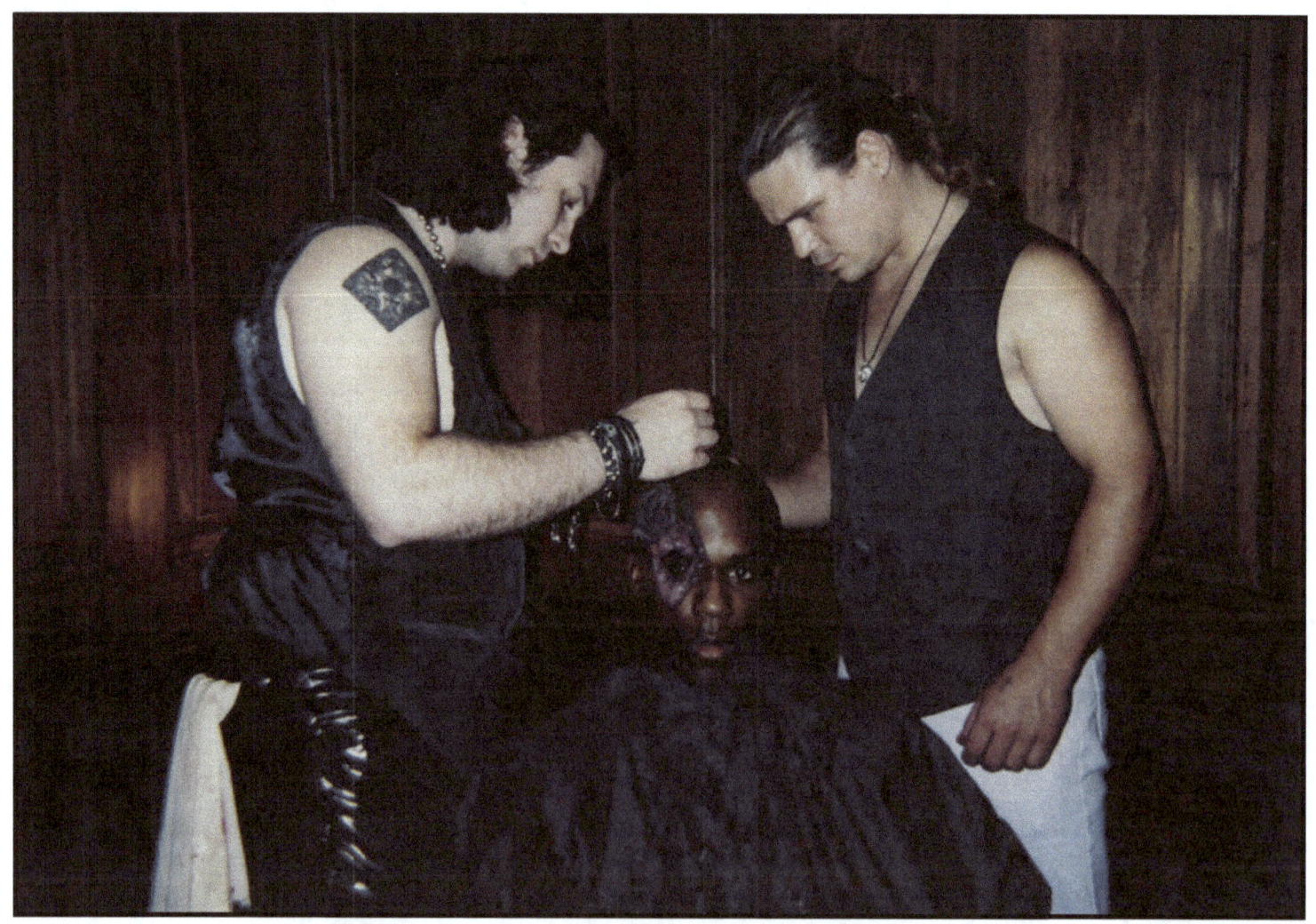

"I'm pretty sure that photo of Glenn and Paul putting the make-up on
Torque was taken by Mike Gingold during his set visit." - Scooter

                         TORQUE (V.O.)
          "In here."

                         ALIK (V.O.)
          "Here?"

The soft image comes into focus, revealing Adrian's confused face
as he looks at himself in the mirror.

                         ALIK (V.O.)
          "Holy shit!"

                         TORQUE (V.O.)
          "I guess I'm not used to visitors..."

                         ALIK (V.O.)
          "I was just on the Web; how the hell
          did I get here?!"

                         TORQUE (V.O.)
          "If you don't like what you see, then
          get the hell out of here!"

                         ALIK (V.O.)
          "Damn; you really are one ugly looking
          mother-fucker, aren't you?"

Adrian suddenly punches the mirror, smashing it into a hundred
shiny pieces that fly all over the room.

                         TORQUE (V.O.)
          "You're just a tenant, girl; don't you
          go trying to fuck with the landlord."

                         ALIK (V.O.)
          "What the hell are you gonna' do about
          it? I'm about to pull the plug on the
          sorriest scumbag that ever was!"

The image becomes a soft blur of color for a moment, and we hear
the sound of Adrian stepping all over the broken glass as the
Voice-Overs continue over streaks of color.

                         TORQUE (V.O.)
          "You've got a lot of nerve trying to
          turn me off from the inside; you've
          got no right being in here!"

                         ALIK (V.O.)
          "You're a dead man, Torque. After
          all you've done to me and my family,

PAGE 66:

Jeezus, did I really type "titsy-poo" and expect an actor to say that line? Thank goodness it never made it past this ill-conceived page portion. In fact, a good deal of this dialogue either got cut or rewritten in an attempt to try and make what was happening slightly more clear to the audience—a point which is still highly debatable to this day.

The eyelids that the EFX guys made were gross, so they did a perfect job. This is exactly the kind of horribly violent scene I normally don't have any interest in writing or shooting, but it was an important detail that needed to be seen.

In my entire (very limited) body of work, this is probably the only time I ever employed a point-of-view shot for a character—at least one that was a handheld P.O.V. shot. It's not something I would do under normal circumstances, but it worked here as it was an integral part of the storytelling.

MIDNIGHTS WITH SCOOTER MCCRAE

By the early '90s, many genre fans took the availability of consumer-grade video equipment as a call to arms, producing massively personal, astoundingly original works; some of which would contain imagery and themes no studio picture would dare touch. Scooter McCrae was on the frontlines of this strange new world, and his debut feature *Shatter Dead* (1994) is at once a staple and a stand-alone slap in the face to the tried pitfalls of the Horror genre, communicating in its own brand of subversive poetry. Several years later McCrae would push the envelope to degrees few others would even dare speak of with his depraved Sci Fi epic *Sixteen Tongues* (1999), a cryptic future-world nightmare with meditation on modern human mentality more brazen than Paul Schader's entire filmography. Join us Sept. 20th and Sept. 27th at Spectacle for two midnights of the extreme, passionate, and undeservedly obscure works of Scooter McCrae. 9/20 & 9/27 midnight -- director in attendance both nights!

These screenings took place at the Spectacle Theater in Brooklyn and were a total blast. I brought along a bottle of very good single malt scotch and plastic cups (sorry, environment) and handed out a decent sized pour to everyone who attended -- which I think added to the fun and also made people a little bit friendlier towards the movies. Midnight shows can be punishing for even the best of movies, but these two especially are not exactly action-packed spectaculars. I'm sure I probably nodded off as well at some point.

you're gonna' pay..."

> TORQUE (V.O.)
> "Revenge doesn't seem like your flavor,
> synapse jockey..."

As the soft image comes into focus, we see Ginny lying unconscious on the floor of the room from Adrian's Point-Of-View towering high above her menacingly.

> ALIK (V.O.)
> "Oh my god; what the fuck is going on?!"

> TORQUE (V.O.)
> "I'm running out of room inside here,
> lady, but you're just in time for a
> very special treat."

> ALIK (V.O.)
> "Jeezus Christ, man; please don't hurt
> her, whatever you do...!!"

> TORQUE (V.O.)
> "Better close your eyes, titsy-poo,
> because you're not about to like what
> you're gonna' be seeing; oh yeah, that's
> right - you can't. They're *my* eyes!"

> ALIK (V.O.)
> "Why don't you leave her alone?! It's
> you and me who've got a score to settle!"

> TORQUE (V.O.)
> "It doesn't work that way in the real
> world; this isn't some kind of fuckin'
> game. This bitch is gonna' suffer and
> die, and then I'm gonna' find you and
> rip your ass inside out. There's no
> bargaining chips here, tough girl..."

> ALIK (V.O.)
> "You god damned sonofabitch!!!"

Adrian leans into Ginny with a sharp piece of the broken mirror in his hand, pinning her arms down under his knees.

He holds down her head and violently slices off her eyelids with sloppy strokes, exposing most of the eyeball beneath.

Still unconscious, Ginny shakes in anguish beneath his tortures as Alik's screams continue.

PAGE 67:

I always get a kick out of watching the footage where Torque pulls the suitcase out from under the bed, pulls out some bagged evidence and grabs the guns—mostly because those are my hands doing all of that. After a long day of shooting Crawford in an outfit that didn't let his skin breathe, under a ton of make-up in a hot room with no air conditioner in August, our good deed for the day was letting him go home when he was done shooting and getting whatever other footage we could get without him needing to be there. I don't think I've ever heard anyone complain that my tiny hands and thin arms looked different than his, yet another testament to the magic of the movies!

BANDIDO'S GOLD:
UNEARTHED SPAGHETTI WESTERN TREASURES

This quartet of lesser known, yet truly great spaghetti westerns is chocked full of gripping action, relentless violence, and brooding intensity with gritty style to spare.

BANDIDOS
Dir: Massimo Dallamano, 1967
Italy, 91 mins.

Outlaw Billy Kane holds up a train only to find his former mentor-of-arms, renowned gunman Richard Martin, is one of the passengers. Kane shoots Martin's hands before letting him escape. Years later Martin meets Ricky Shot (!), an escaped convict who was falsely accused for the robbery. He takes Shot under his wing and together they head on the trail of vengeance.
9/14: 7:30pm • 9/29: 10pm

VENGEANCE IS MINE
Dir: Gianni Fago, 1967
Italy, 91 mins.

Gianni Garko and Claudio Camaso breathe more life into their anti-hero and villain roles from $10,000 Blood Money, here with an added Cain-and-Abel-like classicism. This time it's John the bounty hunter (Garko) versus army deserter-turned-outlaw Clint (Camaso), half-brothers, embittered with extreme mutual hatred. John just served time, falsely accused of his father's murder by none other than Clint. Can John keep his promise to his mother to bring Clint in alive?
9/4: 7:30pm • 9/22: 10pm

$10,000 BLOOD MONEY
Dir: Romolo Guerrieri, 1967
Italy, 94 mins.

Rogue bounty hunter Django mockingly taunts low-life bandit Manuel, who only has a measly $3,000 price on his head. Inspired by spite, hatred and villainous pride, Manuel ups the stakes, first with murder, and then by kidnapping a land baron's daughter, finally netting Django's $10,000 bounty minimum. But when Manuel targets Django's saloon girl lover (Loredana Nusciak from Django), vengeance becomes the main incentive, transforming the hunt into an ornery blood feud.
9/21: 10pm • 9/30: 10pm

CEMETERY WITHOUT CROSSES
Dir: Robert Hossein, 1969
Italy, 85 mins.

After her husband is mercilessly hanged by a ruthless land baron, Maria implores Manuel, an old flame, to infiltrate the killer's ranch and wreak vengeance. Manuel reluctantly leaves the ghost town where he lives to embark on the mission but is never haunted by his unequited affection for Maria.
9/9: 10pm • 9/28: 7:30pm

JOHN BUT NOT FORGOTTEN:
THE DAY WE LOST RITTER AND CASH
A SCREENING TRIBUTE

One bitter fall evening, during a span of three hours caught in the space between September 11 and 12, 2003, we lost two great entertainers; Johnny Cash and John Ritter. One decade after this tragedy, Spectacle celebrates the only way it knows how: by showing an obscure movie in which Johnny Cash plays a psychotic guitar-slinging killer (Five Minutes to Live), and a hilarious made-for-TV cheesefest about John Ritter getting carjacked in front of a Starbucks and moving his family to a techno-totalitarian gated housing community (The Colony).

THE COLONY
Dir: Rob Hedden, 1995
USA, 84 mins.
9/11: 7:30pm

FIVE MINUTES TO LIVE
Dir: Bill Karn, 1961
USA, 75 mins.
9/11: 10pm

SEPT 11TH
ONE NIGHT ONLY!

MOLODOST:
FILMS OF SOVIET YOUTH

Molodost—meaning the time of youth— explores three different coming of age stories from the perestroika era, on the cusp of the Soviet Union's dissolution. The films explore the counterculture & underground music movements that emerged in the late '80s, and represent the first recognition of these movements in the Soviet mainstream.

ASSA
Dir: Sergei Solovyov, 1987
Soviet Union, 153 mins.
Russian with English subtitles

Assa came to cult status as one of the first films to bring underground rock music into the Soviet mainstream. Assa follows the story of a young nurse who is romantically involved with her much older patient and leader of an organized crime group. The nurse starts falling for a young rock musician who introduces her to his eccentric world of music and art.
9/5: 8pm • 9/20: 8pm • 9/24: 10pm

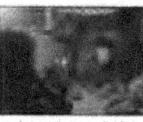

IGLA (THE NEEDLE)
Dir: Rashid Nugmanov, 1988
Soviet Union, 81 mins.
Russian with English subtitles

Igla is often established as a precursor to the Kazakh new wave. Viktor Tsoi, (from the legendary band Kino) plays Moro, a stoic and nonchalant young man who finds himself helping his morphine-addicted ex-girlfriend kick her habit.
9/13: 10pm • 9/21: 7:30pm • 9/29: 7:30pm

KURYER (COURIER)
Dir: Karen Shakhazarov, 1987
Soviet Union, 88 mins.
Russian with English subtitles

Largely ignored on release, Kuryer eventually came to critical acclaim over the years. It tells the story of a high school graduate trying to make sense of his life. With no prospect for a college education, a grim mandatory military service awaits in his future.
9/3: 7:30pm • 9/9: 7:30pm • 9/22: 7:30pm

WOMEN MAKE MOVIES

Spectacle and Women Make Movies, the celebrated non-profit organization and distributor of independent film and video by and about women, are proud to host a new series of collaboratively programmed screenings that will delve widely and deeply into WMM's diverse catalog, showcasing noted classics and underscreened gems.

MADAME X: EINE ABSOLUTE HERRSCHERIN
(Madame X: An Absolute Ruler)
Dir: Ulrike Ottinger, 1977
Germany, 141 mins
In German, with English subtitles

Madame X, the cruelest and most successful pirate of the Far Eastern seas, puts out a call to all women seeking a world full of gold, love, and adventure to join her crew and become marauders on the high seas. But even after their first pitiless attack on a yacht carrying hilarious caricatures of bourgeois male hegemony leaves them awash in plunder, the increasing assertion of the new pirates' identities and desires leads an already chaotic journey into absolute bedlam.
9/26: 8pm

ALSO SHOWING:

FIST CHURCH

The 70s, 80s & early 90s were a wonderful time when a boy or girl could sit down in front of their TV set after Saturday morning cartoons and tune into their local UHF station to catch a helping of hundreds of Kung Fu matinees. Every other Sunday we'll be mining the depths of VHS, VCD, DVD, and the darkest corners of the internet to bring you the wildest post-brunch experience you're likely to have. So, get faded on Bloody Mary's and come kick your feet up while we play fast and loose with the rules and witness people fight vampires, ninjas, swordsmen, and more. The movies won't be announced, but trust us, we wouldn't steer you wrong.
9/1: 3pm • 9/15: 3pm • 9/29: 3pm

IMPACT
Dir: Arthur Lubin, 1949
USA, 111 mins.

Noir-staple Brian Donlevy stars in Arthur Lubin's subtle melodramatic 1949 sleeper Impact. Typically relegated to tough-guy supporting roles, Donlevy plays very successfully against type as love-struck automotive mogul Walter Williams, a sensitive man who unfortunately puts far too much faith in the wrong sort of gal. Despite its B-grade production and modest return, Impact also features an unusual number of on-screen product placements for an era in which the practice remained very uncommon, presenting an illuminating and authentic aspect of late-1940s America not usually seen on the silver screen.
9/3: 10pm • 9/14: 10pm • 9/23: 7:30pm

MIDNIGHTS WITH SCOOTER MCCRAE

By the early '90s, many genre fans took the availability of consumer-grade video equipment as a call to arms, producing massively personal, astoundingly original works; some of which would contain imagery and themes no studio picture would dare touch. Scooter McCrae was on the front-lines of this strange new world, and his debut feature Shatter Dead (1994) is at once a staple and a stand alone slap in the face to the tried pitfalls of the horror genre, communicating in its own brand of subversive poetry. Several years later McCrae would push the envelope to degrees few others would even dare speak of with his depraved Sci-Fi epic Sixteen Tongues (1999), a cryptic future-world nightmare with meditation on modern human mentality more brazen than Paul Schader's entire filmography. Join us Sept. 20th and Sept. 27th at Spectacle for two midnights of the extreme, passionate, and undeservedly obscure works of Scooter McCrae. 9/20 & 9/27 midnight - director in attendance both nights!

20 YEARS OF CUFF

Chicago Underground Film Festival is the longest running underground film festival in the world. Founded the same year as the now defunct NYUFF, it remains a vibrant & evolving home for radically dissenting filmmaking and the defining example for underground film events all over the world. This program brings together legendary shorts from the festival's first twenty years. Running time: 137 mins.
9/13: 6pm • 9/27: 8pm

** For more information on the Portugal Underground Film Festival visit spectacletheater.com

67

> TORQUE (V.O.)
> "There you go; wouldn't want her to
> miss a thing when I find you and fuck
> you to pieces. Closing your eyes to
> all the horrors in this world always
> seemed like a cheat to me..."

Alik screams out in terror as she cries.

> ALIK (V.O.)
> "Nooooh!! You sick fucking scum!!!"

Adrian reaches under his bed and pulls out a beat-up old suitcase;
he snaps it open, revealing that it is full of guns and knives and
all sorts of other obscure and exotic weaponry. He pulls out two
high-powered handguns and loads them up.

> TORQUE (V.O.)
> "You're dead meat, scumbag, cause now
> I'm coming for you. I know you're in
> here somewhere, and now you're gonna'
> die like you never imagined..."

Adrian kicks open the door to his room with the high-powered
weaponry in the air and ready to fire.

29.) INTERIOR MOTEL HALLWAYS - MORNING

Boom! Adrian is charging through the Hallway now, as the lights
and colors of his own perception shift intensity and hue. It has
become as though every move he makes leaves watery trails that
slow him down and confuse him.

> TORQUE (V.O.)
> "I know everything there is to know
> about you now, asshole. You're in
> one of these rooms, aren't you? Well
> I'm gonna' kick in every fucking door
> until I find your ass, and then I'm
> gonna' deep fry it into oblivion."

> ALIK (V.O.)
> "No! Let go of me! Let me out of your
> crazy fucking head, scumbag!!"

Wham! Adrian kicks open the door to one of the rooms...

30.) INTERIOR MOTEL ROOM #A - MORNING

Revealing some Old Guy just standing there in his underwear with a
look of terror on his shriveled face.

SIXTEEN TONGUES Screenplay Notes

PAGE 68:

Torque's rampage is completely different in the movie because we realized that once we had access to a working S&M dungeon, we should take advantage of the various rooms and the scenarios they could provide. Having some rooms that looked different and wellequipped with pricey fetish gear gave us as slight boost in on-screen production value.

One of the fun things we got to do was use a mummification casting that Mistress Rena Mason specialized in; as in, she had clients who paid her to mummify them. This was a new fetish to me, and I found it fascinating. When Torque shoots the mummy in the head, it's my voice that you briefly hear reacting and dying. In fact, the blonde woman in that scene is the wonderful Mistress herself and her reaction to everything is priceless.

Another performer who has branding scars on his arms was a relative of Crawford's; the naughty nun taking care of him is none other than SHATTER DEAD'S Stark Raven in a cameo appearance. It was great to work with her again, although I wish I could have given her more on-screen time. We did shoot some additional footage of her wearing a full latex nun outfit (a $1000.00 work of art that we borrowed for the shoot), but it didn't fit anywhere into the edit. You can see this brief footage in the deleted scenes on both the old DVD and the more recent Blu-Ray release. Stark looks fantastic in a latex nun outfit.

In the regular Sappho Hotel hallway footage, that's pretty much the entire production crew that got squibbed up and shot, and if you'll pardon the pun I think they all had a blast.

"I don't know who took these photos of Stark Raven, unfortunately."

146

                    OLD MAN
         "What the ..."

                    TORQUE
         "It's check out time, old man!"

Adrian opens fire and blows the Old Man to pieces. Before the
body even has time to crumple to the ground, Adrian has turned
around and left.

                    ALIK (V.O.)
         "Oh god, please stop! Please! I'll
         tell you which room I'm in!"

                    TORQUE (V.O.)
         "I don't need you to tell me a fuckin'
         thing, dead bitch! Prepare for justice!"

Moving down the Hall, Adrian kicks open the door to the next room.

31.) INTERIOR MOTEL ROOM #B - MORNING

A Middle-Aged Man with a whip is standing over a Young Woman who
is strapped to the bed. They both look equally shocked to see
Adrian bursting into the room.

                    MAN
         "Huh? Was this your idea, honey?"

The Young Woman writhes in terror and groans as she struggles with
her bonds; the Middle-Aged Man is turned-on, oblivious to the fact
that Adrian has his gun raised and pointed at him.

                    MAN
         "Wow, this is really turning you on,
         isn't it, babe?"

Boom! Adrian opens fire and blows away the Middle-Aged Man; the
shocked Young Woman watches as Adrian turns and points the gun at
her now. She trembles as tears roll down her cheeks.

                    ADRIAN
         "Your license isn't in order, whore."

Boom! Adrian fires, killing the Young Woman. He turns and exits.

32.) INTERIOR MOTEL HALLWAY - MORNING

Adrian administers justice to the people sleeping on the floors;
shooting them as they lie there asleep, kicking bodies out of the
way, moving along to the next door down the Hallway.

SIXTEEN TONGUES Screenplay Notes

PAGE 69:

Alice did this wonderful physical thing when she was plugged into the internet world where she was constantly shaking in reaction to her body taking the electrical current directly from the wall outlet. It was exhausting just to watch her do it while we were shooting, and I could see that it was very draining to do for her for prolonged periods— which is pretty much the entire scene that's spread across this number of pages. So this is just a note of appreciation for her dedication to the role; not just the indignity of the crazy glasses we gave her to wear, or having to be mostly naked for a lot of the shoot and then wearing a stained and loose piece of ugly fabric when she wasn't naked, but also the physical perseverance and endurance she conjured as she lived through the part and the shoot. No performer had it easy on this project, but I think Alice might have had the most physically demanding role overall when it came to stuff like this.

"Sorry, once again have no photo credits for these images."

> ALIK (V.O.)
> "This is like some kind of fucking
> nightmare... Please stop..."

> TORQUE (V.O.)
> "Don't worry, I'll wake you before it's
> all over, dead bitch."

Adrian charges down the Hallway in the heat of his hallucinogenic
rampage, stopping seemingly at random before a closed door.

> TORQUE (V.O.)
> "This is the one, isn't it? I can tell
> this is the right one."

> ALIK (V.O.)
> "Go away."

> TORQUE
> "I can smell you, Alik, cookin' away
> with all that wall current trapped
> inside your body trying to burn it's
> way out of you like a circuit breaker
> that's about to blow. Can you hear me
> out here, about to come inside and kill
> your sorry ass?!"

> ALIK (V.O.)
> "Please go away."

33.) INTERIOR ALIK'S MOTEL ROOM - MORNING

Adrian kicks open the door and finds Alik sitting on the floor in
her electronic gear, plugged into the wall outlet, shaking with
pain and nervousness.

> TORQUE
> "Peek-a-boo, asshole. Time's up for
> you in this world..."

> ALIK (V.O.)
> "Let me go! Let me back into my body
> so I can fight you in the real world!"

Adrian leans into Alik's face, talking to her out-loud as Alik's
voice continues inside his head.

> TORQUE
> "Nope. Ain't gonna' happen, hackette.
> You zapped yourself into my head to

SIXTEEN TONGUES Screenplay Notes

PAGE 70:

Starting on the bottom of this page and continuing on Page 71, Torque kills a hotel guest and uses their cut-off hand to keep the infrared scanner of the sink activated in order to flood the bathroom and the rest of the hotel room.

As much as I wanted to shoot this, there was just no time in the schedule. This would have involved stunt work, special effects make-up, blood squibs and gun firing EFX work, so rushing the shooting of something like this would have jeopardized on-set safety protocols. Also, getting all the correct angles to sell the EFX and the ferocity of the violence would have been difficult without fully choreographing everything completely.

The worst thing in my mind was ignoring established story logic concerning how the sink would overflow if we didn't have something in the path of the infrared sensor to keep the water running. In the end, at this point in the story it didn't seem to hurt anything by ignoring the logic and I've never had anyone complain to me about it. Other stuff? Yes, I get complaints all the time. But thankfully nobody has held my feet to the fire over this minor offense.

"Oh well, at least these are fun photos, whoever took them...!" - Scooter

                    turn me off and it didn't work. So
                    now I'm gonna' get you out of here
                    by turning you off at the source."

Alik's shaking body tries to move, but jerky spasms are the best
that she can achieve.

                    ALIK (V.O.)
                    "You're not gonna' win this one! I'm
                    not gonna' let you!!"

                    TORQUE
                    "Don't hurt yourself too bad; save
                    some for me."

Bullets of sweat begin to pour off of Alik; they crackle into a
shower of sparks as they hit the electrodes that are attached to
her skin. Adrian backs away from Alik.

                    TORQUE
                    "Now *that's* an interesting idea..."

Alik's mouth begins to form a word on it's lips; Adrian leans back
in to her again.

                    TORQUE
                    "Trying one last time to launch a word
                    in your body's dying moments. Strange
                    feeling, isn't it, knowing that you'll
                    be doing something so mundane for the
                    very last time? I remember that feeling
                    just before I woke up wrapped in tongue.
                    But you're not gonna' wake up..."

Alik spits on Adrian, but it is so pathetic that she gets more of
it on herself than on him. Adrian just shakes his head and lets
out a chuckle of understanding.

                    TORQUE
                    "I would have done the same thing if
                    I was as pathetic as you."

Adrian rises and heads towards the door of the room. He steps out
into the hallway.

34.) INTERIOR MOTEL HALLWAY - MORNING

Adrian sees a Motel Guest leaning over the body of a dead man in
the middle of the hallway. Adrian whips out his gun and badge,
pointing it at the Motel Guest as he looks up at him.

                    MOTEL GUEST
        "Shit, man, what the hell happened...?"

                       TORQUE
           "I'll need your help, citizen."

Bang! Adrian fires and blows the brains out of the back of the
head of the now-dead Guest; Adrian walks over to body of the Guest
and pulls out a sharp knife from his boot.

                       TORQUE
           "I'll get this back to you when we've
           gotten everything worked out."

                    TORQUE (V.O.)
           "Better check his wallet; get an address
           and a phone number so he can be contacted
           at a later date."

Adrian cuts off the hand of the Guest just below the wrist.   He
turns around and heads back towards Alik's motel room.

35.) INTERIOR ALIK'S MOTEL BATHROOM - MORNING

Adrian takes the hand, placing it next to sink's infra-red sensor.

                       TORQUE
           "Simple physics is what's gonna' kill
           you, girl. Who says there's no poetic
           justice in the universe anymore?"

Adrian stuffs a towel in the drain, stopping it up to block water.

                    TORQUE (V.O.)
           "You've been so quiet. I would have
           thought you'd have a lot of interesting
           stuff to say before you die."

                     ALIK (V.O.)
           "I've been busy checking up on a few
           things about you while I'm in here."

Finally, Adrian grabs Alik's credit card refreshening apparatus
and slides it through the sink slot. The water suddenly begins to
flow into the bowl of the sink.

                       TORQUE
           "I'm not easily distracted, not that
           it could make any difference at this
           point. It's not me you have to worry
           about, but the water level."

SIXTEEN TONGUES Screenplay Notes

PAGE 72:

"Bacterial psycho-drama". Jeezus, how much was I drinking when I wrote all this? Talk about a pretty serious left-turn to introduce into a screenplay on Page 72 of a 78 page script. As I mentioned before, this is the biological equivalent of the computer SNATCH program that was mentioned and detailed earlier in the story, so they were meant to mirror each other (I've been told that's something writers like to do sometimes in a story....). Since we lost the previous exposition about SNATCH, this story arc feels like a needless complication at this point instead of an interesting thematic expansion.

All that being said, I don't dislike the concept introduced here, but it is rushed out center stage all of a sudden and with no prior introduction of the doubling concept, I think it gets lost in all of the sturm und Drang of the quickly approaching climactic insanity that has been building up and gets suddenly unleashed.

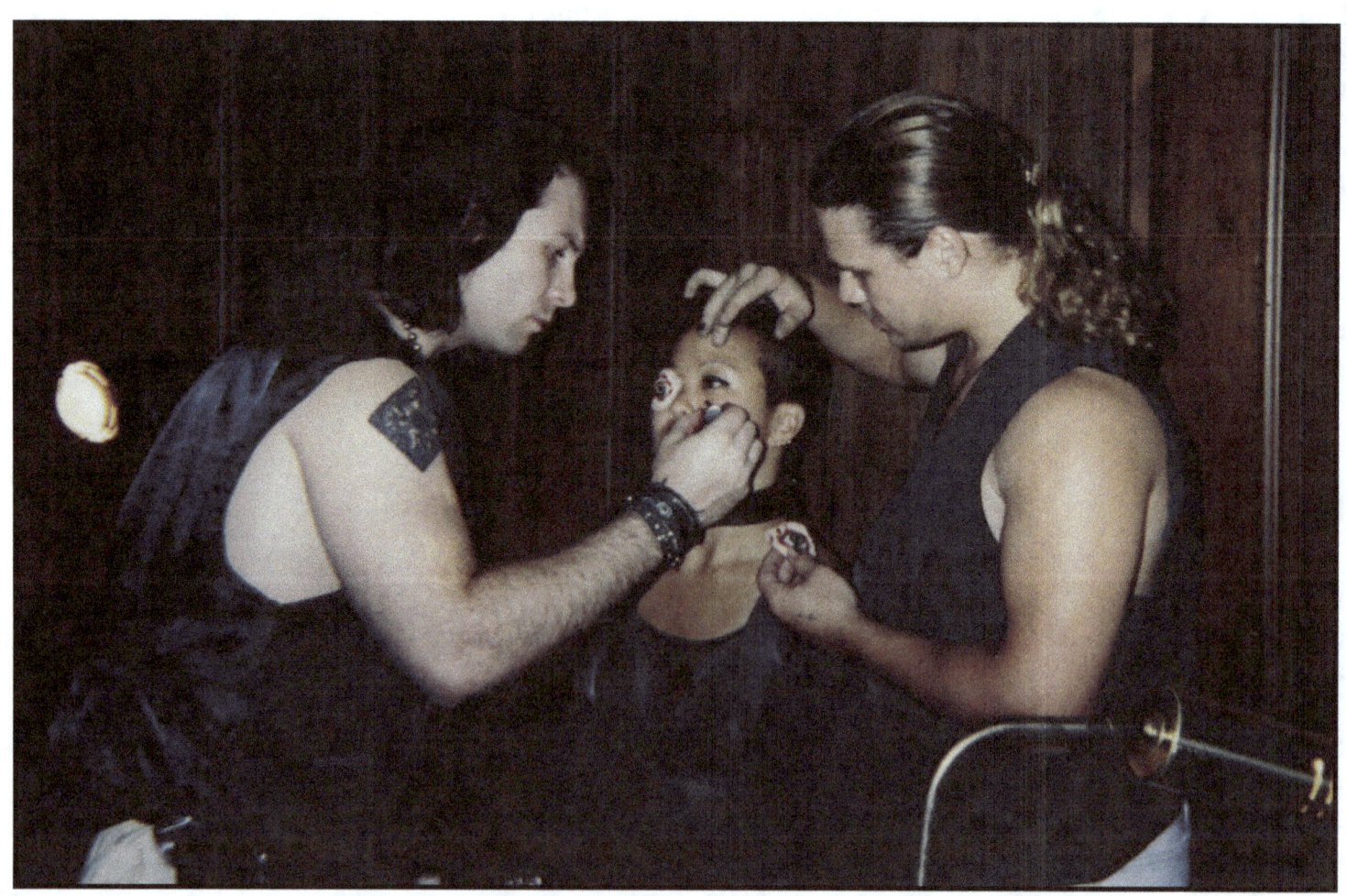

"Also pretty sure these photos of Glenn and Paul with Ginny were taken by Mr. Gingold during his Fangoria set visit." - Scooter

Adrian steps back from the sink and into the room with Alik's struggling body.

36.) INTERIOR ALIK'S MOTEL ROOM - MORNING

Adrian sits down on the edge of the bed, facing Alik to talk.

                    ALIK (V.O.)
          "Lots of files for me to access in
          here. Things I'll bet that even you
          don't know anything about."

                    TORQUE
          "So what? I'm a complicated guy."

                    ALIK (V.O.)
          "Know anything about bacterial psycho-
          drama? You've practically invented the
          fucking field by default."

The sink is now more than half-full of water.

                    TORQUE
          "Those are strange last words to hear
          from a chick who's about to die.."

                    ALIK (V.O.)
          "It's a new field of study that deals
          with infections and virus'. It's what
          happens when a skin graft, like tongue
          meat, and it's recipient, like you, are
          not able to communicate properly."

                    TORQUE
          "Communicate? What's this horse shit?"

                    TORQUE (V.O.)
          "Don't even waste your time listening
          to this crap. Let's get out of here."

Adrian rises and walks to the door; he stands there, in-between the hallway and this room, listening to the voices arguing inside his head. He sees the sink of water is now three-quarters full.

                    ALIK (V.O.)
          "The bacteria have learned to replicate
          body cells in order to move through your
          system undetected. But they've taken over;
          and your stupid body is only beginning
          to figure all this out right now."

SIXTEEN TONGUES Screenplay Notes

PAGE 73:
The screenplay doesn't dwell on Alik's death and the way it's written is almost incidental to the action. But I'm pretty sure I wrote it that way because I just wasn't sure how we were going to shoot it.

On-set, I shot the camera panning up the carpet leading to Alik, and then some close-ups of her reacting to being electrocuted when the water finally reached her. The water creeping along the floor was implied, as we simply could not flood the apartment location we were shooting in.

So Robert Morris saved us by adding a spreading water effect to the panning shot of the floor and then creating a shocking and violent electrical storm effect to fry Alik—giving her the meaningful on-screen death that she so richly earned. We lucked out as it was much better than anything I thought we'd be able to afford to do for this moment.

At the bottom of the page, Ginny is discovering the root of her true self in much the same way that Torque is finding out about the true nature of how his corporeal form has been taken possession of. They may be worlds apart in their character arcs, but they are connected by the pain and circumstances that are beyond their control and have shaped the very different outcomes of their lives. Nice literary aspirations for a dumb schmuck like me.

I love the way we shot this moment with her. It's just a series of simple shots that dissolve from one to another while the camera matches the upward motion of her rising from the bed. Unfussy visual storytelling that delivers the goods and looks cool on-camera can be very satisfying stuff.

                    TORQUE
        "Smart bacteria...?"

                    TORQUE (V.O.)
        "That's ridiculous! You don't believe
        any of this crap for second!!"

Water begins to overflow the sink, spattering against the floor.

                    ALIK (V.O.)
        "Even your brain cells have been replaced.
        There's nothing left of you, Torque, but
        the survival instincts of a spit wad and
        the clothes holding you together."

The water overflows the sink and dribbles into the bedroom carpet.

                    ALIK (V.O.)
        "Tongue is muscle; nothing but pure
        instinct without thought. There's
        more animal life in a pair of shoes
        or a belt than there is in you right
        now..."

                    TORQUE
        "I don't understand..."

                    TORQUE (V.O.)
        "Good; it's better this way..."

                    ALIK (V.O.)
        "Go ahead and kill me, lick stain. At
        least I'll be dying as a human being..."

Adrian steps out of the room and the water catches up with Alik;
she explodes in a burst of sparks and flames.

DISSOLVE TO:

37.) INTERIOR ADRIAN'S MOTEL ROOM - MORNING

A Series of Dissolves as Ginny jerkily wakes up (not showing her
face clearly). She rises and shields her eyes from the ambient
light in the room which is now too painful for her to look at.

                    GINNY (V.O.)
        "Sexual exhaustion to keep me calm.
        That makes sense to me now. The
        thing that was driving me crazy was
        the thing that was supposed to keep
        me calm between assignments..."

SIXTEEN TONGUES Screenplay Notes

PAGE 74:

I suspect I don't need to say this, but I will point out that when we shot the footage of Ginny's hands grabbing the guns from Torque's suitcase, they were hers and not mine. Torque's long sleeves and gloved hands are what made me able to double for him on the previous shot of this suitcase full of marvelous murder toys.

Interesting that I wrote in that Ginny's dialogue would now be voice-over. I don't know if that was an oversight when I was initially typing the screenplay or an on-set decision we made during rehearsal. Either way, making those lines part of the voice-over works better in my mind than having her scream them out on-set.

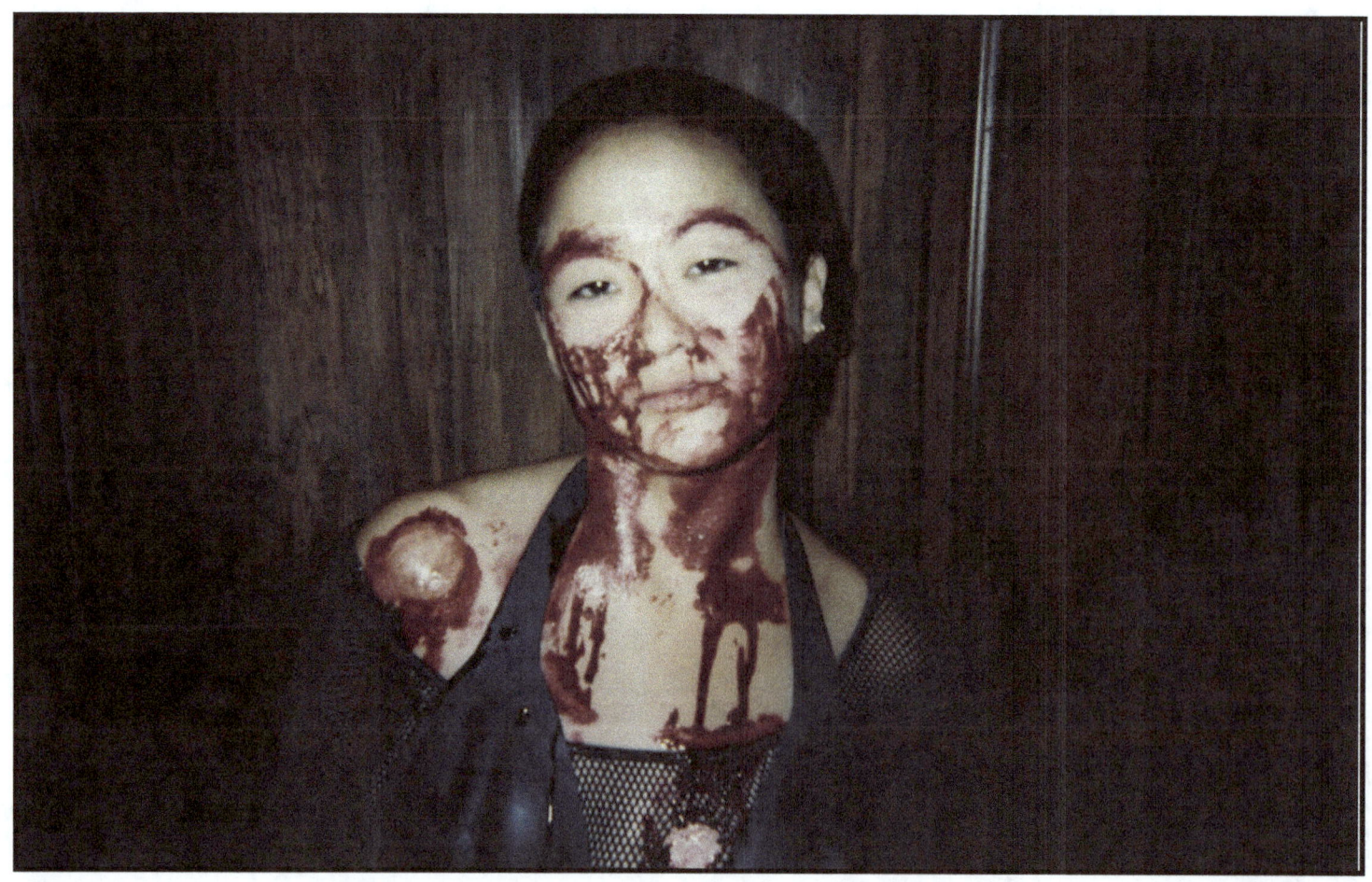

74

Ginny growls and spins around, angrily smashing a lamp on the nearby night stand. It crashes to the floor and breaks, but she continues to kick the broken pieces for a moment.

                    GINNY (V.O.)
       "Now I understand... All the anger
       and urges that blinking kept under
       control. Now it's gone. Nothing
       to distract me from the one thing
       I was made to do... to kill..."

Holding her hands over her eyes, trying to stop the overflow of blood beneath with pressure, Ginny leans her back against the wall and a grimace ripples across her shattered features as she opens her mouth and howls in anger.

                    GINNY *(V.O.)*
       "All this and still no pain! How
       much more am I built to take before
       I begin feeling pain?!"

The blood beneath her hands spills out all over her face like red water out of a squeezed sponge as she falls to her knees.

                    GINNY *(V.O.)*
       "Killer! Killer!! I'm gonna' kill
       you! KILLER!!"

MONTAGE: A series of Quick-Cuts as Ginny's bloody hands open up Torque's suitcase full of weapons, all of which are wrapped up in little plastic bags marked 'Evidence'. She snaps together and loads a few of the more powerful looking weapons and leaves.

DISSOLVE TO:

38.) INTERIOR MOTEL HALLWAY - MORNING

Close-Up of Ginny's bare feet walking through the trash littered hallway; blood is streaming down her legs while the carpet before her is stained by thick airborne droplets of red.

Adrian stops and leans against the wall to reload his weapon; as he does, he hears the footsteps following him coming from around the corner.

                    TORQUE
       "You wanna' know about where you came
       from and who the fuck made you, huh?
       Well listen up, cunt!"

SIXTEEN TONGUES Screenplay Notes

PAGE 75:

Removed just a little bit of dialogue from the bottom of this page, but can't remember exactly why. This was a ton (sixteen tons?) of verbiage for Crawford to memorize, but he did a great job of it and we shot the entire run of it through three or four times, and from those various takes that's what we used in the movie. I asked him to change the intensity on each take, and also made sure to have the camera in a different place each time we shot (it was always me running around him doing my handheld bit on all the takes). So there's a kind of odd discontinuity between the various takes, both visually and in performance, but I wanted that kind of ragged quality as I thought it would better convey the meltdown of his brain and his own sense of first-person self. He did a great job on all of the takes and it was tiring trying to keep up with him with the camera as he threw his body all over the place and bounced off of the hallway walls.

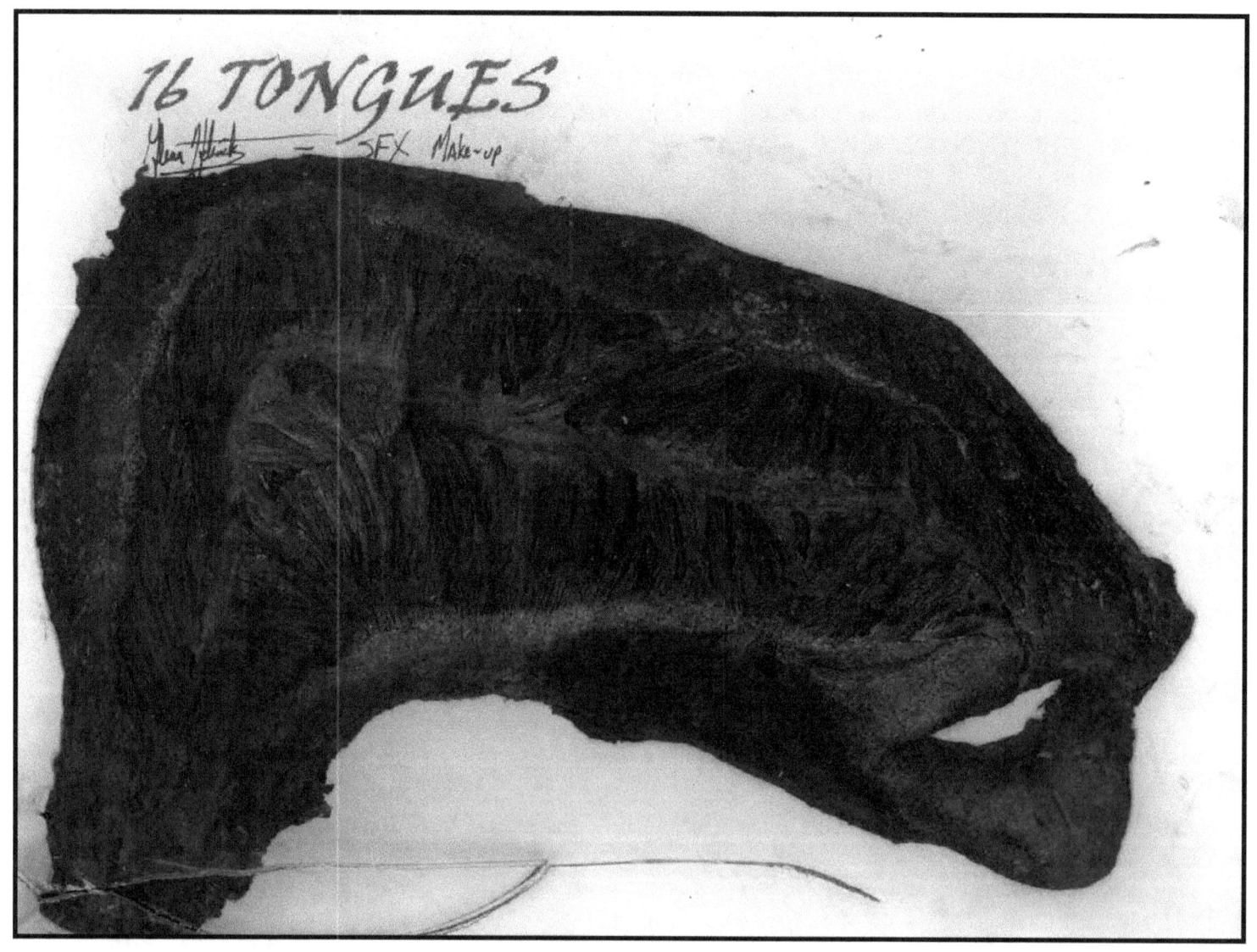

Torque f/x appliance signed by Glenn Hetrick. See p. 162

75

Silence. Adrian finishes reloading and moves cautiously towards
the corner. He is uncomfortable, but in control.

>   TORQUE
>   "Right after you left, I linked up with
>   the big boys and found out everything
>   I'll bet you've ever wanted to know.
>   So I hope you're ready to hear some shit
>   that's gonna' knock you down on your
>   flabby yellow ass!"

Adrian comes barreling around the corner and fires his weapon -
but there is nobody there as the tip of Ginny's shadow slithers
away around the corner. A little flustered, he continues making
his way down the hall.

>   TORQUE
>   "You're momma' was part of a control
>   group; a whole bunch of woman who
>   were pregnant with little defects
>   just like you who were waiting to
>   be born. You know what I mean...?"

We see Adrian's progress down the hallway through a drugged-out
series of Dissolves; Close-Ups of the shakey gun in his hand,
footsteps, his lips moving as he speaks, etc. Various Video EFX
slow-down and blur the image as his mind continues to meltdown.

>   TORQUE
>   "When the Feds found out about this
>   misappropriation of funds and the
>   unauthorized experiments he had
>   operating out of his basement, they
>   tracked down all his belly-up bitches
>   and killed them. Who knows? I'd
>   guess yer' momma' was a whore just
>   like you who needed the money and
>   didn't give a shit how or where she
>   got it from."

Adrian's mosaic of dissolving images continues, now occasionally
interspersed with shots of Ginny's bloody feet and the loaded gun
in her hands moving through the Frame.

>   TORQUE
>   "Couple of hours later down in the
>   morgue, technician hears this muffled
>   crying sound coming from inside a room
>   fulla' dead whores. She opens up the
>   door and finds one of the bagged-up
>   stiffs has got something moving around

PAGE 76:
Some more missing dialogue here as well, but can't remember if we shot it and cut it or excised it on-set. Can't say I miss the term "shit-struedel' too much, but am glad we didn't lose 'cunt-roach' along the way as that one remains in use amongst producer Alex Kuciw and myself in appropriate situations. It's such a joyously childish thing to say and I love it.

~~inside the bag with it. She unzips the~~
~~little fucker outta' there~~, and the
next thing you know some poor minimum-
wage stich-jockey ~~bitch~~ is holding *you*
in her hands..."

Adrian kicks open an ajar door and opens fires, but finds nobody
inside the empty room. He moves back into the hallway.

                         TORQUE
          "Shit! God damn this bullshit!"

Adrian rubs his forehead, trying to pull his mind back into shape.

                         TORQUE
          "So now whadya' think of that, you
          sorry little cunt-roach? They
          pulled you outta' the ass of some *whore*
          ~~dead bitch~~, then they threw you in
          the fuckin' garbage can with all
          the spare parts and crap they dig
          outta' sick people, flush you down
          the toilet into the sewer and now
          here you still fuckin' are, runnin'
          around like a defective piece of
          snot that won't go away, gettin'
          your ass all ripped up outta' shape!"

Adrian hears a noise, points his gun and fires. He stumbles
forward, breathing heavily, and falls to his knees on the floor.
Desperately, his gun shakes as he struggles to re-load it quickly.

                         TORQUE
          "The doctor who made you, by the way,
          was promoted and made head of special
          military projects and is now so high
          up on the feeding chain I can't even
          find his shadow. And I'm a fuckin'
          cop! Is that a shit-struedel or what?"

Rising, Adrian regains his compsosure and moves to the edge of the
next corner. He listens and hears wet movements along the other
side of the wall.

                         TORQUE
          "So daddy's little girl is a grown-up
          kill-freak without a place to play.
          Poor thing. Must really burn you up
          inside, huh? A jolt of juice with
          every blink, and nowhere to cash in
          those itchy murder chips..."

SIXTEEN TONGUES Screenplay Notes

PAGE 77:

The make-up guys did a great job coming up with the lidless eyeball appliances for Ginny. They looked spooky before they even got the blood on them. Poor Jane couldn't see a thing through them once they were put into place, so she had to be escorted onto set and place into position, and then led back to the make-up space when we were done shooting so she could have them removed. I'm sure it was physically uncomfortable to be wearing the appliances and mentally disorienting to not be able to see anything for awhile.

On top of that, Jane had two live weapons loaded with blanks to fire. We did our best to work out with her exactly where to aim them and then cleared the hallway of everyone besides me. The first take went great and Jane nailed the ferocious energy of the moment as she screamed and fired away.

During the second take, I asked her to open up to her anger and anguish even further, and she really let herself fly off the handle—including that wonderfully bonkers moment where she tosses away the empty gun and keeps firing the other one with both hands before falling backwards against the covered radiator behind her. It's the final image of the movie and I always refer to it as our TEXAS CHAIN SAW MASSACRE ending as it feels like the projectionist pulled the plug on the projector instead of turning it off.

At the end of the second take, I noticed some blood on my upper right arm and realized I had gotten so close to her while we were shooting this moment that I got grazed by some shrapnel from the blanks; proof of just how dangerous even a gun loaded only with blanks can still be. Totally my fault, of course, and everything was fine, but a reminder that you can never have enough on-set safety and please don't try this stuff at home, kiddies!

Thanks for reading and I hope these notes provided some interesting context on the writing of the screenplay and the shooting of the movie.

77

Adrian steps away from the wall and fires both his guns into it an angle which would hit whomever might be standing along the other side of the corner.

> TORQUE
> "Bingo..."

He listens for a moment and hears the sound of Ginny sighing in pain on the other side.

> TORQUE
> "There. You happy now, kid? Now come on out and fight, you sorry little fucker. Come on! Stop making me work so hard just to put you out of your fuckin' misery!"

Adrian quickly flings himself around the corner with his guns at the ready, but he finds nobody there. Dumbfounded, he turns his attention back to the bullet holes in the wall.

Adrian, hunched down on one knee, leans in close to the bullet holes and observes the blood that now comes dripping out of them.

> TORQUE
> "What the...?"

SKRUNCH! Ginny's fist comes ripping through the wall and smashes Adrian in the head. As she tears open the wall and pulls the rest of herself through the hole, Ginny slams Adrian flat onto his back on the floor.

Covered in rubble and blood, Adrian looks up at Ginny with terror in his eyes and no weapons within reach.

> TORQUE
> "Holy fuck..."

What's left of Ginny is standing there, her bloody arms stretched out with a gun in each hand, ready to fire. She is grinning from ear-to-ear, the shards of her sliced-off eyelids flapping in her eyes as the blood pours down her cheeks.

Screaming at the top of her lungs, she empties both her weapons into Adrian as he shakes on the floor.

Ginny falls to her knees and lets the smoking guns drop out of her hands as something between a howl of pain and choked laughter rips itself from her mouth.

CUT TO BLACK: THE END

SIXTEEN TONGUES

CAST
JANE CHASE: GINNY CHIN-CHIN
CRAWFORD JAMES: ADRIAN TORQUE
ALICE LIU: ALIK SILENS
JONNY TINGLE: PRISONER ONE
GLENN HETRICK: PRISONER TWO
TINA KRAUSE: BEAR TRAINER
MARIA PEDERSON: DANCING BEAR
TERRY POSTAGE: PISSING MAN
RENA MASON: MISTRESS MUMMY
STARK RAVEN: LATEX NUN
RON SIDDONS: WHIPPING BOY

MUSIC BY CEREBELLION
GEEK MESSIAH
SCOOTER MCCRAE

WRITTEN AND DIRECTED BY SCOOTER MCCRAE
PRODUCED BY ALEX KUCIW

VIDEOGRAPHER: SCOOTER MCCRAE (AS ROBERT FERRAPPLES)
FILM EDITING BY RICK O'SHEA
CO-EDITORS: SCOOTER MCCRAE AND ALEX KUCIW

SPECIAL WEAPON PROP: RON KARKOSKA
SOUND DESIGNER: DOUG JOHNSON
SPECIAL MAKE-UP EFFECTS BY GLENN HETRICK, PAUL SUTT
VISUAL EFFECTS BY ROBERT A. MORRIS

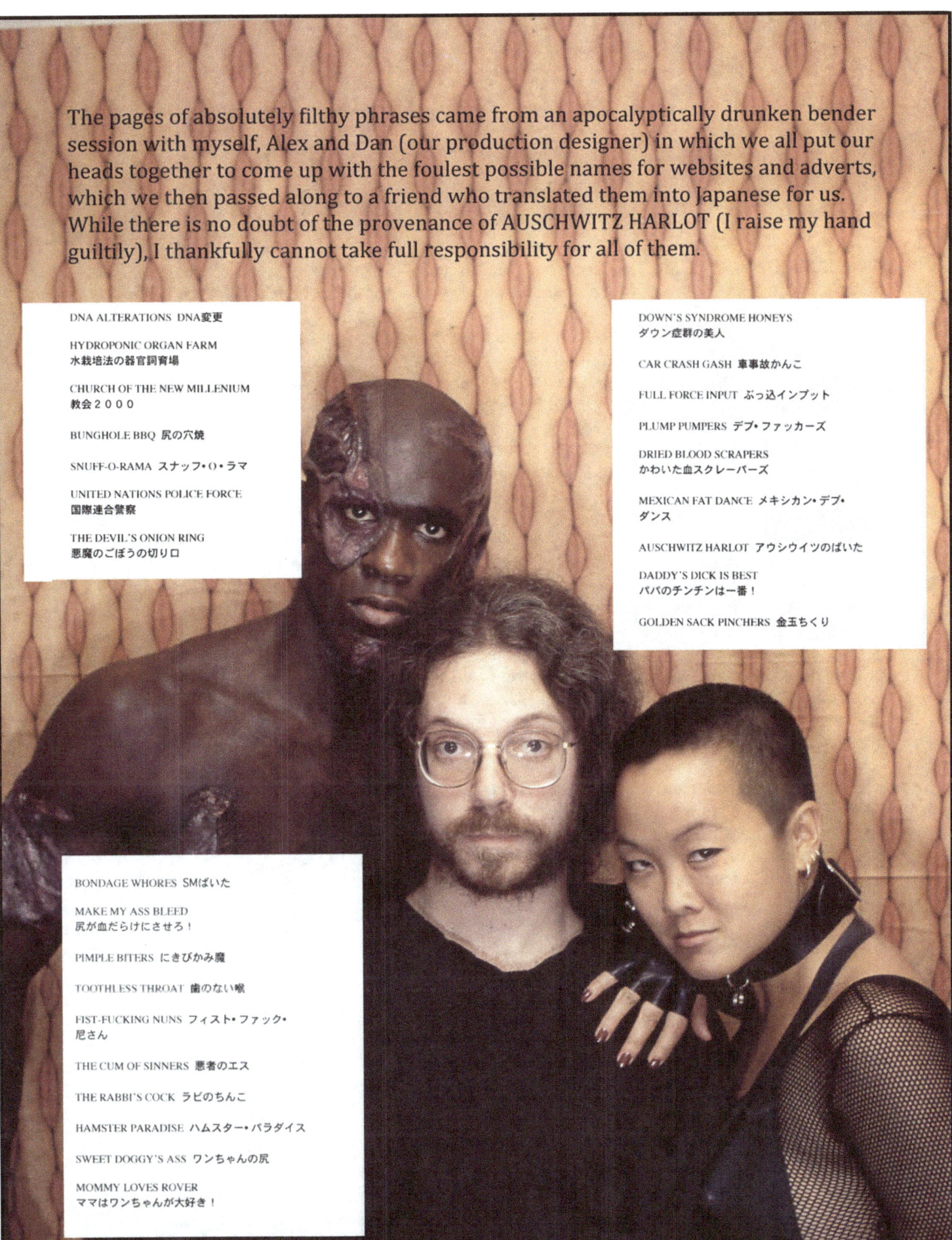

The pages of absolutely filthy phrases came from an apocalyptically drunken bender session with myself, Alex and Dan (our production designer) in which we all put our heads together to come up with the foulest possible names for websites and adverts, which we then passed along to a friend who translated them into Japanese for us. While there is no doubt of the provenance of AUSCHWITZ HARLOT (I raise my hand guiltily), I thankfully cannot take full responsibility for all of them.

DNA ALTERATIONS DNA変更

HYDROPONIC ORGAN FARM
水栽培法の器官詞育場

CHURCH OF THE NEW MILLENIUM
教会2000

BUNGHOLE BBQ 尻の穴焼

SNUFF-O-RAMA スナッフ・O・ラマ

UNITED NATIONS POLICE FORCE
国際連合警察

THE DEVIL'S ONION RING
悪魔のごぼうの切り口

DOWN'S SYNDROME HONEYS
ダウン症群の美人

CAR CRASH GASH 車事故かんこ

FULL FORCE INPUT ぶっ込インプット

PLUMP PUMPERS デブ・ファッカーズ

DRIED BLOOD SCRAPERS
かわいた血スクレーパーズ

MEXICAN FAT DANCE メキシカン・デブ・ダンス

AUSCHWITZ HARLOT アウシウイツのばいた

DADDY'S DICK IS BEST
パパのチンチンは一番！

GOLDEN SACK PINCHERS 金玉ちくり

BONDAGE WHORES SMばいた

MAKE MY ASS BLEED
尻が血だらけにさせろ！

PIMPLE BITERS にきびかみ魔

TOOTHLESS THROAT 歯のない喉

FIST-FUCKING NUNS フィスト・ファック・尼さん

THE CUM OF SINNERS 悪者のエス

THE RABBI'S COCK ラビのちんこ

HAMSTER PARADISE ハムスター・パラダイス

SWEET DOGGY'S ASS ワンちゃんの尻

MOMMY LOVES ROVER
ママはワンちゃんが大好き！

MAKE-UP FX JOURNAL:
"SIXTEEN TONGUES"

BY GLENN HETRICK

SUNDAY, JUNE 22: "O.K. ... so you want the guy to look like he's been in an explosion, lost a lot of skin, and then had it all replaced with human tongue. I got that, but you want the girl's eyelids to look like what?"... "Vaginas, actually vaginas with clitorises beneath them."..."That's what I thought you said...O.K., Cool." So went my first pre-production meeting with Producer Alex Kuciw and Director Scooter McCrea. These guys were sick...I like that. Nestled together at a table in a restaurant located at the mall in Rockaway, New Jersey we spent a few hours going over their concepts and goals for the film's Special FX scenes. We spent a good deal of the time bouncing rough conceptual sketches and verbal descriptions of the films two main characters (Adrian Torque and Ginny) off of one another. Not only were these guys sick but, more importantly, they were both completely original and focused on their vision.

We all found common ground in the fact that we were horror film buffs [I thought that *I* knew a lot until I started talking with them, they taught me a thing or two!], thus making our exchange of ideas simple and fluid. We could all site references whenever we were describing an idea. There was a lot of "Yeah, sort of like when 'so and so' burns that guy up in 'blank' but crossed with the scene in 'whatever' when the creature tears that guys face off...What the fuck was that guy's name?". Needless to say, I fell in love with the project. Prior to this I had met with Alex once before, in Manhattan, when I was bidding on the project. We reviewed my portfolio, discussed budget constraints and went over a few of the basic ideas. At first I was a little weary of undertaking the project. I knew that it would require a tremendous amount of work to pull it all off inside the budget and time allowance, but after this meeting I knew that I just had to be a part of this. It was going to be far too wild a ride for me to miss out on.

MONDAY, JUNE 23–FRIDAY, JUNE 27: With the first installment of the budget in place, I set about the time consuming and completely understated task of budget breakdown and supply ordering. Although this little "step" of FX Make-up for film is not mentioned in any of the "major" books or videos on the topic, I assure you boys and girls it is a BIG part of the work. A few miscalculations and ill-spent dollars here and you'll be up the creek without a paddle before you even get to the first day of shooting. **TID#1:** The words "I need more money" are more sacrilegious to an indie Producer than the nastiest verse of the Necronomicon is to a priest. When you agree to make things happen on a certain budget it is your <u>responsibility</u> to do just that. If you go over budget, you very well may find yourself spending your own money instead of making it.

After carefully comparing prices of every supply from all the different distributors, I placed my orders. It honestly took a full work week to handle this properly. I ordered all of my life-casting materials first and had them delivered by Friday. If I was going to pull all of this stuff together I knew I would have to work fast. I also remained in close contact with Alex and Scooter throughout this week and finalized many of the storyboards for the FX scenes.

SATURDAY, JUNE 28: It is hotter than hell at 7:30 in the morning when I pull up to Scooter's Brooklyn apartment (better known as the set from "Shatter Dead") for the first time. Michele (my assistant / girlfriend/ better half) is already starting to look peaked and I can't help but think to myself "God, please let all of the lifecasts that I do today come out right the <u>first</u> time." Scooter answers the door cheerfully (in his underwear; which, consequently, he remained in for the rest of

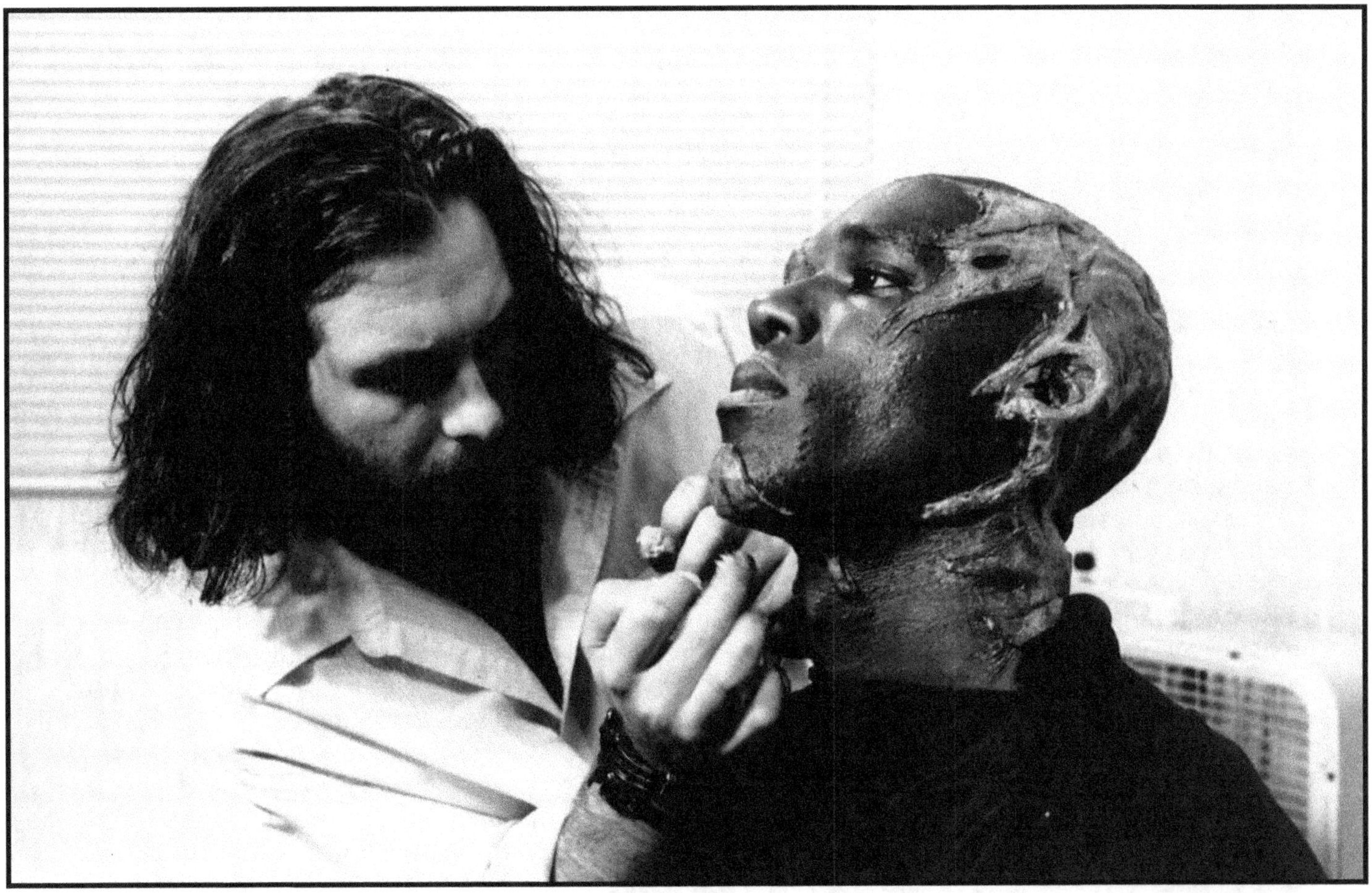

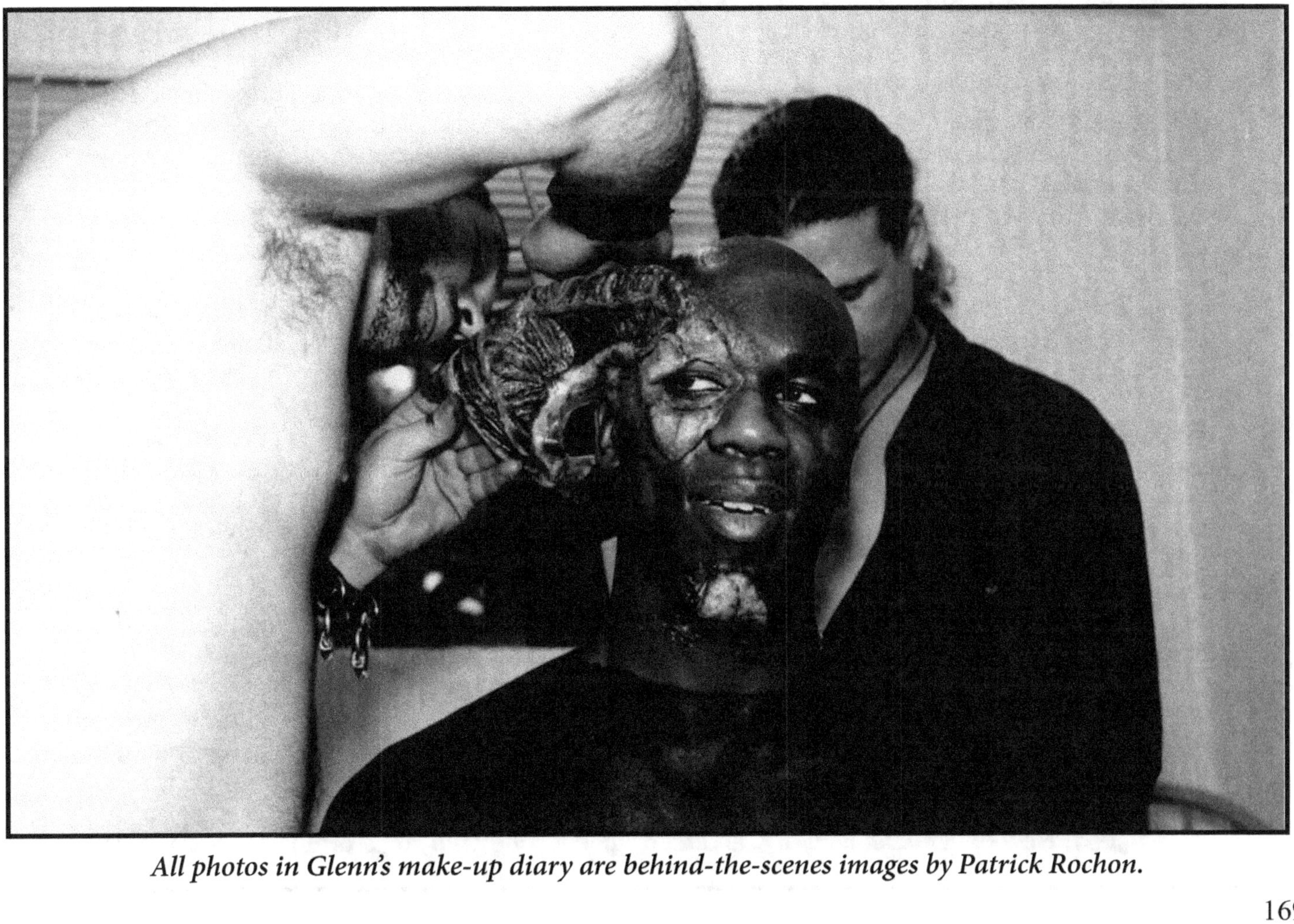

All photos in Glenn's make-up diary are behind-the-scenes images by Patrick Rochon.

the day) and invites us in. We carry the tons of supplies that it takes to do lifecasts on-site into the darkness that is this madman's sanctuary. When my eyes finish adjusting I find myself in a veritable library of laserdiscs.... all horror... from everywhere around the world. Italy, Japan, subtitled, dubbed... practically every one of those movies that you had heard about once or twice and were absolutely dying to see but were never able to find... well; they were all here, imagine my delight! I told you this guy was fuckin' cool. Anyway, back to the point... aside from the massive film library Alex and Crawford James awaited me inside.

Crawford played "Torque" in the film. He was, well...big, bad, and black. He looked like he was ready and willing to kill anyone or anything that looked at him the wrong way (it's called good casting). Despite his appearance, Crawford turned out to be one of the nicest guys I'd ever met. Over the next few hours I buried him beneath a full head lifecast, which he took like a champ. Using Teledyne-Getz Prosthetic Grade alginate and Johnson and Johnson 4" extra fast set bandages (both from Alcone) Michele and I performed a full head lifecast on Crawford. The excessive heat made the alginate set quick, so every second counted. Unfortunately, Crawford suffocated and died beneath the mass because we forgot to leave air holes, so we had to start from scratch with a new actor (just checking to make sure your paying attention here). After three hours of work, I pulled out a perfect ultra-cal reproduction of Crawford's head. Next, I used the same type of alginate to take a mold of Crawford's entire chest. I cast that in plaster while Michele cleaned up and prepared for the next lifecast. After checking the chest cast for problems, Crawford was free to go. I knew that there was no time to redo any of the lifecasts, so the performers had to wait until each of the plaster casts had set until they could leave. By this time actress Jane Chase (Ginny) had arrived. I took a lifecast of her face, from the tip of the nose to her hairline, poured a positive, and we finally sent her on her way. During this all day session Scooter managed to dump two of those movies that I had been dying to see on to a VHS tape for me, but not without a little extra bonus ("Tombs of the Blind Dead" and some vintage "Felix the Cat" cartoons for Michele). I left that day not only completely excited about the project but also about working with the people that were going to make it happen.

MONDAY, JUNE 30-TUESDAY, JULY 8: I immediately began to sculpt the Torque headpieces. The schedule was a little rough because I was also commissioned to produce some Halloween mask prototypes at the same time. I had been doing FX for about six and a half years at this point and I had never had this many things to do at one time. It's amazing how much you can accomplish when you work 18 hours a day, seven days a week. Using roma plastilene (a combo of #1,#2,and#3) I sculpted the right side of Torque's head. I worked with tons of reference photos hanging all around me, most of which came from this great book on reconstructive surgery that focused on burn victims (which Alex had loaned me). I also used a lot of stuff that I found in back issues of horror mags and some other medical reference books. I took a texture stamp from a big strawberry and used it to texture all of the tongue areas of the sculpts. To keep costs at a minimum, I used just one full head life cast and then sculpted, molded and ran each piece separately. I also sculpted Ginny's vaginal eyelids during this time. I then photographed each sculpt extensively, developed the film and had the sculpts reviewed and approved by Scooter and Alex. **TID#2:** Yes, it is a pain in the ass to go through the photography and review for every sculpt and it seems to take up a lot of time but I guarantee it does not take as much time as having to re-sculpt and re-mold a piece that your employers are unhappy with.

During this week I also had a friend of mine (Paul Sutt) who I was working with at the time come to my shop. Paul was handling all of the squib work for me with his associate Russell Oister (who also did all of the weapons work). I also had Paul do the sculpt of the Torque penis for the sure-to-be infamous blow job scene (can I say that in this magazine?!). He showed up with the completed sculpt, which I can't rightfully describe in the pages of this publication. For molding purposes, it was sculpted on a thin wooden dowel. It became affectionately (but not too much so) known as the "Dick-on-a-Stick". Well, we molded it up and poured in a slush layer of mask latex (Alcone's Slush Latex). He took it home, let it dry, and then filled it solid with some ordinary silicone from

Home Depot (which, by the way, worked just fine).

WEDNESDAY, JULY 9-THURSDAY, JULY 17: Next, I molded the head piece and the eyelids in ultra-cal, cleaned the positives that they were sculpted on, (I did the same thing for Ginny; using one lifecast to make both sets of eyelids for her), and began sculpting the next stage. I sculpted the left side of the head and the second set of Ginny appliances (an effect that shows Ginny after Torque cuts off her eyelids). I used a set of glass eyes from Monster Makers and attached them over Ginny's eye area on her lifecast with clay. I then sculpted the surrounding area and gore (from the eyelids being severed) on top of that. I kept it all as thin as possible so as to avoid that fake, built-up look. I then molded everything, cleaned the mold, sculpted the chin piece on Torque and molded that. I took a few days off here to attend the Monster Bash Convention in Pittsburgh (come on, can you blame me...Forry Ackerman was there for Christ's sake?!)

MONDAY, JULY 21-TUESDAY, JULY 29: I had a meeting with Alex on Wednesday and I wanted to show him some tangible examples of the make-ups. I ran slip cast latex tests of all the finished pieces as well as a few pieces (one set of eye appliances and one of the Torque's head pieces) in foam latex. I used Monster Makers foam latex for everything on this project. It is a four part system and is incredible to work with. It's biggest strength is that it is not overly sensitive as far as running goes. If you don't have a triple beam scale you can use a conversion system to measure in cups, tablespoons and teaspoons (something everyone has the capability of doing). As long as you follow the mixing time schedules properly and take in to account the humidity and temperature as they apply to your refine time and gelling agent you should be able to produce near perfect results every time. I highly recommend it for all of you artist out there who are trying foam latex work for the first time. I also mixed a pigment (burnt sienna from Burman) into the gelling agent to tint the foam and to keep track of the gelling agent dispersion while mixing. Further, I added high rise foaming agent (also from Burman, mixed 50/50 with the normal foaming agent) to keep the foam nice and "fluffy" light.

TID#4: Foam latex suggestions- 1. Always bake your mold out for many hours before attempting to run foam latex in it. 2. Always keep a close eye on the size of your mold and all of it's angles while building it to make sure that it will fit inside of the oven that you have access to (this is not mentioned a lot because the "pros" have special ovens that are built big to accommodate foam latex molds; I am fairly certain that is **not** what your mother had in mind when she went to Sears to purchase the one that you are going to be trying to stuff that 200 pound plaster mold into at 3:30 in the morning .) I highly suggest taking interior measurements of your oven before beginning the mold process. You can often keep mold size down if you are making a conservative effort not to over build any of the areas. Another good reason to bake out your mold is to make sure that it fits before filling it. Few things suck worse than making a perfect mold of your sculpture, filling it with an A+ batch of foam and then finding out that the whole enchilada is *not* going to be sliding into your oven or any one else's that you know! (Uhhh...how much was that cold foam kit?) 3. Buy a stop watch before running foam. 4. Try the salvation army and thrift shops for a mixer if you don't have one. 5. If the foam doesn't gel... bake it out anyway because it still may cure properly and if not it will sure as hell be easier to clean out of the mold as one solid mass. 6. Keep records of each and every move you make while running the foam and learn from your mistakes. 7. Buy "Foam Latex Survival Manual" and "Foam Latex 911: The Emergency Manual" (both written by Donna Drexler and both available from Burman) and read them in their entirety. They will pay for themselves the first time they help you avert a major foam latex disaster. 8. Five gallons of foam goes a long way but it is always good to have plenty on hand. You may make mistakes and also may need to run more of each piece than you think you will. You will not have time to reorder and wait for the shipping of more foam. Try to budget a five gallon kit in right from the start. It will make things a lot easier in the long run and you won't have to freak out worrying that you are going to run out of foam if you make a mistake.

I spent the next couple of days running all of the foam pieces (a few runs of each, just in case).

Each piece was washed, trimmed and prepared for painting. I spent quite a few days here running around to local stores collecting other "basic" supplies like tons of cheap paper towels, make-up sponges, powder puffs, Styrofoam bowls and cups, disposable brushes, acetone, rubbing alcohol, etc. **TID#5:** You can keep your supply costs down (and increase your profit margin a bit) by spending the time to find deals on this kind of stuff. The few items that I mentioned here are the tip of the iceberg. You can often find many of the same supplies that you would order from a major supply house at places like Phar-mor Drug Stores or the Home Depot...all at a vastly reduced rate and minus the hefty shipping charges! Just keep your eyes open when you are out doing your normal shopping; remember...an FX artist is *always* working!

Next, I sculpted all of Torque's chest appliances on his chest cast using the same sculpting techniques as on the head pieces and several bullet hit prosthetics for Ginny. After molding those, I also sculpted a large amount of generic tongue pieces, all of varying size and shape, on a flat surface. From this I made two big tray molds of all the generic pieces. These pieces were to be used wherever needed on the days when we were shooting full body stuff. I used this technique so that I didn't have to lifecast every part of Crawford's upper body. Only a few of the pieces ended up being used (on the forearms, shoulders, and hands) but they worked perfectly. This was mainly because I gave myself a lot of options (which made me flexible to customize on-set, an invaluable asset) by sculpting many generic pieces knowing that I would only need a few. Let me make something clear here; this method is definitely inferior to actually designing specific pieces, on lifecasts, for each part of the make-up. The edge-blending of these pieces can be downright nightmarish, but...if you are working with a limited budget and limited time you can get some really impressive results from this "generic pieces" method. I got the idea from Tom Savini's book, "Grande Illusions". He used tray molds of generic pieces for "Dawn of the Dead". I had pulled this off on several other projects and have had great success with it. Just try to sculpt the pieces with a rounded edge that thins out. Keep it from being flat even though you are sculpting on a flat surface.

WEDNESDAY, JULY 30-SATURDAY, AUGUST 2: Each piece was pre-painted to speed the final application process. I used pros-aide adhesive and acrylic paints to create what is known as PAX paint. I thinned it with water for airbrushing and used a combination of both airbrush and paint brush to color the pieces (for the paint that I used with the paint brush, I barely used any water in the PAX mixture). **TID#6:** When mixing PAX I urge you to use small plastic containers with lids (the kind used by restaurants for salad dressings to go, etc.) to do the actual mixing. Make a little more than you need and then when you're done you can just pop a lid on it and save that particular color. This is a must, you will end up using several colors of acrylics to get the realistic PAX paints that you want (I have used more than fifteen tones to achieve a single color) and you must have saved samples so that you can color match if you need to mix more or to do touch ups. If you use more than a few colors, take a second and write the exact colors and approx. ratios used in your project journal (another must have).

On one of the painting days Paul came down to my shop with the finished Torque penis, which was now sporting a PVC tube that ran down the inside, through the silicone, to the tip to allow the prop to "squirt" bodily fluids. This feature was accentuated with three air bladders located between the silicone and the skin which provided a pulsating effect to the thing (just what it needed, right?). He used my mixes of PAX to paint the "Dick-on-a-Stick" so that it would match the color of the other pieces exactly. My original paint scheme used seven different reddish pink PAX tones for the tongue sections and a lightly bruised skin tone (5 PAX mixes) for the rest. I also had another paint scheme in mind, so I painted one of the runs of the big head pieces completely different, following my alternate scheme, in order to show Alex and Scooter the difference. On Saturday I loaded everything up into my sporty (yeah right!) Dodge Neon and headed for Scooter's to do a test make-up session on both leads. After hours of application, blending and coloring we decided to go with my alternate paint scheme. This meant that everything had to be re-painted. I also found problems with the edges of some of the pieces that had to be solved before shooting.

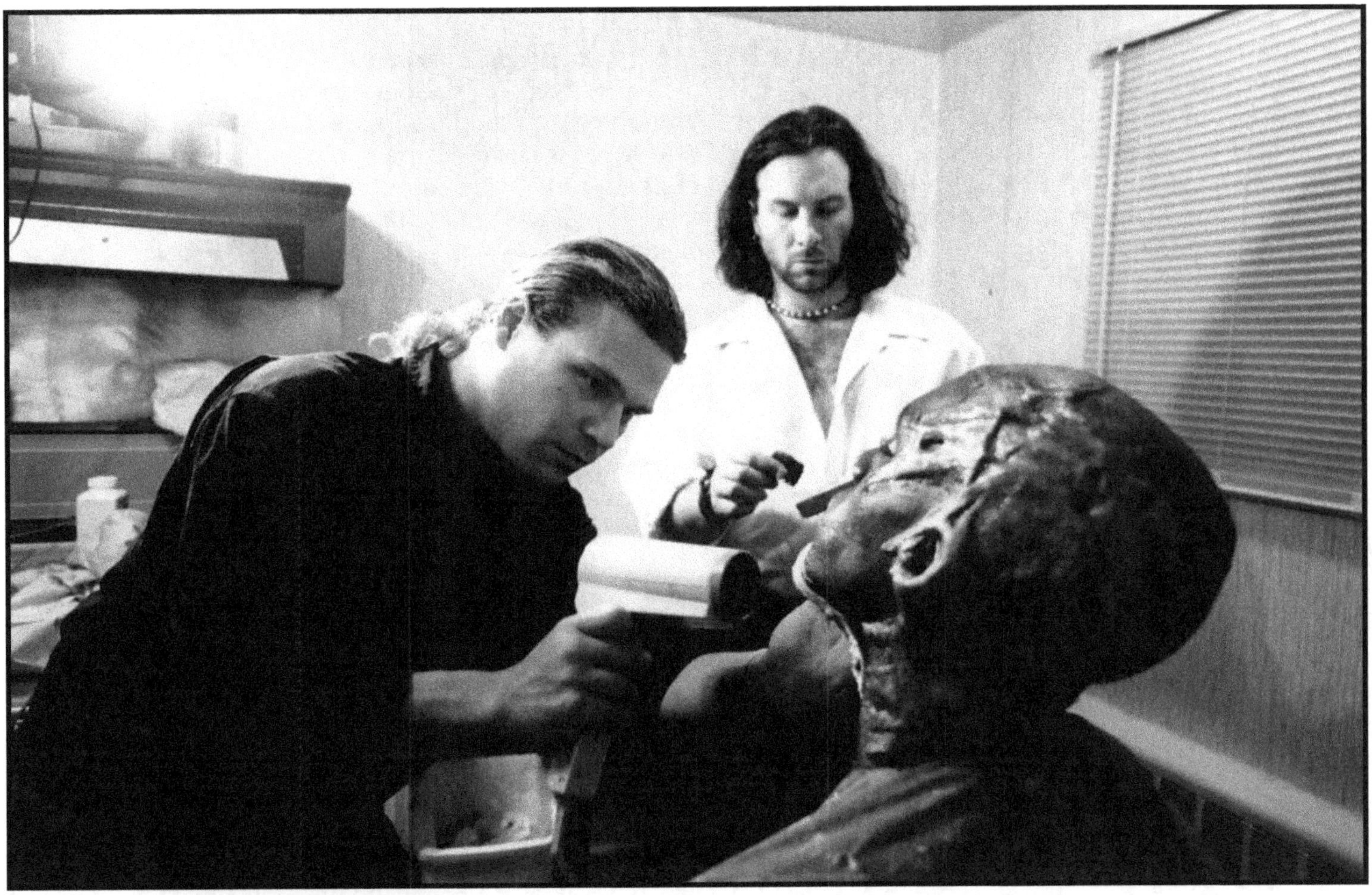

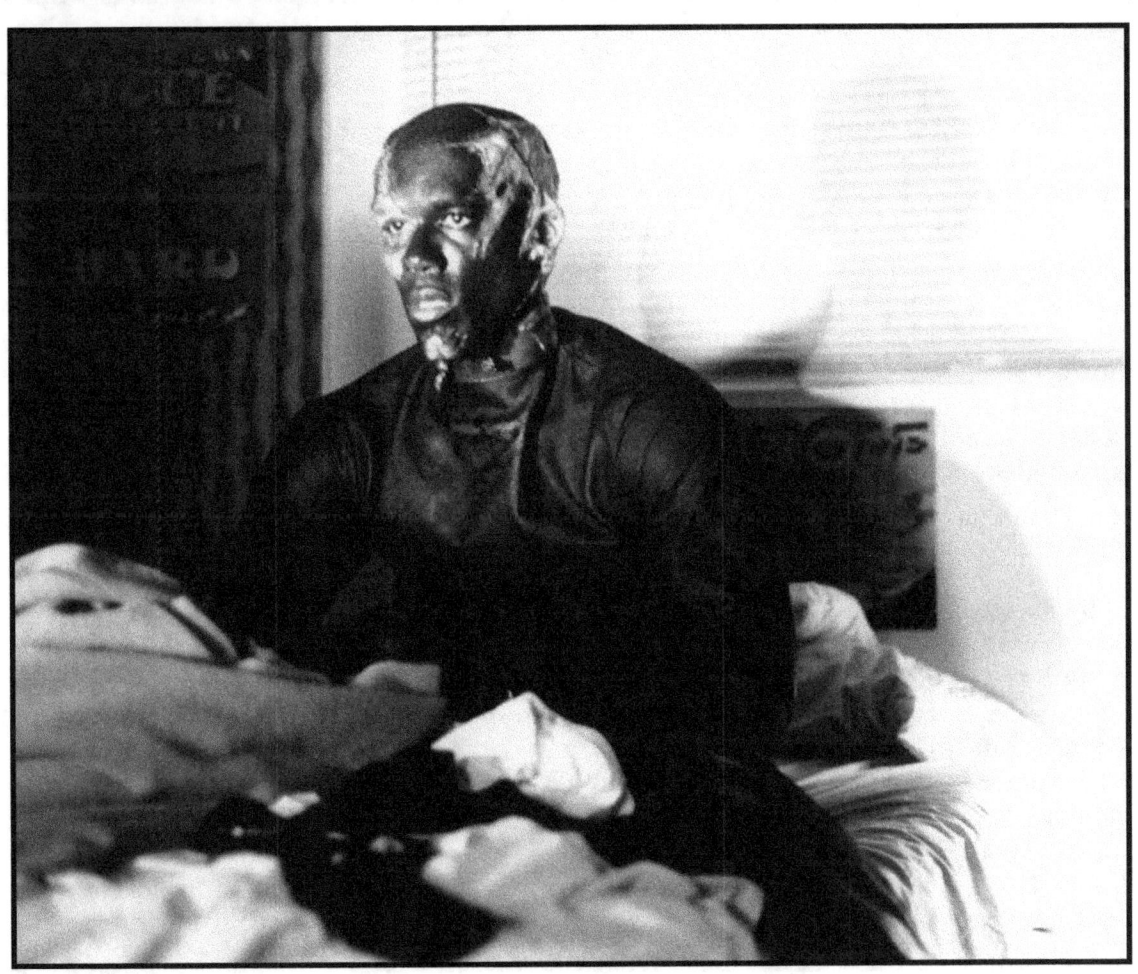

MONDAY, AUGUST 4-THURSDAY, AUGUST 14: I spent this last week and a half tweaking everything, making sure every piece was prepared and ready to go. I also re-painted everything. This time I used three colors (purple, red and yellow) and used paint brushes to put tiny dots all over the tongue areas. I then airbrushed light coats of various shades of pink, red and purple flesh tones; layering them but also keeping them light enough to allow the color from the dots to show through. I used the same technique on the flesh areas. Of course I used different colors (all more fleshy). This breaks up the colors and keeps the paint job from looking flat. With some practice (O.K., a lot of practice) you can begin to approach that life-like translucency that skin has on your foam pieces. I sealed all of the prosthetics with a matte spray sealer.

After checking my supply list (not once but twice; or more realistically thirty times) and making sure I had everything that I would need on-set, I loaded it all up and it was off to the races!

FRIDAY, AUGUST 15-MONDAY, SEPTEMBER 1: All right, on to principal photography. We shot at three different locations; Queens, Manhattan, and Long Island. We started in Queens with a marathon shoot. We did a lot of long days and covered insane amounts in single shooting sessions. I'd say that our average shoot lasted about 18 hours. Torque's make-up took about three hours to apply and blend for the head only. On the days that we shot him without his shirt on it took about 6 1/2-7 hours to apply the twenty three-piece full body make-up. Paul assisted me in doing the applications. It definitely required two sets of hands to get it all done in a reasonable amount of time. I have to add here that Crawford was a perfect patient; I can't recall him bitching even once about the make-up process. We would get in there early (two hours before call time on regular days, about five hours before on full body days) and Crawford would just put in his mini ear phones and zen out for the entire time that we were working on him. When we were finished, he'd go look at himself in the mirror and come back out completely in character and ready to shoot. Scooter would usually start the day shooting some stuff that didn't require Torque while we finished his make-up...it worked out great. This also gave Scooter a chance to come in while we were doing the application and give us his input. Both Scooter and Alex were totally involved in the make-up process, everyday, start to finish.

I used Alcone's PMMA 2004 Adhesive (their replacement for surgical adhesive) to glue all of the pieces down. Once they were secured, I used latex, stippled onto the edges, to blend the seam. On the "bad" seams I used PAX bondo (very simply pros-aide thickened with cabosil to a putty-like consistency) to blend, which I forced dry with my trusty blow-dryer. Once all of the edges were kosher, I used colors from my Kryolan RMGP palette to cover. I was in a situation were so much of Torque's head was covered with prosthetics (well over half) that I ended up giving all of his skin (both real exposed skin and the pros. pieces) a new color value. This was much faster than trying to get the entirety of the foam pieces (all of the edges were to be his normal skin) to match his real skin. I stippled on a few layers of a very dark red and some fleshy yellows all over the pieces and his skin, leaving the tongue sections of the prosthetics alone. I set it all with W. Tuttles finishing powder and then stippled over everything with a creme base African-American flesh tone from Clinique. I used the exact same method when coloring his full body pieces and blending, again covering all of his real skin as well as the pieces.

Once I powdered the entire make-up again to set it, I put the finishing touches on him by going over all of the tongue sections with...you guessed it, Vaseline. That really brought the make-up to life in a big way. The major problem with the Torque make-up was his chin piece. In retrospect, I should have designed this piece differently. It came from the bottom of his lower lip down to his shirt line (near the collarbone). The piece wasn't very wide, that was the mistake. The way I had sculpted the piece caused it to lift up easily from his throat. As soon as he really started to sweat (and sweat he did; two of the locations were sans air conditioning on 90°+ days, not to mention the lights!) the piece would start to peel. There was far too much movement and stress on the piece for it to stay down. Everything that it was glued to was constantly moving. I could have averted this problem by simply having made the piece wrap around the sides of his neck further to stabilize it. Live and learn. As it turned out, that piece required continuous attention and touch-ups, each being more difficult than the last because of the added perspiration and build up of adhesive. There was never time to take it off, clean him up and re-lay the piece so I just kept repairing it. At the beginning of the day it would behave for the first few hours, but between the twelfth and eighteenth hours it was a royal pain in the ass.

Ginny's make-up was much simpler. Originally we had planned to use those vaginal eyelid appliances that I told you about earlier for the entire shoot. I sculpted, molded, ran, and painted two pairs of those foam latex prosthetics but Scooter decided the first day of shooting that he didn't want to lose the expressiveness of her eyes, so they were cut from the make-up roster. So... that only left Ginny's make-up in the final scene. Torque cuts off Ginny's eyelids towards the end of the film so I built two false, bloody, eyelids for him to hold up after he cut them off (off screen). Ginny then wore a two piece prosthetic for her volatile finale after the attack. The foam pieces fit over her eyes and showed the exposed viscera beneath where her eyelids used to be. Glass eyes were inset into the foam pieces prior to the application. I glued the pieces down, blended the edges, and added gel blood to complete the effect. At this point in the story she had also been shot several times in the chest and arm. I built foam latex bullet wound prosthetics for this. They were simply glued down and covered with gel blood; her fishnet costume helped to "sell" the whole thing. Ginny was also a real trooper in the make-up chair. The prosthetics left her completely blind because the glass eyes were directly situated over her own, so she shot the entire last scene (firing off mega-rounds from a powerful hand gun) without being able to see what the hell she was doing. BRAVO! It all worked wonderfully. The effect of seeing these two huge, exposed eyeballs practically popping out of their sockets was far more eerie and affective than even I had expected.

Some of the other FX that I pulled off included; tubing and urination for a scene that I like to refer to as "Pissed Off", an electrocution (I used magicians flash string doused in sparkle additive), and tubing for a bleeding and bullet-ridden living mummy. There was also an acrylic denture (a plate of "real" looking teeth that fit on over the actual teeth) that had a break away tooth built into it for the scene where Torque tortures one of the prisoners (played by yours truly) by smashing one of his teeth to dust with pliers. By the by, that scene was filmed in a real New York City S&M Dungeon, what an experience! On one of the days of the Long Island shoot I had to do several character make-ups on background actors. There was a pair of naked lesbians who were haggard looking and covered with bruises (that was a very time involved task, mainly because there was so much flesh to deal with), a bum, and couple of other assorted oddities. It just so happened that Paul's car broke down that day, so I was left to pump out all of the make-ups without assistance. Thankfully, Michele was there that day. She did all of the powdering and straight stuff that needed doing. It was really tough because that day had the most make-up in it of all the shooting days. I was barely getting a make-up done and the performer would be pulled from my room and put out in front of the camera. Then I would jump right on to another one and barely get him done on time for his scene. It was like that, one after another, for the whole day.

Oh, I almost forgot! There was also a scene were Alice gets shot, PBR, in the forehead. I used the old button, thread, and wax bullet wound trick here. Cunningly positioned at her feet, just out of frame, Paul and I sat crouched with the blood set-up. On action Alex (that's right, Alex the producer) did the honors by pulling the string, the actress snapped her head back (the blood tube ran up her back and along the back of her head facing out towards the wall near the end) and I pumped mondo quantities of blood through the siphon. The thing that I was using was actually for bailing water out of a sinking boat, so you can imagine the urgency and authority with which it heaved forth my crimson concoction of corn syrup blood (which, by the way, made it worse because the blood was a bit too viscous for the pump to siphon smoothly; thus causing this clogged-up, broken damn effect when it finally pushed through). Well, let me tell you...the shower covered the entire room, all of it's contents and all of us as well. Sure, it's funny now but...O.K. it was funny then too, the clean up still sucked. We couldn't get the blood out of the wall paper or the paint. The room actually had to be re-painted, but it was going to be anyway or something like that. Alex was a little vexed about that one (but I think he was laughing on the inside). In addition to my make-up FX, Paul and Russ did a lot of squib work (and a good job of it too) throughout the film. The squibs all worked out perfectly and resulted in some dazzling shots. There was a slight problem with some minimal overspray. Well maybe it wasn't exactly minimal, but let's not split hairs here.

Principal photography flew by, perhaps because of the long days and short rests between. Before I knew it, the fun had already come to an end. We wrapped our last day on the Long Island set at 6:30 in the morning (we had started 20 hours earlier) and headed home for some much needed R&R. Those hour and half drives home on sleep are treacherous! Although I was glad that we had finished shooting and in doing so had accomplished our goal, I couldn't wait to work with these guys again. From what I hear it looks like that will be happening some time around December (here we go again!!!)

PRESENT DAY: I am sitting at this godforsaken word processor, banging out this witty article for all you gore hounds out there (see Mom, I told you that all the money that you and Dad spent on my B.A. in Speech Communications would pay off someday!). Last month I went back and worked on some pick-up shots with Scooter and Alex. One was a scene with two burnt bodies for the opening of the film. Scooter shot that in extra-mega-extreme close-up (you have to see it to believe it). It was shot under blacklight with a "secret" camera technique. Honestly, it ended up being my favorite make-up in it's finished form. I used layers of mud masks which Michele and I forced dry with a blow dryer. We then painstakingly applied color by using dust-off brushes and iridescent charcoal powder (by Ben Nye), filling in the recesses and just "shading" in the highlights.

I also had to make a new penis for Torque. They had decided that the first one that Paul had done looked too much like a normal dildo (whatever that means). It was lacking the techno-organic quality that the original concept sketches by Alex and myself possessed, so I started from scratch. I sculpted "Dick-on-a-Stick 2" using the same "patches of tongue skin" pattern and leaving a huge rut down the center of the underside for metal conduit. I also included several other smaller crevices for wires and the such. I molded it up and ran a skin of slip cast latex in the mold. When it was dry, I removed the skin and cut a hole in the tip to allow for the tubing. I then glued a piece of PVC tubing to the inside of the hole and cut the tube off at about two feet past the edge of the thing. I put the whole mess back into the mold and filled the inside of it with BJB TC-281 Polyfoam, making it solid. My version lacked the bladders that the first one had, I was short on time. When it was set, I removed the mangled member from the mold and painted it with colors that matched the original make-up. I added a big ol' piece of metal electrical conduit, wires and tubes to the proper sculpted in receptacles (which made all of the electronic pieces look inset) and VIOLA! Torque's techno-pecker. It ended up not being used very much due to continuity restrictions. Scooter just got a few shots of the underside to inter-cut with the original footage and that about did it. "Sixteen Tongues" had come to an end for me, but we have immediately gone on to discussing the next project. It's been a blast and I can't wait to do it again.

Well, that about does it for me boils and ghouls (I have *always* wanted to say that!). I hope you have enjoyed my little behind the scenes tour of "Sixteen"'s make-up FX. You may have already seen it by the time you read this. If not... go get it! If anyone reading this article is an Independent Film Producer or Director in need of my Special FX Make-up Services, please feel free to contact me by phone, e-mail or mail at:

REAPERDUCTIONS FX STUDIO
Glenn Hetrick

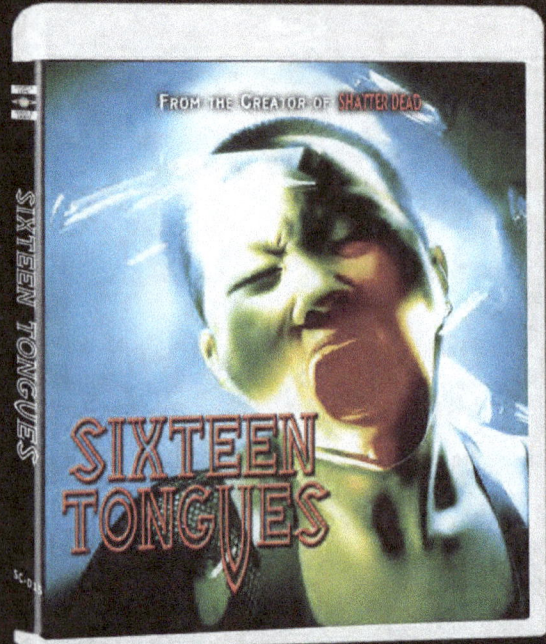

SIXTEEN TONGUES

Adrian Torque is a renegade cop who has lost more than half of his skin in a terrorist explosion. His missing flesh has been replaced with the tongue meat recovered from the sixteen victims that died during the tragedy. Ginny Chin-Chin is a genetically engineered prostitute / assassin chasing down the scientist who implanted her sex organs under the folds of her eyelids. Alik Silens is a wearied computer hacker hunting through the pornographic abyss of cyberspace for the identity of her brother's killer. At a run-down, S&M hotel purgatory where even the strangest desires can be met for a price, the trajectories of this star-crossed trio intersect in a claustrophobic collision of sex, blood, bullets, and personal apocalypse.

The sophomore feature from innovative and visionary New York based video auteur Scooter McCrae (*Shatter Dead*), *Sixteen Tongues* is a transgressive, dystopian chamber piece that fuses cyberpunk imagery, psychosexual malaise, and austere surrealist delirium. Featuring Alice Liu (*She Hate Me*), Tina Krause (*Limbo*), and special makeup FX by Glenn Hetrick (*The Hunger Games*) & Paul Sutt (*Watchmen, Van Helsing*), *Sixteen Tongues* presents a bleak and futuristic vision unlike any other; a subversive and ambitious body-horror epic guaranteed to challenge even the boldest and most daring cinematic explorers.

Special Features

Audio commentary with writer / director Scooter McCrae & producer Alex Kuciw - Audio commentary with writer / director Scooter McCrae, producer Alex Kuciw, & production designer Dan Ouellette - Isolated music track - "Fantasia or Bust"- festival screening featurette - Behind the scenes / bloopers featurette - Visual effects breakdown with post FX supervisor Robert Morris - Makeup and costume tests featurette - Deleted scenes - "I See the Dark" music video - Photo gallery - Video introduction to the student films by director Scooter McCrae - "dB" -16mm student film by Scooter McCrae (1988) with optional director's commentary - "Only Hell" -16mm student film by Scooter McCrae (1987) with optional director's commentary - Trailers - Reversible cover art - English SDH subtitles

Bonus movie: SAINT FRANKENSTEIN -Scooter McCrae's award winning 2015 short film starring Melanie Gaydos & Tina Krause (HD) with optional director's commentary - Isolated score featuring music by legendary composer Fabio Frizzi (*Zombie, The Beyond*) - Behind the scenes stills gallery

1999, United States	**Availabilty: Worldwide**	**Color/B&W: Color**
SKU: SC-015	**Pre-Book Date: September 1, 2022**	**Format: Blu-Ray**
UPC:	**Street Date: October 30, 2022**	**Director: Scooter McCrae**
MSRP: $39.99	**# Discs: 1**	**Rating: NR**
Box Lot: 30 units	**Running Time: 80 min. + Special Features**	**Genre: Horror**
Label: Saturn's Core	**Aspect Ratio: 1.33.1**	**Starring: Jane Chase, Crawford James, Alice Liu, Tina Krause**

OCN Digital Distribution
Jeff Murphy | jmurphy@ocndisital.com | 650.759.4504
100 Congress Street, Bridgeport, CT 06604